VESTIGE OF HOPE

VESTIGE IN TIME SERIES BOOK 1

SARA BLACKARD

Dear Reader,

I hope you enjoy! If you do, would you mind leaving a review on Amazon.com? Thanks & God Bless!

Sara Blackard

DEDICATION

To my husband, who is more selfless than anyone I know.
Thank you for always supporting me through all of this
life's challenges.

CHAPTER 1

JUNE 10, 2019

Hunter Bennett ran flat out as if the hounds of hell pursued him, and, considering he was approaching the Devil's Causeway in the Colorado Flattop Wilderness, the sentiment was fitting. He grunted, pushing himself harder up the snow-covered mountain to the ridge that resembled The Great Wall of China. If only it was just hellhounds chasing him, compelling him to move faster, push harder and not his own demons of failure stalking just over his shoulder. His foot slipped on the talus covering the mountainside, forcing him to put all his focus on the arduous climb, lest he tumbled all the way to the bottom, breaking his neck.

Wouldn't that just be fitting? "US Army Delta Force operator found dead after falling down a mountain in the middle of nowhere Colorado," the newspaper would say. Though they would leave out the Delta Force bit since that part of his life was strictly off the books and didn't exist. The Unit would never let him live it down. No, he needed focus, control. If he couldn't climb a little mountain without screwing up, he didn't deserve to go back to the army, let alone The Unit, after this mandatory R&R finished.

Hunter crested the ridge and slowed as he came to the land bridge. Beautiful, verdant basins filled with aspens unfurling their spring green leaves edged up to the slick talus rocks on either side of the mountain. The snow dotting the mountaintops laughed down on the green in challenge. The Bear River flowed on the side he'd hiked up from. Lakes dotted the land where he planned to camp on the opposite side, glittering like sapphires and emeralds sewn into the lush fabric of God's creation.

Hunter sat on the three-foot middle of the Devil's Causeway, letting the crisp early morning air cool him, and grabbed his canteen and an energy bar. While being ten thousand feet above sea level didn't bother him too much, he knew if he didn't keep hydrated, he'd be hurting later. He pulled out his detailed topographical map he'd printed from the satellite before leaving and surveyed the lakes below, wondering which one would provide his dinner. He took a deep breath in, his heart already slowed to normal, and closed his eyes as the sun warmed the back of his neck.

Hunter needed this—the quiet of the wind blowing across the mountain ridge. The whisper of birds singing in the trees far below. Maybe he would hear God speak with him again in the wilderness's solitude. Maybe He'd forgive Hunter for his failure to protect those whom He'd entrusted Hunter to protect.

A hawk screamed in the sky above, yanking Hunter back to a moment three weeks before when the screams were from a filthy and bloodied little blonde-headed girl in the humid jungle of Colombia. Hope Isaac. He could still feel her skinny arms and legs wrapped tightly around him, as he'd rushed her from the barn the kidnappers kept her and her parents in. The kidnappers had executed her diplomatic missionary parents mere seconds before his team could neutralize the situation. Hunter had hesitated too long, not listening to God's silent urging within him to hustle, wanting everything to be perfect, controlled. Because of his hesitation, he'd not only failed God, but also that beautiful, sweet, orphaned Hope, whose screams of terror and anguish still echoed within his brain. Hope. Hope no longer existed. The hawk screamed overhead again. The demons had caught up.

Hunter stood abruptly, slung his pack over his back, and took off at a run across the ridge. He found a path of descent that looked particularly dangerous and worked his way down, forcing himself to focus on the snow, the slippery rocks, the trees, the placement of his feet, the maximum effort he could execute without killing himself, all while keeping quiet like he'd been trained to do. He rounded a large boulder about three-quarters of the way down the mountainside and ran straight into the biggest mountain lion he'd ever seen, not that he'd ever really seen any mountain lions this up close and personal. The startled cat swiped at him as Hunter spun away, catching him across the chest in searing pain as the contact pushed him off balance and down the mountain. He'd always hated cats.

He tumbled through the sharp talus straight toward the little ravine he was hoping to skirt at the bottom. With the angry lion chasing him from up top, he half laughed, half shouted in pain at the irony of it all. Not only would the newspaper report about him falling down a hill, but now he'd allowed himself to be kitty lunch. *That's just fantastic*, he thought, as he slid to the bottom of the mountain, flipping headlong into the ravine and into blackness.

∼

JUNE 10, 1877

Viola Thomas wiped the back of her arm across her forehead to remove the pesky strand of hair that was forever escaping her braid and falling in front of her face, at the same time keeping the deer's blood covering her hands out of her hair. As the strand fell immediately back in front of her eyes, she huffed in resignation.

"It's useless," Beatrice, her younger sister, said with a laugh. Beatrice would look as beautiful smeared in blood and wrapped in furs as she did in her one nice calico dress she refused to wear. Beatrice's exquisite looks—her spring green eyes, hair the color of the chestnuts her father brought from the trading post each year, and delicate features that appeared so much like their mother, God rest her soul—caused Viola's heart to cry just a bit sometimes when she peered at her, and always made Viola more envious than she knew was right.

"What's useless?" Viola asked as she came out of her musing.

"We are both going to need a bath after dealing with this carcass," Beatrice grimaced as she finished wrapping the organs they would take home in the muslin bags they'd sewn. Beatrice's muddy brown calico blouse, which had once been a pretty rust colored fabric with tiny white flowers, and her buckskin breeches were much cleaner than Viola's own breeches and blouse, which appeared to have gathered every bit of blood possible.

Viola shook her head as she finished deboning the mule deer and laying the meat on the fur they'd skinned from the animal. Wrapped with the fur out, the skin would make the perfect pack for the short two-hour ride home.

"You won't need a bath. You look just as you did when we left the cabin before sunrise," Viola said with a moan. "I, on the other hand, appear to have wrestled with the animal before butchering him."

"You're beautiful like always," Beatrice said with mischief. "Filthy, but beautiful. Not that it matters much with us out here in the middle of nowhere. Although, there is the slight possibility River Daniels will be in the area. Then you might worry about your appearance. There is no one of consequence ever in these wretched mountains for me to worry about. I must leave for that to happen."

Viola blushed at her sister's not-so-subtle reference to Viola's potential husband. Potential because he was the only man within a hundred miles who wasn't old, missing teeth or mean-hearted. In fact, he was just about the most handsome man she'd ever seen with his dark, brooding eyes and his sharp cheekbones reflecting the strength that wrapped his entire body and spirit. Though his grand-mother came from the Ute tribe, it didn't bother Viola one bit, since most men in the area were a combination of

SARA BLACKARD

many backgrounds. Viola and River's discussions the past fall had hinted at a match, he'd given her no promises. It hadn't stopped her mind from daydreaming through the long winter.

Why Beatrice was so intent on leaving the mountain was beyond Viola. She looked up at the towering mountainside, ending in a ridge along the sky some said resembled some wall in China, and marveled at the splendor of God's creation. She loved her life in the middle of the Rocky Mountains, though, in honesty, it got a little lonely. Especially now with her older brother, Orlando, away looking for their father. Pa hadn't returned from their gold mine after the winter trapping was over in March. And, yes, the choices of husband material were limited to some old mountain men, a few Ute warriors who passed through occasionally, and the riffraff miners like Linc Sweeney and his brothers, whose thick skulls couldn't comprehend the little word "no." But with Colorado gaining statehood last year, Viola thought God would bring the right men into their neck of the woods if they weren't already there.

"That was an amazing shot you made today," Viola said, in an attempt to change the always touchy subject. Her sister had shot the arrow through the trees to the buck they'd spotted grazing the meadow grass, an incredibly difficult shot. "All your practicing sure is coming in handy. Now we will save the bullets and gunpowder for when we really need them."

"I guess something good has come from my neglect of those womanly chores you keep pushing onto me," Beatrice said with chagrin.

"Well," Viola teased softly, "since you enjoy being

6

outdoors so much, I will let you tan the hide." Viola shivered dramatically as she thought of smearing the brains on the hide to get it soft and useable for leather, coats, or blankets.

Beatrice laughed loudly, the joyous sound lifting Viola's lips into a large smile.

"Come on." Viola laughed along. "Let's hurry before the bears or lions take notice and join us."

The two worked in tandem, wrapping the meat in the fur and strapping it onto Viola's mountain-bred mare Cocoa. The chocolate-colored beauty never balked as they placed the meat behind the saddle.

"You're such a good girl, aren't you my sweet thing?" Viola crooned as she rubbed Cocoa's nose and kissed her softly.

Viola led Cocoa to the creek for a drink where Viola washed her hands and scrubbed her face, hoping she'd wash any blood off she'd inevitably smeared there. As she turned to join her sister, a loud anguished shout came from the direction of the mountain.

Mounting Cocoa, Viola hollered at Beatrice. "Bea, did you hear that? It sounded like it came from the base of the talus slide."

"Yeah, I heard it," Beatrice answered from atop her painted stallion, Firestorm. Beatrice pulled her Colt Navy from her holster. An edginess that always surprised Viola shuttered Beatrice's normally pleasant face.

"Honestly, Beatrice, the shout sounded like someone in trouble, not someone looking to make trouble," Viola joked as she made her way through the woods towards the mountainside.

"You and I both know that there are all kinds of

vermin scurrying about these mountains that would love nothing more than to make trouble for us, especially with Pa and Orlando gone, which is exactly why I'd rather go in prepared for the worse than wishing I had," Beatrice whispered harshly and pointed to the left as they reached the base of the mountain. "I'll go that way a few hundred yards. You go the opposite. If you find nothing in the next ten minutes, turn around and we'll meet up and head out. I don't want to stay around here with that fresh kill attracting who knows what."

"Sounds like a good plan. The shout didn't sound too far off, and we'll still be close enough to signal," Viola answered, trying to keep the nervousness from her voice that Beatrice's little speech induced. "Three whistles if you find something."

"Like always." Beatrice nodded as she turned Firestorm and took off along the tree line.

Viola breathed in deeply and let out a shaky breath. Her sweaty palms slipped along the reins, and her heart thumped somewhere within her throat instead of her chest where it belonged. Mad at herself for letting Beatrice's paranoia affect her, she yanked out her own Colt, checked the bullets, then held it across her lap where she could get it into action quickly.

Her eyes constantly scanning the grasses and under the bushes, she prayed aloud, hoping God would calm her nerves, "Lord, thank You for being here with me now. That though I walk through this dark valley, You are by my side." A peace that always calmed and comforted her settled upon her spirit as she continued, "Lord, I know that I heard what sounded like someone in trouble.

8

Please open my eyes to the one in need. Guide our direction to their side."

A whisper upon her soul had Viola confident that God was telling her she wasn't in any immediate danger. She holstered her gun, and eased Cocoa up to a little ditch that was forming from the watershed. As she came around a large sagebrush, she pulled up short at the sight of a man crumpled in a heap within the ditch.

Viola dismounted and tethered Cocoa to the sagebrush before she slowly approached the man, not only watching for any sudden movement that might prove Beatrice right but also taking in his unusual apparel. He had on a dark undershirt with the sleeves cut very short, long pants with several pockets, boots that had strings laced up the front, and a large pack on his back made of an odd-patterned cloth that appeared delicate. He dressed like no man she had ever seen, even when her family had travelled to visit her grandfather in cities across the nation.

Viola put her fingers in her mouth and whistled sharply three times. The man jerked, then moaned. She pushed her fear aside and rushed forward, kneeling beside him.

"Mister, I'm here to help. Let's roll you over and see just how bad off you are." Viola spoke calmly while gently rolling the man over onto his side. She inhaled sharply. She'd been wrong. Despite having a multitude of scrapes upon his unconscious face, he was, without a doubt, the most handsome man she had ever laid eyes on, far more so than River

Daniels. Though, if truthful, her exposure to the opposite sex remained limited in her twenty-six years. His face was tanned dark from the sun with strong lines and what appeared to be a beard he was just growing in. His dark, short brown hair the color of rich soil, proved he must be a city dandy since men of the mountain wore their hair longer, and when it received a cut, it was uneven, like a bear hacked it off with his claws. The man's dark blue shirt left no room for imagination as it sculpted tightly to every muscle.

Blood ran crimson from claw marks across his chest, snapping Viola out of her inappropriate perusal. She scanned the area for any predators while pulling her Colt out of her holster. It would be ironic if the animal that got this man pounced on her all because a handsome face distracted her. Thank heavens Beatrice hadn't caught her gawking like a fool.

Hearing a horse approaching, Viola tried to push the man over onto his back to assess his injuries more closely. The man cried out in pain as his pack forced his back to arch. Viola moved him back and fumbled with the fancy straps and buckles holding the odd pack onto the man. The buckles weren't metal, but some strange, smooth material she'd never seen before. She unlatched the buckles across his chest and waist as Beatrice slid Firestorm to a stop, slapped the reins around the same big sage Cocoa stood tethered to, and quickly approached.

"Help me figure out how to get these straps off," Viola said, pointing at the frustrating things. She leaned over the man's face and calmly spoke. "Mister, we need to get your pack off, and I apologize if this upsets you, but if we can't figure it out, we must cut those fancy straps of yours off."

"Here!" Beatrice shouted in triumph as she manipulated the strap by the man's hip. "Look, Viola, the strap is wrapped around this hard piece here, holding it in place. All you have to do is maneuver the strap through and around it."

As Beatrice worked on the exposed strap, Viola scanned the area again. Dark, menacing storm clouds brewed to the west. She noticed the temperature had also dropped considerably since they'd finished with cutting up the deer. If they didn't hurry, they'd all get soaked, or worse, stuck in a spring blizzard that the area was notorious for.

"We need to hurry," Viola said. "If we roll him towards me, do you think you can get the other strap off?"

"Should be able to," Beatrice replied. "If not, I'll cut it. No use wasting time fiddling with a silly strap when a storm's moving in."

Viola rolled the still unconscious man to her, cradling him as best as she could. He smelled incredible, a spicy musk that urged her to inhale it deep within her. Before Viola made an idiot of herself by burying her face into his neck and breathing in, Beatrice grunted and sat up with the pack.

"I got it. You can roll him over now." Beatrice smirked, causing Viola's face to flame in embarrassment.

"Good work," Viola said, ignoring her sister's knowing look as she laid the man as gently as she could onto his back. "You check his legs. I'll check if he has any broken ribs and see if I figure out what got a swipe at him from the claw marks."

The two worked quickly, pushing and prodding as gently as possible. The man's arms seemed to be fine, except some abrasions and a rather nasty cut along his forearm. The claw marks appeared to be from a mountain lion, which meant they'd need to make sure it got cleaned out well when they got home. Animal claws were filthy, lions worse than most, and might cause infection if not cleaned thoroughly. When Viola got to his ribs, the man moaned in agony at the pressure she applied.

"He's got some broken ribs, a nasty scratch by a mountain lion and some cuts and bruises." Viola reported as she sat back and peered at Beatrice.

"I think he might have a sprained ankle." Beatrice looked up at Viola. "I don't think it's broken, but I don't want to take off these fancy boots to check before we get home."

Viola nodded in agreement as she glanced from the man, to the sky, to their horses, and back again.

"We don't have time to make up a travois, not with your fresh kill through those trees and the storm building," Viola decided aloud. "Go move that meat to Firestorm, then bring Cocoa here. I'll see if I can wake him up enough to get him to help us hoist him onto her."

Beatrice raced over to the horses and shifted the items around. There was no way the feisty stallion would ride double. That loco animal only allowed Beatrice to ride him and only because Viola fancied him enamored with her.

Viola bent back over the man, brushing her hand down the side of his face and speaking loudly yet soothingly, "Sir, I need you to wake up. There's a storm coming, and we need to get you onto my horse. But you're so big and strapping I don't think my sister and I can do it without your help."

The man moaned as he scrunched his forehead in concern and leaned his head into her hand. Viola placed both hands on either side of his face and leaned closer.

"Sir, please," Viola pleaded. "We don't have much time. If we have to lift you on our own, I'm afraid we'll injure you even more."

His eyes fluttered and his face worked in concentration. Slowly, his lids opened and startling blue eyes, the color of the summer sky on a clear day, gazed at her with more focus than she thought possible in the circumstance.

"Mountain lion." The man muttered in apprehension.

"It appears the lion left or at least didn't want to finish his handiwork. I'm Viola Thomas. What's your name?" Viola asked as Beatrice came beside her with Cocoa.

"Hunter." The man groaned as he grimaced in pain.

"Mr. Hunter, we need to get you on my horse and to our home before this storm settles in on us," Viola said. "Do you think you can help us get you up?"

Hunter breathed in deeply and winced before answering. "First name's Hunter. Please help me sit up and clear my head a minute. It's spinning faster than a rollercoaster ride."

Viola peeked at Beatrice in confusion. Beatrice shrugged her shoulders and mouthed, "Loco." Viola motioned for Beatrice to go to his other side, and they both helped him up by the shoulders. He slowly raised his hands to his face, pushing his palms into his eyes and pulling his hands through his hair.

"He can't ride in front of you." Beatrice talked over him. "He's too tall, even taller than Orlando, I'd guess. You won't be able to see."

"We'll put him behind me," Viola answered.

"What if he falls off?" Beatrice examined him as if it wasn't a possibility, but a given. "If he passes out and falls, we'll be right back where we started and probably worse off."

"We'll tie him to me," Viola said, trying to be nonchalant to save the poor man's pride.

Hunter sighed and rolled onto his knees. After a few breaths that seemed to settle him, he looked at Viola and said, "I'm ready."

Viola and Beatrice helped Hunter to his feet as best they could. When he tried to put weight on his right leg, Viola watched him wince and pull it off the ground quickly. His forehead dripped with sweat and his shirt clung even more to his body.

Viola said, "Though this will hurt, you must put your right foot in the stirrup and swing yourself up. We'll help you as much as possible."

Hunter nodded, a drop of sweat rolling down his cheek.

"Beatrice, once we get Hunter up, I want you to duck under Cocoa's neck just in case his momentum takes him off the other side." Viola hoped she didn't sound as condescending as Beatrice had, though in honesty, she pictured that happening in his weakened state.

Hunter pulled her a little closer to him, almost as if he was tucking her into his side. When she peered up into those perfectly blue eyes, she stood still, stunned.

"Don't worry," Hunter whispered, his breath dancing with that stubborn strand of her hair and skittering down her spine. "I promise I won't fall off."

All Viola could do was nod her head in idiocy as she stared up at him.

Beatrice cleared her throat. "I'd rather get at least part of the way home before we get drenched."

Viola nodded, ducking her head lest anyone notice the blush rising her cheeks.

CHAPTER 2

HUNTER HAD WOKEN to the most beautiful vision he'd ever seen, an angel with long dark blonde hair trailing over her shoulder in a braid and eyes colored somewhere between blue and green that reminded him of his favorite fishing hole growing up. Her eyes were calm, yet gorgeous. She'd had her small hands placed upon his cheeks and a look of immense concern marred her blood-smeared forehead. Then the nightmare invaded in a cascade of pain.

He didn't know how he'd pushed through the pain without passing out as the two little women hiked him up onto the horse. He would say under oath it was a testament to his years of military training, but it was more likely the bruise to his ego the jabbing comments and looks of doubt the sprite of a sister threw at him that kept him clinging to consciousness.

Even now, after successfully mounting the horse and riding for a good while, Beatrice, if he remembered her name correctly, still glanced at him from time to time, as if to make sure he wasn't about to drag her sister off the horse. He didn't blame her though, since each step of the horse sent excruciating pain radiating from his chest to his outer limbs. He should've accepted his brother Chase's offer to hang out, rather than hike, especially since he'd been away on missions for so long. Rescue by horseback was definitely not his first choice of extraction. He'd have to catalogue this intel for future missions.

Though forced to hold tight to the captivating Viola might make the experience worth it. Her hair smelled so sweet and clean, like the pastures and woodlands that surrounded them permeated into her very cells. It was intoxicating and threatened to lull him back into sleep. He adjusted his position and caught a whiff of something putrid, like she'd rolled in something dead. He moved back to where he'd been, figuring if he kept his face in her hair, he wouldn't smell the rest of her.

Something, however, kept tugging at his brain, that little part of his mind that shouted something was not right, preventing him from diving headfirst into the comfort that Viola's presence infused into him. Maybe it was the odd clothing the women wore or the gear strapped upon their horses. Nothing appeared wrong with it. It just was overly old fashioned. From the blouses and buckskin pants to the antiquated revolvers holstered at their hips, even the blanket-like jacket they'd called a capote they'd gently pulled over him reminded him of all those mountain-men movies he and his brother used to watch growing up. The thick material scratched his neck wear it rubbed and the buttons holding it closed appeared to be made out of antlers. The whole scenario screamed Jeremiah Johnson, though beautiful feminine versions. It caused unease to skitter up and down his spine, making him force unconsciousness away until he could assess the situation.

"I don't remember any houses close by on the map," Hunter said, hoping to get information without raising suspicions. "In fact, with this being a designated wilderness area, the only structure I know of is an old settler cabin on a lake about five miles from the causeway."

"I sure hope you didn't pay too much for that map," Viola said, shaking her head. "There aren't any cabins abandoned in this area. In fact, the only permanent place for at least twenty miles in either direction is our place, unless you call the shack the Sweeney clan threw up as permanent."

"Don't forget about the gold mines up on Hahns Peak," Beatrice said. "And didn't Orlando say something about a Crawford family that moved in a summer or two ago over by the mineral springs?"

Viola answered, "I forgot all about them. You know, if time allows, we should have Orlando take us over to meet them this summer. It'd sure be nice to chat with some other ladies."

"But, what about the town of Steamboat Springs or Yampa? Together they are pushing thirteen thousand residents." Hunter asked with caution.

Their exchange did nothing to settle the unease. In fact, his mind was now racing double-time and his heart banged away like a fifty-cal machine gun. Had he knocked his brains completely loose? There was no way these women wouldn't know that Steamboat Springs, a population of over twelve thousand, was a quick drive away once you crossed the causeway.

THE POOR MAN had completely knocked his brains loose. That was the only explanation Viola could think of as the beat-up, half-conscious man wrapped around her back jabbered on about thousands of people living in these rugged mountains. What nonsense! The only reason there'd be that many people sticking around through the rough, long winters was gold. The only gold found in the area was Hahns Peak, and that had played out about as quick as they found it.

"The only place that big in Colorado is Denver, though I suppose it's closer to thirty thousand people now," Viola said cautiously, not wanting to upset him more than he already was.

His heartbeat increased upon her back from that of a woodpecker pounding on a tree to the wings of a hummingbird violently flapping. His hot breath came quick and choppy on the back of her neck.

"Denver's population is over six hundred thousand people," Hunter whispered harshly, his body leaning more and more on her each second.

Viola glanced at Beatrice, who mouthed "Loco" not so subtly. From Beatrice's concerned expression as she watched Hunter, Viola knew they needed to calm him down or he'd pass out again, though that might not be a bad idea. All this talk of hundreds of thousands of people had her heart beating about as fast as a hummingbird's wings as well.

"Hunter," Viola said, praying God infused her voice and words with calm and peace. "You've had a trying morning, what with your tangle with the lion and falling down the mountainside. We've had a long morning with our hunting trip. We are all exhausted, a little anxious, and you are definitely hurting. We are almost home, a half an hour more. Why don't you try to rest, and after we get you taken care of, we can figure out what's going on?"

"Yeah. Sure. You're right." Hunter answered tersely. "I'll understand things clearer after I get some shuteye."

With that, Hunter took several long, shallow breaths. His heartbeat slowed until she could no longer sense it, and his head nuzzled into her neck, which got her heart racing for an entirely different reason. After a minute or two, his body went lax, and she could tell he was sound asleep.

"How did he do that, just fall asleep on the spot?" Viola asked, looking at Beatrice in amazement.

"He's a strange one. I'll give you that." Beatrice shook her head and examined him like she used to examine bugs as a child. "What I don't get is his insistence that there are thousands of people living in these mountains. If we have a hundred, not counting the Indians, I'd be mighty surprised."

"Possibly locations got jumbled in his head during his fall, and he's remembering some place back east." Viola spoke softly, not wanting to wake him. "Whatever the case, we need to take this time to pray before he wakes back up."

Beatrice snorted, "He will definitely need a lot of prayer."

Viola threw her a reproachful look, then focused her thoughts on God. Viola thanked God for letting them find Hunter. She prayed for healing and wisdom since the situation didn't seem to add up. She finished and glanced at the sky behind them.

"Lord," Beatrice prayed, surprising Viola since she rarely shared her prayers. "Please help open my heart to be more trusting. I'm torn and conflicted at the moment. One part of me wants to raise a shield to protect me and mine from this man who is so strange. Yet, I sense Your presence with him, that You had him fall in our path for a purpose. Help me rest in Your peace, to recognize when my sense of fear is from You for our protection. In Jesus' name, amen."

"Amen," whispered Viola as she wiped the tears from her eyes. She focused on the task coming before them, on the best way to get Hunter into the cabin without harming him more. She thought through what she'd need to gather to treat his wounds. However no matter how hard she tried to focus and plan, the man's arms around her waist and his breath upon her neck pulled her thoughts astray.

HUNTER WOKE in a little piece of heaven. Viola's intoxicating perfume enveloped him in its freshness. He pulled her slender body closer to him, her back pressing to his chest. She fit perfectly. He snuggled his face closer to her neck and exhaled. This was by far the strangest, most wonderful place he'd ever napped, and with his military career, there'd been some doozies. Extraction by horseback wasn't such a bad means of rescue after all.

"Um, Hunter?" Viola whispered, a slight tremor coursing through her.

He took one last inhale and hugged just a little tighter, hoping to imprint this memory. Maybe once he got released from the hospital he'd hike on out here and spend the rest of his R&R getting to know Viola better. If things went well enough, he wouldn't mind spending his leave time in Colorado. The mountains were refreshing when they weren't chewing you up.

"Hunter, we're here," Viola said.

Was her voice huskier or was he imagining it? Yep, definitely spending some days in the wilderness after the hospital. He sat up, every part of his body burning in pain. His ribs seared him in white hot agony, as if the dumb cat hadn't left him be but was chowing down.

Hunter looked at Viola's delicate lines as she turned in the saddle, a slight blush pinked her neck. She lifted her eyes to his. They were kind and bore an expression of worry. Hunter smiled, or rather hoped it was a smile and not a grimace that would scare the sweet thing away. Just for good measure he winked, reveling in the crimson blush racing up her cheeks and the slight movement that lifted her lips before she turned back around.

"Let's get you in," she said, swinging her leg over the horse's head and dismounting.

A small cabin sat fifty yards from an emerald blue lake fed by a creek that danced through the mountain meadow. The cabin's back side butted up against a steep, smooth rock face of the mountains that stretched behind it as though grafted to it. From a strategical standpoint, the position was brilliant. The rock face was smooth and stretched on forever with a outward bend that created a natural awning up high that would protect it from weather and anyone who attempted to drop something nefarious onto the cabin. Whoever was inside would only have to worry about three sides, and with the lake so close, actually only two. The large meadow stretched out past the cabin and was lined with fluttering aspen trees, towering pines and magnificent mountains jutting up like sentry as they horseshoed around the luscious wide valley. Someone had built a log barn with a corral attached that held a handful of horses and a dairy cow. The cabin, which appeared from the outside to be one room, had only one window on the front and a sod roof.

As the unease of before tried to claw its way up his throat, Hunter pushed it down with difficulty. *Lord, what is going on?* Hunter was a Delta Force captain. The US government trained him to remain calm, assess the situation, and find a solution. He had commanded more successful missions in the most bizarre and dangerous situations possible than any other operator, ever. He could figure this out. All he had to do was remain calm, in control. He closed his eyes and forced his mind to focus, to push past the fear and concentrate on what needed done posthaste. He had to get off this horse, have his injuries dressed, and then set up communications. Once he reached Search and Rescue and got someone on their way out here, he could look at the situation more clearly.

"Okay, here's what's going to happen," Hunter said as he took charge of the situation. He ignored the look of surprised amusement that passed between the sisters. "If you ladies would stand here next to this horse, I'll lean forward and dismount. I can tell you it's not going to be the prettiest dismount you've ever witnessed, but if you help me keep steady and not fall on my face, I think we can get it done. Would you mind looking at my injuries and see to anything that needs addressed before Search and Rescue make it out here?" he asked looking at Viola and ignoring the petulant smirk that seemed a permanent feature upon Beatrice's face.

"I think we can handle that," Viola answered as they came up alongside him. "Will your party be looking for you then?"

"Without a doubt, once I get in contact with them." Hunter grunted in pain as he leaned over the front of the horse and lifted his leg back and over. The agony of before ratcheted up to hellish torture as his entire body protested the movement. He clamped his teeth tight, more than likely breaking some, to keep the scream from ripping out of his throat. Once off the horse, he stood supported between the sisters, shaking like a leaf and breathing as deeply as his ribs would allow to keep the black tunnel of unconsciousness threatening his line of vision at bay.

After a few minutes, Hunter nodded his head and said, "Alright, let's go."

The short walk to the cabin had his grip on the tunnel loosening. By the time they reached the threshold and made their way to the bed shoved in the room's dark corner, the women almost completely supported him. Four more steps and he'd rest. *Control, hold it together.*

Two more steps, but the tunnel was winning. He mumbled an apology before his consciousness tumbled down the tunnel into darkness.

CHAPTER 3

Viola and Beatrice had just gotten Hunter to the bed when he went limp and tumbled into a pile, thankfully on the bed. Goodness, that man was heavy. Two hundred plus pounds of solid muscle had gotten heavier the instant he'd passed out with an apology. Hunter had impressed her with his strength and ability with just a grunt of sound to press through what had to have been immense pain .

"Okay," Beatrice said with resignation. "Now I'm impressed. What do we need to do?"

Viola shook her head at her sister's candidness. "Let me catch my breath, then we'll roll him flat on his back."

"Well, let's hurry." Beatrice humphed in impatience. "I have work to do outside before the storm hits."

"Help me roll him over, and if I still need you after you're done outside, you can help," Viola answered.

After they got Hunter positioned onto his back, Beatrice left to take care of the horses and other animals. Viola set to work getting the fire going to boil water from where they'd banked it before they left. She lit a lantern on the table and the lantern her father had mounted on the wall by the bed. Viola glanced down at her blood-crusted clothes and over at the unconscious Hunter. She quickly ducked into Beatrice's and her room off the back of the house and changed. Though she reached for the favorite forest green dress with the intricate embroidery upon the collar and sleeves, she chastised herself as a ninny and yanked her serviceable faded yellow dress on over her head before she allowed her romantic musings to run rampant. But could anyone blame a girl if her imagination was running amok with the way he'd pulled her tight to him? His breath blowing from lips that barely grazed her neck where he nuzzled had sent delicious spirals of warmth straight to her core.

"Good grief, Viola," she scolded herself as she fanned her warmed face with her hand. "The man's passed out, in severe pain, and touched in the head. He was doing nothing but holding on, so you best snap out of it."

She marched out of her room, ignoring the desire to brush and rebraid her hair. She checked the fire and water, then went to the still unconscious Hunter. Realizing she should have had Beatrice help her with the capote and his shirt before she left, Viola decided she'd start at his feet, checking more thoroughly for injuries. That would also keep her from becoming distracted by his handsome face and getting caught gawking again. Maybe she was the one touched in the head. Prayer. She needed to pray. She asked God to focus her mind and keep the daydreams at bay.

Viola loosened the boot laces as much as possible, marveling that they were a string bound at the ends with some kind of casing. She pulled the left shoe off gently and examined the boot with awe and a bit of trepidation. The craftsmanship far exceeded any she had ever seen, with the sole made from some hard material that had words and a design carved into it. She pulled out an insert located inside the boot. When she saw it up close, her hands shook with unease. What was this strange unnaturally blue-colored thing that squished but made no mess? She assumed it was for comfort, but she had never seen or heard of such an invention. She put it back within the boot and placed the boot on the floor.

Viola reached for the right foot and carefully began to pull it off. Hunter moaned in pain. Viola thought for a moment on how to get the boot off without hurting him more. She picked up the one from the floor and examined the laces and area behind the laces. She puffed up in triumph, set the boot down and began unlacing the boot still stuck on Hunter's foot. When finished, she pulled a flap hidden behind the laces open all the way and, with a grin, released the foot from its hold.

"That was a rather smart addition to boots," Viola said to herself as she closed the flap and shoved the laces within the boot so they wouldn't get lost.

Viola placed a chair at the foot of the bed and set to peeling Hunter's socks off. With that done, she examined his right foot more closely. It appeared swollen and bruised, but as she manipulated it and felt the bones, she noticed nothing broken. Though a sprained ankle would take a while to heal, it was better than it being broken.

She moved the chair to the bed's side and grabbed a bowl and cloth for the shelf and water from the stove. After adding enough cold water to make it tolerable, she sat and carefully began washing his hands and face. The fall had battered his face and his cheek under his left eye was so swollen, Viola doubted he'd be able to open that eye fully. The palms of his hands were full of cuts and scrapes from where he'd tried catching himself. As she cleaned his hands, she realized they weren't the soft hands of a city dandy, but the marred and scarred hands from physical labor. Yet they weren't hands of a farmer or even a miner. They were hands that had seen violence and struggle, much like a mountain man's hands, evidenced by the few knife scars and an odd patterned scar upon both palms. The mysteries and puzzles of this man kept stacking up.

Viola stood and retrieved the muslin they kept for bandages and calendula salve when Beatrice came through the door, bringing a violent, frigid wind with her that soaked the entryway.

"It's going to be a big one." Beatrice placed a bag of meat on the table and hung her coat. "I won't be surprised if we wake up to snow in the morning."

"Are the animals settled?"

"Yes, though I'm sure glad Maybelle won't calf for another couple of weeks." Beatrice said. "It might be lazy, but I wouldn't want to be going out there to milk in this, or worse yet, calf."

"Sorry I wasn't able to help you get everything settled." Viola dumped the dirty water in the bucket to take out later.

"Don't worry." Beatrice laughed as she leaned over Hunter. "How is he?"

Viola rubbed her eyes tiredly. "I don't think he broke his ankle, just sprained real bad. The bruise on his face and cuts and scratches are nothing serious. But I couldn't get the capote or shirt off alone. I will need your help."

Beatrice leaned closer to his face and sniffed. "Even with his face all scratched, he's a mighty handsome fellow. Smells nice, too." She stood and teased. "But you already know that don't you? I see you freshened up."

Viola's face heated as her annoying sister chuckled. Viola huffed in exasperation. "Well I couldn't tend him covered in blood and guts could I? Now if you're done poking fun, help me take off his clothes."

Beatrice doubled over in loud laughter. As Viola realized what she'd said, the scorch of the blush raced the rest of the way to her forehead and threatened to consume her in humiliation.

HUNTER WOKE in a haze of pain and confusion. Whispered words spoken from somewhere in the room told him he wasn't alone. Intense pain consumed his body. Had he gotten captured and tortured again? His heartbeat threatened to hitch into overdrive, but he couldn't let those who whispered know he was awake. He focused his energy on breathing as in sleep, opening his senses to what was around him, and remaining in control, waiting for the most opportune time to escape. The wind was blowing fiercely outside. Warmth surrounded him, and it didn't smell antiseptic like a military base. It smelled earthy.

"Let's get this over with," a voice hissed from the corner, followed by two sets of footsteps approaching.

Hunter waited, preparing to lash out. Though the pain ebbing from his ribs and ankle would slow him, he hoped the adrenalin that coursed through his body, like in every mission, would get him away. Then he'd focus on getting to safety.

His captors surrounded his head. One on the side began tugging on his shirt hem. The other leaned down over his head. His hands struck out simultaneously, grabbing the one pulling his shirt by the wrist and the other by the neck. He opened his eyes, but everything was blurry. He shook his head, trying to clear it. He heard a knife leave a scabbard. His hands tightened.

A squeak and a garbled, "No, Beatrice." brought his attention by his head. His eyes focused and filled with Viola, her neck clamped tightly in his hand. He wasn't under threat. He dropped his hands, wincing at the movement.

"I'm sorry," he said. "I thought I'd been captured again." He closed his eyes and took in several calming breaths in. Looking at Beatrice then returning his gaze to Viola. "Please forgive me."

Viola touched her neck, her eyes still tinged in shock and fear. She nodded. "It's all right, Hunter. We forgive you. You've been through a lot. It's understandable that you're confused."

"I'll forgive you, considering the circumstances," Beatrice snarled as she slid what Hunter now saw was a large hunting knife into its sheath at her back. She leaned over him, anger, and what Hunter recognized as fear, burned from her eyes. "But if you ever grab me or my sister like that again, you'll wish that lion had finished you off on the mountain."

Viola gasped. "Beatrice,"

"Understood," Hunter spoke over Viola.

Beatrice spun around and stomped to the door. After jerking on her coat, she yanked the door open, letting a frigid gale race through the cabin, and slammed it. Viola came around his side where Beatrice had left, wringing her hands in her apron.

"Don't worry about her." Viola shrugged as she sat in the chair pulled beside the bed. "She needs time to cool down."

Hunter nodded, taking in the woman sitting next to him. Her dress was a soft yellow, the color of butter. Her hands picked at a string that frayed from the cuff. The slight bruising discoloring her slender neck pained him more than his burning ribs. He'd make it up to her. He didn't know how, but he would. She lowered her head, blocking her face from him. He had the crazy urge to talk to her so she'd look at him.

"So," he said, his voice croaking. He cleared his throat before continuing, "How bad off am I?"

Hunter inwardly cheered in success as she lifted her eyes filled with compassion to gaze at him. He smiled at her, hoping to coax one from her. He had yet to see one grace her lips, and his curiosity had him wondering if it would be as alluring as the rest of her. The right corner of her mouth lifted before she started talking. It wasn't enough, but he'd take it for now.

"You have some bruises and cuts on your face." She listed off his injuries with sympathy. "Your cheek is pretty swollen. I'm guessing that you'll have a nasty black eye by tonight. You scraped the palms of your hands, so they'll be tender for a few days. You sprained your ankle pretty bad. It's swollen, but didn't appear to have any breaks. Can you try to move your foot?"

Hunter nodded and, gritting his teeth, moved his ankle up and down. She nodded her head in encouragement and both corners of her full lips lifted slightly.

"You're right," he said with a moan. "It hurts like the dickens, and I'll not be able to put pressure on it for a while, but it's not broken."

"Beatrice and I were getting ready to check your ribs and clean out that claw swipe when you woke." Viola continued in her assessment of him. "Now that you're awake, you might sit so I can take off the capote and your shirt."

"Sure, no problem," Hunter answered, holding in the smart remark on his lips about her wanting to take off his clothes, something his brother would say without missing a beat. She seemed so pure and innocent; he didn't want to embarrass her with bawdy male humor.

Viola leaned over him to help. Her closeness enveloped him with peace, like it had on the horse. He stared into her eyes and wondered what it was about her that caused this reaction, because if all his brain waves were firing, peace would be the last emotion felt at the moment.

She breathed out, covering him in honey and clove, and whispered, "Ready?"

Hunter could do nothing more than nod. She slid her arm beneath his shoulder, grabbed his forearm with the other hand, and helped him sit up. He clamped his lips and his teeth so the scream that built within his chest wouldn't reach freedom.

His breath came out fast and shallow as the pain almost consumed him. He closed his eyes tightly and willed himself to stay conscious. Just when he thought he'd lose control, soft fingers brushed through his hair, landing on his shoulder. He glanced over to where she sat on a chair pulled next to the bed. Her eyes shone with empathy and admiration. The first comforted. The second bolstered.

"I have some willow bark tea for you to drink, if you think you can," Viola said.

"Don't you have some ibuprofen or something?" Hunter asked, hoping these ladies weren't some kind of all-natural hippies who chewed leaves for medicine and rolled in mud for bruises. He only had a couple of travel packets of pain killers in his pack and knew those would barely put a dent in the pain.

Viola gaped at him in confusion. "I just have willow bark tea."

Hunter sighed and nodded. She reached behind her to the table stacked with the supplies needed to doctor him. She placed it in his hands, then guided them up to his mouth. The bitter and nasty taste caused him to grimace.

"I know it's not very palatable. But it will help ease the pain."

"It's fine." Hunter drank the rest in as few gulps as he could.

"All right," Viola said in a way that said she was boosting his confidence. "If you're ready, you can lift your arms, and I'll slip off your shirts. I'll try and make it so you don't hurt more."

"Definitely don't want to hurt more," Hunter said, smirking. "If that's even possible."

Viola returned his smile, a little bigger this time. He was getting there. Soon he'd have her lips curving up. He lifted his arms with great effort, and she took off his shirts.

She cast down her eyes with a slight pink blush creeping up her neck. "Let me check your back before we lay you back down," she said in a rush.

She disappeared behind him. A shocked gasp brought his mind to his back, mentally searching for pain he'd lumped with the rest.

"What?" Hunter asked with hesitation.

"These scars." He heard her gulp as he felt her fingers feather across his lower back and then up to his shoulder. "What caused such scarring?"

"So, I didn't bust up anything new back there?" he asked in relief.

"Oh, goodness, sorry I got distracted." Her hands swept the rest of his back. "Nothing new. Your pack protected your back."

Viola came from behind him and turned her back to him. She began gathering some items from the table, but not before he saw her swiping her hand across her face. Disappearing behind him again, she messed with the bedding, before she faced him.

"Let's lay you down," Viola said, her eyes still gleaming.

He reached out and grabbed her hand. "They happened a long time ago. They don't hurt anymore."

"It's just that they don't look like anything I've ever seen before. Your shoulder looks like a burn, but it's different, more intense somehow. The cluster on your lower back looks like bullet wounds, but they're too small, too concise." Viola turned her head to the side and stared across the room. She took a deep breath and resolutely turned back to him. "Let's get the rest of you looked at."

Hunter let her help him back down on the bed, admiring her ability to push through her emotions and curiosity to focus on what needed done.

WHILE VIOLA'S admiration for Hunter's strength and character increased with each passing minute, she tried to control the emotions rolling inside her, threatening to spill out in useless tears. The massive scars on Hunter's back had filled her with such pain and sympathy for him that she wanted to hug him close.

They'd also filled her with an intense apprehension. She'd lived in the mountains her whole life, surrounded by men who lived a lifestyle that liked to eat you for dinner, chew you up, and then spit you out again. If you survived, you did so with the scars to boast about it. She'd seen everything from animal maulings, gunshots, arrow wounds, and fire burns. The scars on Hunter's back were not the savage scars of the wilderness but calculated and sophisticated somehow. The sight of them sent fear coursing through her body, chilling her to the bone.

"I will have to push on your ribs to figure out if you broke any," Viola said, hoping she'd sounded more confident than she felt as she started systematically pressing his ribs for any that moved. When she reached the bottom right side she paused, lightly touching the cluster of scars that matched the scars on his back.

"An insurgent shot me during an extraction of a US diplomat kidnapped while in Yemen," Hunter explained through pained breaths. "Thankfully, the bullets missed any major organs, and they patched me up and sent me back out to save the world, or at least the US interests in the world." He chuckled, the sound tight with pain. "The other scar, well, let's just say the Taliban captured me during a reconnaissance mission, and when I wouldn't give them the information they wanted by the traditional beating-you-to-a-pulp interrogations, they resorted to other measures."

Hoping to cover the shock she knew must be clear on her face, Viola pointed her face towards his feet as she placed her ear to his lungs to listen for a punctured lung. She had never heard of the tribes he talked about. She thought she knew all the names of the tribes east of the Rocky Mountains where any government interest would be. Had the United States acquired more territories she wasn't aware of? As she lay listening, she detected a minuscule tug on her braid from Hunter and wondered if she had something stuck in her hair. She turned to the table and brought the bowl of hot water to her feet and placed some clean rags on her lap. Her face scrunched in confusion as she started cleaning his wound from the mountain lion.

"You have at least two cracked or broken ribs on your right side and three on your left. It doesn't sound like you have a punctured lung, praise God. After I get this taken care of, we'll wrap your ribs and get you as comfortable as we can."

"Why do you look so concerned?" Hunter asked, regarding her. "Are you worried my injuries are worse than you think? Between my tours with the Army and my all the adventures my brother Chase and I had growing up, I'm sure I'll be alright."

"No," Viola hesitated. "I guess I'm trying to make sense

of your story. I've never heard of Yemen or even the Towa Band. Are they Indian nations? You say these are gunshot wounds, but they are so small and precise. There should be more scarring, and someone surviving such an attack would be next to impossible. Even if you had the finest city surgeon out here in the wilderness with you when you received the shot, you'd bleed out before the doctor could clean and close all the shots. I just don't understand. Did your attack happen in a city back east?"

Hunter gave her a look that clearly expressed he thought her dimwitted. She wondered if every word out of his mouth would send her brain to spinning or if they'd find some ground that was common to both of them.

CHAPTER 4

HUNTER KNEW the look he gave Viola could only be described as dumbfounded. She was either clueless or a great liar. His eyes sharpened in distrust. He answered, "Maybe you've lived secluded in these mountains a bit too long. It's simple modern medicine. We can temporarily stop bleeding of most wounds long enough with Quik-Clot to get medical help, especially in the military. Yemen and the Taliban aren't here in the US, but in the Middle East."

Hunter watched as Viola's head shook back and forth, her forehead scrunched in confusion. She dabbed at the lion's claws' marks, intent on cleansing the entire area. It stung like the dickens, but he ignored it, focusing only of her obvious confusion and, in his intensely trained opinion, lack of lying.

"I've heard of the Ottoman Empire, Rashidian Emirate, Persia." Viola listed as she rubbed her head as if trying to remember a learned fact from long ago. "I even recall a Zaidi Imamate and Afghanistan. But I don't remember even something similar to what you're saying."

"Afghanistan is correct, but the others are no longer in power." Hunter dredged his Arabic nations' history from his memory bank. "The Ottoman Empire dissolved in 1924, and the Persian monarchy hasn't been in power since the Iranian revolution in 1979."

Viola's hands began to shake violently and her face became impossibly pale. She started shaking her head and stuttered, "Wh… what? I… I… I don't understand."

Hunter took the cloth from her hand and held her hands to his chest to stop them from shaking. He'd seen this kind of reaction before, usually from some greenhorn who'd just had his first mission with unfriendlies. Her body pulsed with fear.

"You mean 1824, not 1924, right?" Viola asked in a hoarse whisper.

"Why would you say that?"

"You can't mean 1924," Viola said, as she pulled her hands from his grip and stood up. "It's only 1877."

Hunter felt the blood rush from his head. He sat up and swung his legs over the side of the bed. "What are you talking about?"

Viola backed up away from the bed and pulled a calendar from the wall and handed it to him, "Today is June tenth, 1877, well as close to the tenth as we can reckon."

Hunter studied the homemade calendar in his hand. They had painted it over a newspaper. The newspaper had the date of August 13, 1876. Now his hands began to shake so violently they threatened to tear the calendar in half. He placed it on the bed beside him.

"No." Hunter's head fell into his hands. There had to be an explanation. Viola must be lying or something. Or maybe her and Beatrice were part of a terrorist group sent to get information from him. Hunter shook his head. How would a terrorist group know where he was when he just picked this location on a whim? How would they get this cabin and buildings set up in such a short time? No, Viola must just be lying, but why?

He stared up at Viola, her hands twisting in her apron. Maybe these two were just some nature-loving, flower-child type of people, getting back to the basics, living off the grid in their own little world. Viola didn't seem dangerous or even to be lying. Maybe she'd lived up here so long she'd truly forgotten what year it was. Or maybe this was some kind of commune where the kids grew up never exposed to reality and have been told it was the 1800s.

He spoke softly, hoping he'd be able to convince her he was right. "No, I'm sorry, but you're wrong."

He stood as fast as his injuries allowed and hobbled to his boots. His body screamed in protest at the movement. He tried reaching for his socks and almost toppled over. He sat down at the end of the bed in frustration.

"Where's my pack?" Hunter asked, his voice low and strained with pain, "I need to use the SAT phone and get an evac... stat."

"It's right here," Viola said, pointing to the corner, her face riddled with confusion. "Let me get it for you. I know we can figure this out."

As she crossed the room to retrieve the pack, the door opened. Beatrice followed a blast of frigid air into the cabin. She closed the door and stopped in the middle of taking off her coat, looking between the two of them.

"What's going on here?" Beatrice asked as she slid her coat onto the antler hook and rested her hand on her holster.

"Hunter's just a little confused," Viola answered, sympathy laced in her voice. "He might have hit his head a little too hard."

Hunter took his pack from her outstretched hands as the two sisters glanced at each other in worry. He figured keeping his mouth shut would be the best plan of action. Anything he said would probably only make things worse. He'd get a call out for rescue, then figure out a way to convince these ladies they've been lied to and it was really the twenty-first century. He dug through his pack, tossing things to the bed in a very unDelta Force manner. The disorder of the mess almost distracted him to organize it. To control something in this screwed up situation. He grabbed the SAT phone and pointed it at Viola. Beatrice's gun was out of the holster in a second and pointed directly at his chest.

"Hunter." Viola's voice shook, the calm gone. "You can put the weapon away. We aren't going to hurt you."

"Weapon?" Hunter looked at the phone in his hand and shook his head. He decided he would bring these two off this mountain with him. He could help them adjust to a normal life living in the modern world. He had contacts that could get them the necessary documents they'd need. He could even help them find housing and connect them with a church. "This is a phone, not a weapon. You use it to call people. In fact, I'm going to call Search and Rescue right now."

"What is he rambling about?" Beatrice demanded, still holding her Colt, but at least now she was pointing it to the floor. "What is that phone contraption?"

"You know... phone, as in telephone. You talk to people over long distances with it," Hunter said. When Viola and Beatrice glanced at each other and shared a look that said they thought he might be crazy, Hunter squeezed his forehead, trying to think of a way to explain. "It's like a telegraph but with sound. You can talk to another person located somewhere else and hear them."

Beatrice's face lit up with recognition. "Oh, I read about a display of Alexander Graham Bell's first telephone at the World Fair last year. It's an amazing invention, but far from being in use. How can your's possibly work? There are no wires to transmit sound?"

"Phones haven't needed wires for over thirty years," Hunter answered, his frustration with the situation fraying his already threadbare nerves.

"But—" Beatrice started asking when Viola interrupted.

"Hunter says he's from the future," Viola answered, inching closer to the bed. Her eyes riveted onto the items strewn across it. "The 1980s, I believe."

"I think you ladies have been lied to by someone, made to believe a truth that doesn't exist," Hunter said as he turned on the phone. "You were right about it being June tenth, but it's June tenth, 2019, not 1877."

"What are you playing at, mister?" Beatrice asked, her grip on the gun tightening. He'd have to watch her closely. She probably wouldn't take the news very well.

The phone's screen blinked on, and Viola jerked back,. Hunter ignored her as he waited for a signal to register.

The phone beeped. Both ladies jumped at the noise, and a message that no signal was available came onto the screen.

"Storm must be interfering with the signal," Hunter said in disgust, as he turned it off and tossed it onto the bed.

The room had gone quiet. Quiet except for Viola's short, quick breaths as she inched her way closer. Her trembling hand reached for the headlamp he had tossed onto the edge of the bed..

"The material," Viola murmured. "The material is strange, off…"

She shook her head as if trying to clear it. Hunter moved his legs around the corner of the bed so he didn't have to twist to see her. She reached her hand again towards the headlamp. It shook so hard Hunter was surprised she could move it at all.

"Here, let me show you," Hunter said as he reached over and clicked the light on, causing both women to inhale sharply.

"Dear Lord God, help us all," she prayed before fainting dead away. Hunter barely had time to catch her before she hit the floor, the bottom of his heart dropping out of his chest.

VIOLA WOKE to a soft slapping on her cheek and Beatrice's concerned voice echoing in her ears.

"Viola, please wake up," Beatrice pleaded. A cold cloth dabbed upon Viola's forehead. She began registering her surroundings, the fire crackling in the stove, the hard floor beneath her, the musk of Hunter's scent teasing her nostrils. Hunter. Her eyes flew opened and locked onto his staring at her.

"Sorry, I had to lie you on the floor," Hunter sheepishly stated. "I couldn't lift you to the bed with these busted ribs."

"Oh dear." Viola pushed her sister's hands away and kneeled beside Hunter. She pressed her hands against his broken ribs. "I didn't hurt you, did I?"

Hunter's hands stilled hers and pulled them in front of him. He slowly rubbed a comforting circle upon her wrist. She gazed into his eyes. Concern and tenderness replaced the distrust that had been there before she'd embarrassed herself and fainted.

"I'm sorry," she said. "I normally am not so weak-hearted. It's just... everything is too much. I'm so confused." Viola eased her hands out of Hunter's and sat in the chair next to the bed. Maybe if they talked things through, they could figure out this puzzle. "Beatrice, why don't you pull up a chair so we can talk this out?" Viola asked.

"No," Beatrice answered, throwing a cautious glance at Hunter. "I'll stand."

"Well, in that case, can you make your pacing useful and pour me a cup of tea, please?"

Beatrice huffed but stalked towards the stove. Viola's gaze moved from her hands that clung together to the items haphazardly lying on the bed. Her trepidation threatened to cause her to faint away again.

"Do you mind if we pray?" Viola asked, needing God's presence and direction. "We're going to need His help if we want to figure this out."

"I'm not opposed to praying," Hunter answered. "It should probably come from you, since He's not exactly on speaking terms with me."

The pain in Hunter's statement baffled her, but she pushed that mystery aside to deal with the present one, "Father God, I'm not even sure how to pray at the moment. This situation we find ourselves in is disorienting and unsettling. Please Lord, calm our hearts and give peace to our minds. Give us understanding and wisdom to the puzzle before us. Help us work together in harmony without contention. And Lord, heal Hunter. Keep his body strong to fight against infection and mend what is broken. Help him find his way home. Amen."

Viola studied at Hunter's items strewn upon the bed. She reached for a small rectangular object about the size of her palm that appeared innocuous. It was black with a smooth glass surface on one side and a material that was rough and bumpy on the other. Her thumb hit a circular indention at the bottom of the glass. The black glass became vibrant with faces of people. Hunter and another man who was similar smiled from the contraption at her. The number 15:13 showed above the people with *June 10* written smaller below. Viola heard Beatrice's sharp intake of breath moments before a tea cup rattled to the table. Viola looked to Hunter in confusion as Beatrice snatched the thing from her hands.

"It's my eye phone," Hunter said, watching their reactions like a hawk, searching within their faces for something. Truth, maybe? Whatever he searched for, his look was intent, and she determined to be as open as possible. "Slide your finger across the bottom from left to right.

You'll be able to see my apps, contacts… an official calendar. The passcode is 089300."

Viola watched as Beatrice did what he said. Her sister's face lit up in a mixture of amazement and fright. She moved closer so Viola could see. Viola slowly reached a finger towards the little square that read "calendar." When she tapped it a new image popped up. A miniature calendar with the year 2019 in red at the top.

"How is this possible?" Viola asked. "You say it's the year 2019. Your clothing, pack, shoes, this eye phone are not the kinds of items available now. But, despite what you may think, we are not insane. It is the year 1877."

"I believe you believe it's 1877," Hunter stated.

"Please, Hunter, let's not be condescending," Viola retorted, infusing as much patience in her voice as possible. "I'm not some backwoods nitwit. We may live in the middle of nowhere, but we've surrounded ourselves with books of all categories and studies. We've all delved deep into the knowledge of the world as we know it."

Viola had always prided herself in her family's propensity to gather books. They didn't limit themselves on topic, purchasing books from all disciplines. Their mother had been intent on them learning as much as they could despite their limited surroundings. She had always been so fascinated with learning about new discoveries and cultures around the world. Grandfather used to bring boxes of books for them when they'd visit him before he'd died in an accident at one of his steel factories. She may be from the isolated wilderness, but she was intelligent. No stranger, no matter how handsome or confused would tell her different.

～

HUNTER CONSIDERED THE LITTLE CABIN. Books or weapons covered every available space on the walls. There was a Lancaster rifle he itched to get his fingers on propped within a gun stand . He'd only ever read about them or seen them on his and Chase's favorite TV show *Top Shot*.

"I'm sorry," Hunter apologized, again. He'd apologized more today than he could remember ever apologizing in one day. "You're right. That was a low blow. I'm a little out of my element at the moment."

"You and me both," Viola retorted. "Maybe if you tell us what happened, starting first thing this morning, we can figure out what is going on. But why don't you let me wrap your ribs while you tell us. No use of me sitting here looking at you talk when you still need patched up."

Beatrice snorted, drawing his attention to her. He mentally chastised himself for how he'd all but forgotten she was there, his attention so focused on Viola. That's how people ended up killed. He knew that firsthand, the devastating consequences of an operator with tunnel vision. Beatrice had already proven she wouldn't hesitate to mark a bead on him. He needed to remember to keep his wits about him.

"If you press the button on the bottom, you'll be able to open the other apps," Hunter instructed, pointing to the phone. He watched Viola out of the corner of his eye as she rummaged for what he assumed was cloth to wrap his ribs.

"What's the purpose of this device and what's an 'app'?" Beatrice asked, as she clicked the button.

"The main purpose is to communicate with others via

48

the phone function," Hunter answered. "The subsequent purpose is whatever you want it to do. Apps allow you to play music, keep records, read books, and tells the weather."

"Why would you need that when you can peek outside and see what the weather is doing?" Beatrice said with a snort of indignation. Hunter wondered if she realized she snorted a lot or if that was a recent development. "What kind of instrument is it? There's no strings to strum or holes to blow through."

"Not what the weather is doing now but what it's forecasted to do in the next few hours, even days, and not just here but anywhere, even China." Hunter shook his head in disbelief. "And you aren't performing the music, only listening to it. Tap the app with the music note, and you'll see."

Hunter watched as her eyes lit up in amazement as a country song's chorus about just a kiss came singing out of the speaker. Both ladies stared at the phone as Beatrice turned it over and over, looking for where the sound came from. Hunter peeked up at Viola as the chorus repeated. He slowly smiled as a pink blush crept up her neck to her cheeks. She ducked her head, looking down at the bandages in her hands as she approached him.

"Here, let's get you wrapped."

"All right," he whispered as her hand placed a bandage on his chest. He decided he wouldn't mind helping Viola and her sister adjust to life in the real world, especially since it would mean getting to know Viola better. Maybe he could talk Chase into helping out, keep Beatrice busy.

"Beatrice, can you please come help? I can't hold the bandage and wrap," Viola asked over her shoulder.

Looking back at him, she said, "Can you tell us what you remember of today?"

"This morning I left the hotel in Yampa before dawn to get to the trailhead early. I'm going on an extended camping trip," he explained, though he left out the reason for the trip. "I left my Jeep in the parking lot at about 0600, grabbed my gear, then took off up to Devil's Causeway. The plan was to hike into the wilderness from that access point."

Viola leaned forward. "I'm sorry to interrupt, but where is this Yampa and Devil's Causeway? There isn't a hotel anywhere near here. The closest is Denver and that'd take you weeks on foot. Unless you have a horse—"

"Mister, you didn't say anything about a horse being tied up somewhere. If that poor critter dies because of your not having the brains to remember, I'll push you off the mountain again." Beatrice placed her hands on her hips, her face a menacing glare.

"I don't have a horse. I drove a vehicle from Yampa, a town about a forty minute drive to the parking lot for the trailhead to the causeway, that big mountain top that looks like China's Great Wall I fell down this morning," Hunter said, exhausted at how this conversation circled nowhere.

Viola and Beatrice exchanged another puzzled look. Beatrice opened her mouth to say something when Viola spoke over her. "I don't think we are going to understand what Hunter is talking about completely. Why don't we let him finish telling us what happened."

Hunter eyed her with gratitude. "Thanks, Viola. So, I reached the land bridge right at dawn, watched the sun crest the horizon, and then took off down the opposite side at a fast clip. I got maybe three-quarters of the way down when I came around a boulder right into the mountain lion. I was booking it fast and didn't have any time to do anything but dodge the best I could." He peered down at his chest they wrapped tight. He shrugged sheepishly. "Guess I didn't dodge fast enough. When he got me, my momentum took me tumbling straight down through the talus. The last thing I remember is heading headlong into the ravine at the bottom of the mountain."

"Thank God you didn't break your neck," Viola said as she finished tying the bandage. "Do you want to try to eat a little something before you lay down?"

"Yeah." Hunter pushed back so he leaned against the cabin wall. "That'd probably be smart."

As Viola went to the cookstove, Beatrice returned to the phone, enthralled with it. Viola ladled what appeared to be stew from a pot at the back of the stove and brought it to him. It seemed delicious, full of meat in a thick sauce.

"There's no ravine anywhere near where we found you," Viola said, shaking her head as she sat back down in the chair. "There's only the runoff ditch you were laying in."

"No," Hunter said, taking a bite and sighing as the savory flavor hit his tongue. "I definitely fell into a ravine. I remember thinking it would hurt."

"I don't understand." Viola touched her neck, pulling on the collar of her dress.

"What if you travelled through time like that Rip Van Winkle fellow from Washington Irving's story," Beatrice suggested as she gaped at the phone, turning it to face Hunter. "Who are these men?"

"That's my army unit, and what do you mean by Rip Van Winkle?"

"Don't you remember how he fell asleep next to a tree and woke up twenty years later?" Beatrice answered as she flipped through the pictures on his phone. "But instead of you waking up twenty years in the future, maybe you woke up 142 years in the past."

"What? That's crazy!" Hunter replied, the stew he ate soured at the thought of being in the 1800s.

"Bea, why would you say that?" Viola asked, her eyes as wide as saucers.

"Think about it," Beatrice said, looking up from the phone. "We know for a fact that it is 1877. He's convinced, and by the look of his outfit, I'm pretty convinced myself, that he's from the year 2019. So either this is some kind of outlandish dream or he travelled back in time."

"But that's impossible!" Viola whispered, sounding only slightly unconvinced. She stood up fast and began to pace.

Hunter nodded his head in agreement and ran his hands down his face, weariness settling upon him. There had to be an explanation that made sense. If he could get his SAT phone to work, he'd call for help. Or maybe he needed to rest, recharge, then look at the problem with a clear head. Because there was no possibility what Beatrice was suggesting had happened. People didn't just jump through time. This wasn't *Dr. Who*, for Pete's sake.

"Why is it so hard to imagine? God did it to Philip," Beatrice shrugged, looking back at the phone.

"What are you talking about?" Hunter asked in impatience.

"In Acts, chapter eight, Philip is one moment baptizing

the Ethiopian, the next moment in a town over thirty miles away," Beatrice explained. "One minute he's dunking the man in the water, the next, poof, he's gone. It shouldn't be so hard for you to imagine, Viola. It happened to Pa, after all. One minute he walked along the creek here in Colorado, the next he laid in an alley in Pittsburgh. Why couldn't it happen to Hunter?"

"I'm sorry, did you just say your dad time traveled?" Hunter's voice full of doubt he couldn't hide.

"Yes, but Pa didn't travel through time. He just traveled to a different location, like Philip did," Viola pointed out.

That distinction made this whole situation so much easier to believe. Hunter tapped his fingers on his leg in frustration.

Beatrice looked at Hunter with a new excitement in her eyes, an excitement that put dread in his. She had a look of admiration that didn't quite add up.

"I've always read that story in the Bible and thought about Pa's adventure and imagined that God would take me somewhere off this mountain. Somewhere not so isolated from all mankind." She sighed, looking down at the phone. The longing in her voice tugged at his core.

How many times had he wished to get away from it all? To have a life that was simpler, more wholesome. But his responsibilities were too great, those to his country, his unit, his brother. How could he leave knowing the threat that existed, always looking to attack the country he loved? No. He may have wished to get away, to start anew, but his conscience would never allow him to leave.

"Why would God do that? I'm no one special," Hunter argued. His head was spinning so quickly he thought he might pass out again and wouldn't that just be the embarrassing icing on the cake.

"He must have a reason," Beatrice said. "He has a plan for you here. You are special. There must be something about you that makes you uniquely equipped for what He needs you for."

"Beatrice, this is nonsense," Viola said, not sounding at all convinced that it was in fact nonsense and looking washed-out as she sank to the chair.

"It's not nonsense, in fact I find it fascinating," Beatrice said with a confidence that threatened to crumble the thin hold Hunter had on consciousness. "God is the author of time and space. If he can move Pa over thousands of miles in the blink of an eye, what's stopping Him from moving someone back or forward through time? Time and space are all relative to Him."

Hunter's vision began to tunnel and his head throbbed as the room spun. With that completely logical stream of crazy talk, Hunter lost the battle with oblivion.

CHAPTER 5

VIOLA STARED at Hunter as he slumped sideways onto the bed into unconsciousness. She knew how he felt and wished she could just pass out into oblivion too. But there was work needing done.

Turning to Beatrice, Viola shook her head, "How can you be so sure?"

Beatrice turned the telephone around so that Viola could see the image. It was an image of Hunter and a man that was younger than him but very similar, maybe his brother. They were standing next to a shiny red machine with wheels. The younger man smiled broadly, while Hunter's grin seemed more amused.

"This is how I'm sure," Beatrice answered. "There are too many advancements in his gear and things we've never even dreamed of, like this eye phone, for him to be from this time. There is no way this invention wouldn't have spread through all the papers, even if we got it late, someone would've heard and spread the news at the outpost."

"But how is it even possible?" Viola questioned as she started grabbing Hunter's clothes from the pile on the bed, folding them and placing them on the table.

"Why is it so hard to believe that anything is possible with God?" Beatrice countered. "God stopped the sun and moon for Joshua, gave Elijah superhuman speed, brought Lazarus out of the grave after three days, and I've already mentioned Phillip. It makes perfect sense that the Creator of time could bend it to His needs."

Viola picked up the sat phone and turned it over in her hands. It was bigger than the eye phone Beatrice was once again fiddling with, but it still resembled nothing she'd ever read or seen. She stared at the pile of items still laying on the bed and realized Beatrice's crazy suggestion was just about the only thing that made sense. Which opened up a completely new problem. If Hunter was from the future, how could he get back? And what if he couldn't?

"Who do you think he is?" Beatrice asked as she turned the little box to face Viola again. The same man from the first picture with Hunter was there. Though he looked much younger and his hair was different, he appeared to be laughing at some hilarious joke.

"He might be a relative of Hunter's, like his brother," Viola answered. "They look very similar, especially in the image you showed me earlier."

Beatrice whispered so soft Viola almost missed it. "Of course he's from the future, while I'm stuck here."

"Come." Viola reached for more of Hunter's items, ignoring the comment she was sure her sister hadn't meant for her to hear. "Help me clear off the bed and get him comfortable. I don't want him to wake up hurting anymore than he is now."

They placed his items on the table, often stopping to show each other a shiny package here and there. Beatrice found a small square item made of leather. When she opened it, they found paper money printed in the future and a thin hard card that had Hunter's picture on it with his birthdate showing March 22, 1990.

"This is just so hard to believe. I know it happened with Pa, but honestly, I haven't thought much about his story since we were little. Plus traveling to a different location seems much more plausible than traveling through time," Viola said as she put the last of the items on the table.

If she were honest, she hadn't thought much about it since her mother's death when she was fourteen. She couldn't understand why God would go through such amazing lengths to bring them together, only to take her away much too early. She'd been angry with God for a long time after that, until Pa had spoken to her about life being too short to be angry with God. So she had forgiven God, and chosen to remember the joy and love their family had for each other. Viola grabbed Hunter's calves and swung them onto the bed.

"I think it's exciting," Beatrice said. "What does God have planned for him that no one here could do?"

"Help me get him onto his back. I don't want him to remain scrunched over like he is with those broken ribs," Viola said as she grabbed under his shoulders. After they got him laid out with only a few moans of pain from him, they both sat to catch their breath.

"We will have to help him adjust and when he gets

better, search for a way back," Viola said as she stared at his face.

"What if he can't get back?"

"I can't imagine how upsetting this will be for him," Viola said, pointing to the eye phone. "Especially if he has family back home." Viola bit her lip. "What if he has a wife and children?"

Beatrice shook her head. "I don't think he does. There were only images of him, that man I showed you, the military men, and different places. No family images."

Viola shoulders sagged in relief. "Thank God. At least he won't have to worry about a wife or children. We must help him in whatever way we can. Be praying for him, Bea. He will need a lot of prayer."

Viola turned to the table and started methodically packing his supplies into his bag, anything to keep Beatrice from seeing the emotion she might see on Viola's face. Viola knew the joy she felt at the likelihood of him being single shone from her. She attempted to keep her thoughts in check, but maybe God had brought Hunter back for her. Viola scoffed at herself, snorting a laugh at that ridiculous thought. She huffed and shoved the last of the items in the bag. She would do well not to count her chickens before they hatched. She understood too intimately those eggs could easily be crushed.

HUNTER WOKE to the sound of soft breathing rhythmically going in and out as it blew across his hand. He opened his eyes against the headache that fired rapid rounds behind his eyes. The light was dim that shone from an old time oil lamp and glowed softly onto Viola.

She was on her knees with her hands clasped upon the bed as in prayer and her cheek resting upon her hands. Her mouth was slightly open and a stray section of hair blew forward and back with her breath. Hunter lifted his hand and tucked the errant hair behind her ear, taking his time and rubbing the golden strands between his fingers. It was soft, like silk sliding over his fingers, and he couldn't resist sliding them through the strand again, just like he had when he'd grabbed her braid earlier. The breathing stopped and Hunter gazed into eyes that were wide awake.

"Sorry," he whispered. "I didn't mean to wake you."

Viola sat up and brushed the hair from her face. Even in the dim light, Hunter could see an adorable flush climbing up her neck.

"Oh goodness, I didn't mean to fall asleep. How are you feeling?"

"Besides my head trying to explode, my ribs clawing from my chest, my ankle throbbing a two-step, and the lion's mark stinging like crazy, pretty good." Hunter chuckled then breathed in at the reminder he shouldn't do that. "What time is it?"

"It's almost dawn. Do you want to eat something? If not, I can make you some willow bark tea," Viola asked, a look of extreme concern marring her beautiful face.

"Yeah, tea would be helpful," Hunter replied as he attempted to push himself up to sit. "Though Vicodin would be better."

"Please, Hunter, just lay there." Viola placed her hand

upon his shoulder. "I don't want you hurt more than you are."

Hunter laid back down and sighed. "I'm not very good with lying still."

Viola got up and moved to the cookstove. Pulling the kettle off the back, she poured hot water into a pan she had waiting on the table.

"My brother and Pa aren't very good at sticking to bed either," she said with a shake of her head and a smirk. "Pa once busted his leg when his horse got spooked and threw him. Just about drove him crazy staying in bed the four weeks Orlando forced on him. Orlando said it should've been more like eight weeks with the break he had, but Pa would hear nothing of it. Orlando sure had his hands full that time."

"Is Orlando the doctor or your husband?" Hunter asked, a jealous anxiousness prompting the question in response to Viola's smile when talking about Orlando.

"No, he's my older brother," she replied. "Though with all his studying of medical books and Indian healers, he's about as good as anyone could ever hope for by way of a doctor in these parts. Better, if you ask me."

"Why aren't they here now? Your dad and brother? Did they get stuck in the storm?"

Viola grabbed the pan and strained the tea through a cloth into a mug. She spooned a dollop of honey into the concoction and brought it to the bed. She was quiet. Too quiet. A line of concern creased her forehead as she sat down on the edge of the bed and helped Hunter lean forward enough to drink the tea. The stuff was still nasty with a sweetness of honey that did little to help it. After he had drank it all, she sighed and set the cup on the table.

She gave him a small, sad smile, got up, and sat in the chair next to the bed. "My father never returned from his winter trapping, so Orlando took off about six weeks ago to find him at his normal trapping area."

Viola began ringing her hands within her apron again, a habit Hunter recognized as nervousness.

"Does this happen often?" Hunter questioned.

"Never." Viola sighed. "Which is why I'm so worried. I have a bad feeling something terrible happened this winter."

Hunter reached out and placed his hand over hers. "I'm sorry. And now here I am, just another stress to add on."

"Oh no, you aren't a stress," she said, sincerity shining from her face. "Well, maybe a little, but I'm just thankful we were there to find you. Plus, it's nice having a man around again." Viola gslapped her hand over her mouth. Her face turned a fantastic shade of red.

"Even one laid up and useless?" Hunter teased.

"Oh dear Lord, please hold my tongue," Viola whispered in a prayer Hunter was sure she didn't want him to hear. "I apologize for being so forward. That was unseemly of me."

"That was nowhere near unseemly." Hunter shook his head. "You forget, I'm in the Army. I'm surrounded by unseemly. You … you're refreshing."

Hunter watched as a full smile bloomed across her face, brightening her eyes and cheeks. It was as magnificent as he imagined it would be. He inwardly sighed and basked in success. Viola's forehead knit in thought and the expression he'd worked so hard to coax out disappeared. *So much for basking*, he thought.

"Hunter ... " Viola began as if afraid he'd pass out again, which he determined would not happen. "I know this sounds loco, but what if Beatrice is right and God brought you back here, to our time?"

Hunter gaped at her and shook his head. He'd witnessed a lot of crazy things his eleven years in the military, especially after joining Delta Force, but time travel? That was a bit too far-fetched, even for him.

"You are definitely from the future," Viola insisted. "Your things are too far advanced to be anything remotely from now, plus your identification card says you were born in 1990. So, unless this is some kind of elaborate hoax, somehow when you tumbled into the ravine, you tumbled back in time."

"What if you're part of the hoax?" Hunter responded, rushing on when Viola looked to protest. "I've read about it before where children are born in a family or community and aren't told the truth about how life really is. They're kept apart from society, never knowing the real world is out there. Shoot, there was even a great movie on that very idea made about fifteen years ago. With your location here in the middle of the mountains, it wouldn't be hard to sell you the lie."

Viola shook her head, her forehead scrunched in concentration. "But in order for that to be, wouldn't we have to remain here, in the mountains? We may look like we live isolated and stay isolated, but we've traveled before. We've gone multiple times to Denver, and when my grandfather was still alive, we travelled to Chicago, New Orleans, St. Louis, and other cities to visit him. We haven't been sheltered or lied to, Hunter. There's no way entire cities and months of travel could be fabricated all so me and my siblings would believe we lived in a different time."

Hunter's stomach dropped, making him want to vomit. He tried to keep the anxiety building within him at bay. "Say for a second I believe you, how is it even possible? I may be from the future, but even in my time we don't have time machines."

"I don't understand it either." Viola sighed and reached for her Bible on the table. "It does happen though. God sent my pa that way. One minute he was falling into the swollen creek here in Colorado, the next he'd landed in Pittsburg and was able to save my mother from a kidnapping attempt. I seemed to have focused on the romantic part of Pa and Ma's story of how they met, where Beatrice focused on the supernatural. I went back and read the part Beatrice was talking about with Phillip, including some others she brought up after you'd fallen asleep. There's a lot of evidence supporting the fact that it's possible for God to bend time and space."

"Ok, so it's possible, not probable, but possible," Hunter conceded. "Why in the world would He want a nobody who's failed Him so completely that He has closed communication down? No, if He was going to do something this spectacular, He'd choose someone worthy."

"If I remember right, God specializes in working with the nobodies," Viola whispered. "Think about Moses, Joshua, David, Elijah, even the disciples, all nobodies used by God to do great things through the miraculous wonders God did for them to succeed. God hasn't changed in the few thousands of years since then. If He could stop time for Joshua and the Israelites, He could manipulate time to bring you here."

Hunter's brain threatened to explode at any moment. His logical mind kept going through the situation, looking for inconsistencies, searching for the logic in this illogical yet seemingly evident circumstance. His emotions kept vacillating between elation that God would deem him worthy of such a miracle and anger at the possibility this might all be a joke. If this was a reality, his heart gripped with terror that he'd never see his brother again, never live up to God's desire for him, remain stuck in this wilderness for the rest of his life, which according to historical statistics wouldn't be long in the 1800s.

"No," Hunter said, his throat clogged with conflicting emotions. "Hand me my SAT phone so I can get out of here and get back to reality."

Viola grabbed the phone from the top of a pile of his clothes which sat on a crude homemade table. The table's legs wobbled on the split log floor of the small cabin that was far too rustic to be a hunting cabin. Bile rose up his throat as reality was starting to appear to be 1877. He snatched the phone and prayed desperately that it would work.

VIOLA STOOD as Hunter started pushing buttons on his contraption. She'd seen the desperation upon his face as the wide range of emotions had flitted across it. She ached to comfort him, to reach over and just hold him close, which was inappropriate and dangerous. So, to keep herself from doing something idiotic, she decided some distance was necessary.

Viola crossed to the stove, picking up dishes and medical supplies as she passed. She dumped the dishes in the dry sink and placed the medical supplies on their shelf, all the while very aware of the man lying on the bed, muttering in frustration and pushing button after button on his "sat," as he kept calling it. She made herself busy with gathering the ingredients for breakfast, knowing that while Hunter might not be up for eating, her stomach rubbed her backbone after forgetting to eat supper the night before.

"I don't hear the wind." Hunter's voice brought her attention back too him. "Has the storm passed?"

Viola walked to the door and opened it. A few inches of snow covered the ground, but the wind had stopped and the sky was clear.

"Yes," Viola answered. "The storm has passed. We didn't get as much snow as I was thinking we would. If it warms up enough, this will all melt off fast enough."

"Yeah, that's nice," Hunter muttered. "I need to get outside to the open air to make sure there's no interference for the phone."

Before Viola could protest, Hunter was sitting up and attempting to stand. She hurried to his side and eased in under his right arm. He groaned as he attempted to put weight on his ankle.

"Hunter, you shouldn't be out of bed," Viola said.

"Are you going to help me outside or do I need to make it on my own?" Hunter asked, a bit terse.

Viola smirked at Hunter's resemblance to her father and brother when they were sick and helped him across the floor to the door. He stopped at the threshold and stared at the snow that covered the ground, indecision marking his countenance. He glanced at his bare feet, then back to the snow and shrugged.

Before he could take a step, Viola realized the problem and stopped him. "Wait a moment."

She left him leaning upon the doorjamb and went into her father's room. She opened the trunk at the bottom of his bed and dug to the bottom. In triumph, she pulled the old pair of moccasins her father had put there after she'd made him a new pair last year for his birthday. She closed the lid and rushed to the front room where Hunter still stood in the doorway, looking into the sky.

"I have my pa's old moccasins here," she said as she knelt before him and slipped them onto his feet. "They're worn and falling apart, but they'll work to get you out to the yard and back without your feet getting too cold."

Hunter peeked down at his feet and then over to her. His voice was tight and gruff as he said, "Thank you."

"You're welcome," Viola said. "Will the fencing by the corral work? It's away from the buildings but will give you something to lean on."

"Yeah, that will work," Hunter took a deep breath as if to prepare himself for the short walk.

"All right, let's go," Viola said, taking more and more of his weight as they approached the fence.

By the time they made it to the fence, Hunter was panting and sweat dripped from his forehead. His face appeared etched in pain and had drained white as clouds. He leaned upon the fence and collected his breath.

"That was worse than I expected." Hunter sighed.

"I told you it was too soon," Viola softly scolded.

"Well, at least I didn't pass out again." Hunter joked, then sobered as he pulled the phone out of his waistband.

Hunter stared at the phone for a few seconds then regarded her, apology written clear on his face. "This is going to sound horribly rude after everything you've done for me, but do you think I can just have a few minutes alone. My brain is so scrambled right now, and you're a distraction that scrambles it more, a great distraction. A wonderful distraction ... I mean, geesh, I'm really screwing this up."

"If you think you'll be okay here, I'll just go get breakfast started," Viola said as she backed away, his stumbling words making her heart skip and beat erratically.

When he nodded sheepishly, Viola made a quick escape back to the cabin. She closed the door and leaned against it. Tears pricked her eyes. What was Hunter going to think when his sat phone didn't work?

She bowed her head as she wiped her eyes. "Father God, please help him. Give a peace that surpasses all knowledge. Help him accept the fact that You've brought him here."

"Viola?" Beatrice asked from the doorway to their room, causing Viola to squeak in surprise. "Where is he?"

"He's outside trying to use that phone thing of his," Viola answered as she crossed the cabin to start breakfast.

She peeled and chopped a potato to fry. They were getting to the bottom of their supply, so Viola only prepared one, knowing Hunter might not eat. After it was sizzling in the pan, she mixed up a batch of pancakes. The entire time her hands were busy, her mind raced with wondering how Hunter was doing. Should she go help him? Should she leave him alone? Had he fainted again? If he did, would they be able to get him into the house or would he be ok with a blanket thrown over him? Questions raced over each other like the rabbits that played in the fields. She looked back towards the table and sighed in frustration.

"Would you put that silly thing away and help?" Viola admonished Beatrice, who was once again messing with the eye phone. "I need more eggs, and the animals need checked on."

Beatrice grimaced and put it down. "You're right. This device is just so interesting, I can't seem to help it. I'm sorry Vi. I'll get out to the barn, check the animals and be right back to help."

By the time Viola had the potatoes finished cooking and a stack of pancakes piling up, Beatrice had returned with a basket of eggs. She placed the basket on the counter, shaking her head.

"What?" Viola asked. "What's wrong? Is Hunter all right?"

"He's still upright, but 'all right' is relative." Beatrice snorted. "He's just standing out there staring up at the sky as if he's expecting something to happen."

"Can you finish up here and I'll go check on him?" Viola asked, as hundreds of questions romping through her head began running so fast she could hardly think.

Why hadn't she checked on him earlier? She flew to the door, forgetting to take off her splattered apron. She headed outside and sent up a silent prayer for help.

CHAPTER 6

"GOD, PLEASE HELP ME," Hunter prayed, knowing there wouldn't be an answer, but desiring one anyway. As he stood there, staring into the sky with his heart beating so hard he might choke, a calm settled over him. Its familiarity surprised and comforted him, as a tear trekked down his cheek.

"Thank you," he whispered, knowing that, though he was completely out of his element and beyond confused, God was here with him and had revealed Himself to him again.

Hunter stared up at the clear blue sky. The trepidation was still there, but a resignation that felt right was there as well. He would complete this mission God had put him on and get back home. He heard soft footsteps coming towards him, and he quickly wiped his eyes of all evidence.

"Hunter?" Viola's sweet voice spoke with such compassion and concern he wondered if she had an endless supply of it. "Are you okay?"

She came up beside where he stood with his back to the corral fence. Her hands were wringing her apron into knots. Her presence, even with her nervousness, brought him another comfort he couldn't help but thank God for. He grabbed her hand and pulled her to turn and stand beside him against the fence.

He knew he should let her hand go, but he needed a point of contact in this insane circumstance. So instead, he threaded his fingers through hers and held tight. A crazy sense of home rushed through his heart as he gazed down into her face. Why she would elicit such feelings confused him just as much as this whole time travel thing, though in a more pleasant way.

"Are you all right?" she whispered again.

"There are no jet streams," he answered as he cleared his throat and observed the sky.

"What?" Viola asked, looking to the sky with a look of confusion.

"Jet streams," Hunter answered. "I've been out here for over thirty minutes and haven't seen a single jet stream. My phone doesn't work, which makes sense, but it was the lack of jet streams that convinced me. By now there should have been at least one, if not more, marking the sky. But there's nothing. It's clear."

"I don't understand."

"In my time, 2019, we have this mode of transportation called airplanes," Hunter answered, breathing out slowly in an attempt to stay in control. "They are large metal vehicles with wings that carry passengers all over the world through the sky."

Viola gasped and tightened her grip on his hand. "No. It's not possible."

"I might have a picture in my phone I can show you," Hunter replied. "Anyway, the planes fly so high most of the time you can't even see them, but they leave a trail, a line through the sky with their exhaust, called a jet stream. There should be some here in the sky. Denver is a hub and has a major international airport with flights coming and going twenty-four-seven, yet the sky is completely clear. In fact, it's clearer than I've ever seen it, probably because of the lack of pollution."

Viola stood staring into the sky, shaking her head. She inched closer as she brought her other hand over to hold on to his arm. She looked horrified and pale.

"I don't understand most of what you just said, but people can't fly," she whispered. "That's impossible."

"It's very possible," Hunter said, shifting as the pain of standing there became unbearable. "In fact, people have flown all the way into space and landed on the moon."

"No!" She gasped. Her slight hands were shaking. He realized this whole time travel stuff or whatever had happened to him would disconcert Viola and Beatrice too, though Beatrice seemed to take it better than any of them.

"I think I need to go lay down," Hunter said as he shifted on the fence. Viola might need to sit down as well, maybe even more than he needed to. "I'm not sure how much longer I can stand here."

"Oh goodness, yes, I'm sorry." Viola rushed quickly through her words, letting go of his hand and shifting under his arm. "We made breakfast if you are up to eating something."

Hunter grunted an agreement and then took the first of many agonizing steps back to the cabin. By the time they made it to the door, he had sweat dripping down his face and back and his breath was coming out in sharp knifing gusts. He knew if the walk took much longer he'd probably pass out again, so he tried to hurry, though each step got slower and heavier.

"Beatrice, come help." Viola spoke out in obvious strain as they came into the cabin that smelled of pancakes and eggs.

He realized the little sprite was probably taking just about as much of his weight as she could, but, try as he might, he didn't have the strength to help her. Beatrice came up to his other side and the two ladies practically carried him to the bed. They definitely made women strong in 1877, or whatever year this was. They even attempted to get him on the bed gently, though he was sure with his weight they wanted to just drop him.

He laid back upon the pillow, the dark edges of sleep pulling him under. "I think I'll just rest for a bit."

As the strong fingers of unconsciousness tugged him into darkness, Hunter had another moment of panic. How would Chase take Hunter's disappearance? Would it throw Chase over the edge of no return he'd been tittering on since their parents' deaths? *Lord, please, help him.*

"SURE GLAD HE made it to the bed." Beatrice chuckled. "Otherwise we would've had to keep him where he landed."

Viola nodded as she sucked air into her lungs to gain her breath. Though, to be honest, she didn't know if it was the walk to the cabin or Hunter's realization and explanation that had her out of breath.

"Breakfast is done," Beatrice said, going to the stove and bringing two platters to set on table.

"Good." Viola huffed as she straightened from where she'd bent over. "We'll need to eat quickly so I can help you outside before he wakes up again."

They sat down and served up. Beatrice offered a quick prayer and ate. Viola looked across the table at Beatrice and sighed.

"It's true," she said as Beatrice peeked up from her plate. "He's from the future."

"So his sat phone thing didn't work, and he's realized he's here instead of there?" Beatrice asked.

"No, he said it was the absence of what they call jet streams in the air that made him realize." Talking about people flying in the air made Viola's heart rate hitch higher again. The idea of being encased in metal traveling through the air terrified her.

"What's that?" Beatrice asked in fascination.

"It's these lines in the sky made by some kind of machine with wings which flies people around the world," Viola answered, her lack of belief evident even to her own ears.

"No! That's impossible." Beatrice gasped in amazement, as opposed to Viola's own gasp of horror earlier. She realized her sister was taking the idea of time travel much better than Viola was. A little too much better, if you asked her.

"Apparently, they can fly all the way into space and have landed on the moon." Viola shuddered at the thought.

"That's amazing." Beatrice sighed and sat back in her chair. "Imagine, if they can land on the moon, what other incredible things are possible in his time? I can't wait to hear him tell us all about it."

"Bea, you'll need to pay attention and observe his reactions," Viola cautioned. "He's gonna be overwhelmed and hurting by being here, at least that's how I would feel. It might be hard for him to talk about his time, especially if we can't figure out how to get him back."

Beatrice studied Hunter on the bed. "He might also need to talk about his time, his people, in order to adjust."

"Just be careful. I don't want you so enamored with the future that you become discontented with the present."

Beatrice exhaled as she got up from the table and took her plate to the washstand. She walked away, and Viola heard a whisper. "I can't get any more discontented than I already am."

Viola began to answer, but Beatrice turned with a forced smile. "You're right. I'll be careful, and I'll watch him for cues I'm pushing too hard. I'm going to go let the animals out and get busy on smoking the meat."

She left the cabin before Viola could even form a response. She bowed her head and prayed for Beatrice, for Hunter and this entire situation that threatened to drown her in anxiety.

LINC SWEENEY WATCHED NERVOUSLY as his brother Robert knelt next to the unconscious, bloody lump that earlier that day was a man of legends, a mighty mountain man birthed from the mountains themselves. Robert's shoulders slumped. Linc cursed violently and kicked the pot that sat on the log they'd set up as a makeshift table, sending it flying into the forest.

"You killed him." The accusation thick in Robert's voice and disgust clear in his eyes where he turned, still kneeling on the ground.

"The stupid idiot wouldn't give," Linc yelled in rage and frustration. "How was I supposed to know he was such a weakling?"

Robert shook his head in disbelief before he stood and went to the horses.

"Wh-wh-what are we going to do now?" his other brother, William, stuttered in fright from the other side of camp. The spineless sound brought the rage back up, making Linc's fists to squeeze tight.

"We'll drop him in the forest and let the mountain lions drag him off." Linc shrugged, getting a rise out of the way his sissy brother's face turned green. "Then we move onto the next plan. There's another way to get what's ours than through this stupid old man."

He smiled in wicked delight as he turned to pack his saddlebags. His next plan was much more desirable than following the dead man ever was.

AFTER CLEANING THE BREAKFAST DISHES, picking up the house, and helping Beatrice with what outside chores she wanted help with, Viola decided that mending some of her brother's clothes he'd left behind would not only keep her busy so she didn't fret and hover over Hunter while he slept. She'd noticed the night before while folding and putting Hunter's things back into his pack that he wasn't at all prepared with clothing appropriate for the harsh Colorado mountains. All he had was a few shirts, an extra pair of pants with more pockets than one could ever need, some admittedly nice wool socks, and a thin jacket that was slick and puffy with the words North Face on the front. She had no clue how something so silky and cool kept one warm.

Viola paused her needle in the air as a thought came to her that perhaps in the future they had a manufacturing that created warmth in material that seemed contrary to the job. She shrugged at the possibility, knowing that in the here and now, there was no such thing. He'd need this buckskin shirt much more than some flimsy jacket. For Pete's sake, one snag on a branch and the thing would rip wide open. She snorted at the realization that maybe not all things were better in his time. In fact, if he'd been wearing buckskin, there was a good possibility that mountain lion wouldn't have even gotten through the material in the first place. She nodded in pride at her deduction that she still found satisfaction in the things of the present.

She realized with Beatrice's fascination of the eye phone and everything about the future that she herself would need to follow her own advice about becoming discontent. Though the experience was still so frightening, she had to admit when she allowed her thoughts to linger on flying around the world in some contraption in the sky, the fear faded to the background of wonder. Then she'd think of all the amazing things she'd read about in her books: the wall in China, Venice, Egyptian pyramids, the White House, Ireland … so many things she'd read about but never dreamed she'd be able to see in person. If one could fly around the world, those things would be available to experience. Though she supposed if it cost anything like train and stagecoach tickets' prices, one probably couldn't afford to travel by the flying machine often.

Which brought her right back to the reality of now, in 1877 where she had work to do. She finished mending the seam in the shirt with a flourish of determination and grabbed the next item in the basket. As she pulled the buckskin pants out and held them up, she wondered if she'd have to adjust them any. Hunter seemed taller than Orlando, though Hunter's waist tapering from his muscled chest seemed much trimmer than Orlando's.

Hunter moaned and mumbled from the bed, and Viola wondered if she should go check him. She'd wanted to look at his wound earlier but decided it'd be better to let him sleep. Now she began to doubt her decision.

Hunter thrashed his head and groaned. Viola sent the mending flying into the basket and raced to his side. His face was flushed and sweaty, the sheet sticking to his skin. Viola felt his cheek and chest. His forehead burned her fingers where they laid.

Viola sat in the chair now stationed by the bed, uncovered the lion wound, and sucked in a sharp breath. The skin had turned bright red and angry with pus. Tears stung her eyes at her idiocy for not checking this wound sooner. Animal claws were known to be filthy, lions more so than others, and she had needed to keep a close eye on it.

"I'm so sorry." She choked out as she placed her hand upon his cheek.

The door opened, and Beatrice walked in. Viola sprang from the chair and rushed for the medicine box. On the way she said, "He has a raging fever. Run to the creek for fresh, cold water."

Beatrice grabbed the bucket and hurried out the door. Viola brought the box to the table and started rifling through it, setting things aside and trying to remember all that Orlando had told her. Oh, why couldn't he be here? He'd know what to do.

Viola's hands shook so violently as she read the labels on the bottles that the words blurred, making it difficult to read. She took a deep breath and closed her eyes and prayed. The shaking stopped in her hands and her mind seemed clearer than just a second before. *Thank You.* She grabbed the yarrow, sage, and plantain herbs stored in jars, added the plantain salve she'd found in a tin, and put the rest back in the chest. Beatrice ran back in with a fresh bucket of water.

"Thank you," Viola said, "Please grab a cloth and bathe his forehead while I work on a poultice for his wound."

Beatrice nodded her agreement. As Beatrice bathed his forehead and whispered prayers of healing, Viola brought a bowl of steaming water over to cleanse the wound again. She leaned close and sniffed, relieved that while it was red and leaking pus, it didn't smell pungent.

After cleaning the wound with hot water, Viola mixed the dried herbs she'd gathered in a bowl. She took a spoonful and chewed it in her mouth like she remembered Orlando doing before and placed it on the wound. She continued to do that until the mixture covered the wound. She then checked his other scratches and scrapes to make sure none of them looked infected. While they didn't show signs of infection, she smeared plantain salve on them just to be safe.

"I'm going to make a comfrey poultice for his ankle and re-wrap it," Viola stated with a sigh. "I should've checked him sooner."

"Well, considering all the excitement we've had in the last twenty-four hours, I'm not surprised this slipped past you," Beatrice replied. "Don't worry about it too much. He probably would've gotten infected anyway, with lion's claws being so nasty and all. Besides, I doubt God would bring him all the way here then kill him off before he could be of any use."

Viola mouth gaped in shock at her sister's lack of care. She sputtered a reprimand. "Well... I... I... don't..."

"Sister, calm down," Beatrice said as she placed one hand on Viola's lap and used the other to push the strand of hair forever in Viola's face behind her ear. It was a move their mother had done so often in comfort that the resemblance caught tears in her throat.

"I understand the dangers of infection and fever," Beatrice continued softly. "But I also know deep in my heart that God brought this man here for a purpose beyond this sickbed. Otherwise, what would be the point of that amazing miracle? Yes, we should do everything we can to help his healing, but God will heal him because Hunter hasn't fulfilled his purpose here yet."

"And what's that purpose?" Viola asked in a hushed voice of reverence at her little sister's proclamation.

"How am I supposed to know that?" she said with a shake of her head and a snort. "I'm not a prophet!"

Viola chuckled. "Okay, okay. But I guess you make sense."

"Of course I do," Beatrice said cheekily. "Why don't you work on his ankle, and I'll make a batch of cornbread?"

Viola turned back to Hunter and placed a cold cloth on his forehead. She then turned back to the medicine chest and pulled out the dried comfrey. She chewed and placed the wet herb into a cloth. When she'd gotten a good amount into it, she folded the cotton into a pack and then placed it onto his ankle. She wrapped a long strip of cloth around his ankle and the pack to hold the pack against the skin and his ankle tight.

With that done, she went back to the head of the bed and began to bathe his forehead, cheeks, and what remained unwrapped on his chest and arms with cold water. As the minutes stretched into hours, she prayed for wisdom, healing, and peace.

CHAPTER 7

VIOLA WOKE with a start as her head slipped off her hand. Jerking her head up, she glanced around in confusion. What had woken her up?

Hunter moaned and thrashed on the bed, the sheets a tangled mess around his legs. How she hadn't woken up through what appeared to have been some intense thrashing was a testament to her exhaustion. After hours of bathing his body with cold water, she thought his fever had gone down some, and he finally slept peacefully. So, since she could barely keep her eyes opened, she'd moved to the only comfortable chair in the small cabin, her mother's rocker, to take a quick nap.

Viola rushed to the bed and touched his forehead. It burned hot again. He thrashed his arms and mumbled incoherently. Viola sat in the chair beside him and washed his skin with cold water again.

"No, no hope." Hunter groaned as he moved his legs within the sheets.

Viola placed the cloth in the bucket and moved to

unwrap the sheets from the tangled mess they'd become. All the while, he groaned and moved as if attempting to run.

"Hope, no hope," he voiced in such anguish that Viola's tears almost fell.

"Shhh, it's okay," she said as she wiped the cloth across his forehead. "There's always hope. Our hope comes from the Lord."

"No hope!" Hunter yelled, swinging his arms and hitting Viola, knocking her to the floor.

She got up and hugged his arms and whispered into his ear, "Shhh, Hunter. It's okay. You're okay. Dear Lord, help him calm. Give him peace in his heart and hope."

"Hope, hope." Hunter started crying. "Hope, I'm so sorry."

As Viola realized that Hope was a person, her heart broke in two at his anguish. Who was she? His wife? What happened to her? Viola whispered comfort into his ear, wiped his tears and sweat from his face and just held him. She knew it was improper, but he needed comfort, what she'd want if the situation was reversed. So she whispered and held him until the tears and the groans stopped.

Then she held him, placed her head in the fold of his neck, and silently cried. Cried for this man whose cries were heartbreaking. Cried for this strange and unnerving situation they found themselves in. Cried for her father and brother, who remained away too long. She didn't know how long she'd laid there and bawled like a newborn calf.

~

HUNTER WOKE, his muscles aching and his body hot with fever. But that wasn't what woke him. The weight of Viola's face curled into his shoulder, her body shaking in silent sobs brought his mind from the foggy depths of fever he'd been stuck in. His brain was still muddled, but Viola's anguish tore at him.

"Shh, it's going to be alright," Hunter whispered, lifting his arm that seemed to weigh a hundred pounds and rubbed her back.

Viola sat up with a gasp. Hunter looked into the emerald eyes bright with tears and knew in that instant he'd do anything to make her happy. Though he was weak with fever, in a time he knew nothing about, and a situation way beyond whatever training the Army had given him, he would keep her safe and fill her life with joy. That was his new mission, as crazy and illogical as it sounded. He knew deep within his soul that God had assigned it and when he completed this mission successfully, it'd restore the past and give hope to the future.

"Don't worry," he whispered. He ran his hand over her braid that hung over her shoulder. "I'm not going to die."

"I know, it's just ..." She took a shuddering breath and continued between sobs. "You are burning up. You started thrashing and moaning. You were yelling for Hope and started crying. I thought my heart was ripping out of my chest over your anguish. There's also the fact that my father and brother still aren't home, which more than likely means that one or both of them are gravely injured or dead. And you come falling here from the future and now you're sick with fever, which is all my fault. And ... and it's too much."

"It's going to be okay," he said as he pulled her to him.

She came easily, which was good since what little strength he had, he'd used in keeping her from jumping away when he first woke up.

He whispered softly and stroked her back as she cried into his neck, soaking him and his pillow. He had no sisters and spent most of his time in the service around a bunch of tough men. He wasn't sure if this was normal behavior, but if she was busy crying, she wouldn't notice that he was holding her.

He focused on what he could decipher of her blubbering speech. He had been out of his mind with fever. He'd seen it before in a few injured soldiers during missions where extraction wasn't immediate and fever had set in. He wasn't sure, but he figured servicemen who'd seen action reacted more intensely during fever. Perhaps it was PTSD or something, but he hoped he hadn't hurt her in his thrashing. She'd said he'd called out for Hope and had cried. How embarrassing. He was an elite member of The Unit, not some weakling. Hopefully she'd just forget about that part.

Her crying slowed, and he knew the pleasure of holding her was over. She took a deep breath and sat up. She wiped her face on her apron and then stared at her hands, twisting in her apron.

"Sorry," she whispered. "That was highly unseemly of me."

"No worries." He shrugged and tried to sound nonchalant. "You needed a shoulder to cry on. I have one convenient for use. It's about the only thing I can do in this state."

Her ears turned red as touched his forehead with the

back of her hand. "You don't look so flushed, and your fever isn't as hot, praise God. How do you feel?"

"Better," he answered, shaking his head. "Honestly though, I still feel horrible. The chills have disappeared, but my ribs are killing me. I think all that thrashing might've hurt them more. I got a headache the size of Alaska, and my throat's parched."

"Oh dear." She jumped up and brought over a cup of water. "Let's get you a drink."

She sat on the bed and eased an arm behind his shoulders. Her small delicate hands lifted the drink to his mouth. The cool sweetness eased down his throat until he drained the entire cup.

"I have some willow bark tea ready on the stove," she said as she laid him back down. "It'll help with the pain and the fever."

He grimaced in anticipation of the nasty drink. He knew he had ibuprofen in his pack, but also knew without antibiotics, his body needed the fever to fight the infection. He supposed drinking nasty concoctions were a necessary evil of this time, and he should belly up and stop complaining. Besides, he should save the pills for the next few weeks of recovery that he knew would be painful.

She came back to the bed and repeated helping him drink. Once he laid down, she began to wipe off some green junk that had caked onto his chest where the lion had got him. The rough texture of the cloth against the tender skin caused Hunter's fists to bunch into the bedding to keep from embarrassing himself again.

"I need to change the poultice," she said in explanation.

"Okay, do whatever you need to do. I'm going to lay

here and rest." He hoped his voice sounded more nonchalant than agonized.

He watched her as she combined three dried herbs into a bowl. In a mixture of fascination and disgust, he observed as she spooned it into her mouth, chewed, then spit it onto her fingers. As she came towards him as if to put it on him, he held up his hand.

"Whoa, there," he said, his eyes warily shifting from the gunk on her fingers to her face. "What do you think you're doing?"

Her forehead scrunched in confusion as she glanced from her fingers to his face to his wound. "I'm putting on a poultice. It will help draw out the infection that's set in from the claws."

"I know that's what you're doing. What I don't understand is why you are chewing it up like a mama bird and spitting it out. That's gross! Why not just use water?" Hunter asked.

"It doesn't work as well when you do it that way. Orlando said that when you chew up the herbs, it works much better than with water alone. No one knows why, but it does."

She moved to place it on the wound, and he blocked her again.

"In my time we know that the mouth has germs that cause infection. There are better ways to treat this," he said.

"Well, you aren't in your time." She huffed in frustration. "And there may be other, better ways to treat your wound here now, but you managed to fall in the middle of the mountains where we treat with medicine the natives have used successfully for hundreds of years. Now stop being a weak-bellied city dandy and let me treat this the only way available!"

Hunter laid his head back in exhaustion and replied, "Fine. By all means, use your spit medicine."

Viola placed the poultice on Hunter's wound, not looking him in the face. Keeping her head down, she turned back to the table for more herbs, but not before he saw her swipe her hand across her eyes. He'd made her cry, and all because he was acting like a … what did she call him? A weak-bellied city dandy. She'd been wonderful this entire time, taking care of him, praying for him. Shoot, even with the whole time-travel thing and him crying, she hadn't freaked out like a lot of women he knew. He had to upset her, all over a little spit.

If she was kissing him, he wouldn't have a problem with her spit. Wouldn't have a problem at all. In fact, it would be downright pleasant. He'd take her braid out and run her hair through his fingers, kissing her deeply to show how much he cared for her, grown to love her.

Hunter shook his head. This fever was making him loopy. He'd just met her, for Pete's sake. He shouldn't even be considering kissing her, let alone love. If he kept it up, he'd be writing sonnets or sappy romance novels.

Get it together, commander, he chided himself.

He closed his eyes, took a deep breath, and said, "It could be the enzymes in the saliva that helps break down the herbs to make them work better."

Viola peeked up at him in wariness. "What?"

"They've discovered that saliva has different components in it that help us digest food." Hunter gestured toward the poultice. "Maybe those components break-down the herb in a way that helps it do the job."

"Maybe." Viola shrugged, still not looking at him.

"Listen, Viola …" Hunter sighed. "I'm sorry I acted like a city dandy. I mean, the things I've had to do and places I've been, a little spit should've never affected me. This fever and pain and crazy circumstance has me a little freaked out and out of sorts. I should know better than to question your expertise in this situation. I was trained better, and I apologize."

Viola scrutinized his face for a long time. Her shoulders relaxed, and she exhaled. "This situation is crazy. I'll give you that. You've had such amazing strength through all of this. I know if I was in your place I'd be more than a little—how did you put it?—freaked out?" Hunter nodded and the tightness in his chest loosening as she continued. "I forgive you, and I pray that you forgive me too for my harshness and unkind attitude."

"You have nothing to apologize for," Hunter answered. "I was out of line. Sometimes us grunts need a little yelling at to get us to listen. I blame it on basic, since we're conditioned with shouting."

Viola looked confused. Confused and adorable. Hunter shook his head.

"Never mind," he said as he closed his eyes. "I believe I'll have a lot of time to explain while I recover. For now, I'm beat. Thank you, Viola, for taking care of me."

"You're welcome, Hunter," Viola whispered softly.

With her sweet voice lingering in his ears, he drifted off to sleep.

LINC SWEENEY SAT atop his mangy horse and examined

the lush green meadow below that held his dreams. Well, if he was being honest with himself, his dreams were held in the elusive gold mine owned by the uptight family who lived in the solid cabin nestled in the meadow below. He was positive that cabin wouldn't let the harsh Rocky Mountain wind sweep through in the winter like the shack him and his brothers built did. Linc shivered in remembrance.

He had spent months, no years, plotting and planning on how to figure out the location of the Thomas's mine. He knew they owned one. Linc had figured out that little doozy right quick, being the intelligent man he is. The old man, Joseph, and his son, Orlando, used gold too often at the trading post and bought too many supplies and mail-order goods on trapping alone, especially now that trapping in the area had pretty near played out. After he and his brothers had spent a miserable first winter and bust of a summer mining, Linc had started trying to figure out how to get his hands on the Thomas' gold.

Linc and his brothers scouted around everywhere they knew the Thomas men frequented. They trailed and spied on them more hours than he'd care to dwell on. When his youngest brother William whined about it being easier and more profitable to trap or go find another place to mine, Linc quickly beat that stupid logic out of him. It was too bad their pa had gotten himself shot when William was so young, otherwise he wouldn't be such weakling. Linc had tried to do right by his brother, but the heavy hand of a brother just didn't produce the same caliber of citizen as the heavy hand of a father. So when William got to bellyaching, Linc would have to help him remember that the Sweeneys don't whine.

SARA BLACKARD

Sure if they thought with their stomachs, him and his brothers could spend their time hunting up some pelts or go mine down Silverton way, but that wasn't thinking long term. He knew his middle brother Robert doubted, but acknowledged in his quiet way that Linc was right. Which was good since there was no way he could beat sense into the Goliath.

Linc wasn't dumb, though, and saw the determination wavering in Robert's resolution, so Linc upped the ante. This last winter when Joseph left the cabin for his trapping grounds, the Sweeneys followed, not to spy, but to stalk. They'd waited for the opportune time and caught Joseph unawares, which proved more difficult than Linc anticipated since the geezer was a true mountain man. Linc rubbed his side where Joseph's knife had gone before they overpowered him. Three against one and the old coot still injured all three of them.

Linc's plan hadn't worked out like he expected, though. Instead of giving in and telling them where the mine was, the idiot allowed Linc to beat and torture him until he succumbed to his injuries. If Linc was honest with himself, and he always was, he may have gotten a little out of control when the old man hadn't given in.

Linc loved the energy and power that flowed through him when he let his rage go. It fed him, exhilarated him and frightened him enough that he kept it reined in most times. He knew the rage came straight from the devil, but he figured that him and the devil were on closer terms than him and God, so if he accepted the gift offered, what was it between friends?

But that gift held consequences. When he killed Joseph Thomas, his plans changed. Following Orlando proved

90

pointless. That man was even more savvy than his pa, which was why Linc now stared down upon a sturdy cabin in a lush green meadow.

Linc's dreams may be in the gold mine, but his fantasies, the ones that kept him up at night in rapturous agony, were of Viola Thomas, the beautiful blonde vixen born to be his wife. He wiped his mouth in anticipation of the passion he imagined having with her. All those nights in the woods and filthy shack he spent fantasizing about her would become a reality by the end of the day. Linc praised the powers that be that Colorado didn't require a couple to stand before a preacher to get married. A common law marriage was perfect for him, better than perfect since it meant they could start their wedded bliss tonight without having to travel days to find a preacher.

Once Linc told Viola the unfortunate news of her father and brother dying, she'd fall into his arms in grief. Though truthfully, Orlando wasn't dead ... yet. Sure, she ignored his advances in the past. Linc was convinced her pa had talked bad about him, and Viola, being a dutiful female, wouldn't defy her father. Now with her pa dead and out of the way, his proposal of marriage would be both logical and heroic, to his way of thinking. His brothers could fight over the other sister. Shoot, they could share her, for all he cared.

Linc smiled in glee and turned to his brothers. "Come on boys, our future awaits."

In a few short moments, Viola would be his. The mine would be his. All the torment and agony of the last two years would be over, and his plans fulfilled.

CHAPTER 8

VIOLA CHOPPED herbs to go into the hearty stew she was making. Hunter was still sleeping, his fever no longer so high it required constant attention, which gave her time to make a good meal and get to the chores she'd missed yesterday. Her first focus of the morning was the meal. Hunter would be hungry when he woke up, and she wanted to be ready.

Viola paused in her chopping, remembering the sweet murmurings Hunter had said as she'd bawled like a newborn lamb on his shoulder. She placed her hands on her cheeks as they heated in both embarrassment and blush. How mortifying that this strong man who, when conscious, fought against his intense pain with barely a grunt, and there she was, tears running from her eyes like a snowmelt stream, fast and erratic.

Hunter must think her some soft-witted, nonsense girl who couldn't handle a thing. Well, she'd just have to prove that she wasn't. For goodness' sake, she'd only cried a handful of times since turning fourteen, at the death of her mother and her two baby siblings being born. She could only explain her momentary lapse in sensibility at being overwhelmed. They had copious amounts of situations they were dealing with at the moment, not including Hunter's surprise visit. Now that she'd purged herself of more tears than necessary, she could continue in a more fitting manner.

Though, if she were truthful, the tears generated a pleasant side effect. She never imagined it would feel so good being held and comforted by a man. Sure, Pa would give out hugs and affection to his daughters in abundance, and Orlando was gentle and compassionate when one of them became upset. Yet Viola felt cherished and protected when Hunter held her close, whispering in her ear and stroking her hair, which was complete hogwash since she'd barely met the man, and he'd been mostly unconscious during their time together. Still, she'd relished the sentiment, God forgive her, and couldn't help imagining what it would be like being cherished by this man from the future.

A hard knock on the door brought her out of her ridiculous musings. Instantaneous awareness focused her thoughts. For shame, her distraction had cost her diligence, allowing someone to walk right up to the door without her even noticing. Of course, it could also be Trapper Dan. He hadn't come through yet for his spring visit. Viola stilled her breathing and thoughts and listened. Three horses snorted outside and separate feet shuffled at the door. Definitely not Trapper Dan. She grabbed the shotgun from its rack, and keeping the gun hidden, she cracked the door and peered out.

An involuntary shiver of dread raced up her body as

she stared into Linc Sweeney's cold, calculating eyes. His two brothers were standing a bit to the side of Linc looking half starved and rugged, as if the mountain had taken more than it's due out of them. She turned her attention back to Linc and suppressed the desire to slam the door in his gleaming face.

"Hello Linc, Robert, William," she said as she nodded to each, hoping to warn her sister, who Viola had heard coming in from the bedroom.

"Good morning, my sweet Viola," Linc crooned, his voice slithering down her back like a snake.

Viola swallowed the breakfast that rose involuntary to her throat. While his brothers seemed to be decent, Linc had always rubbed her wrong, always made her skin twitch as if something slimy crawled up it. Why was he here in the first place? How would she ever convince Linc to leave without being downright rude?

"WE COME BEARING NEWS. Can we come in?" the strange voice asked, reminding Hunter of a jackal, high and a bit unbalanced.

Hunter had pushed himself into a sitting position after the hard knock had jarred him awake. Now, after hearing that slimy voice call Viola his sweet and expressing his wish to come in, Hunter's consciousness came to complete awareness. Something wasn't right. He could tell by the tension in Viola's shoulders the instant she'd opened the door and the shiver he'd seen course through her body. Beatrice confirmed his suspicions when she came rushing in silently with her gun drawn and whispered, "Sweeneys!"

He motioned her over, "Quick! Help me get a shirt on."

She nodded and grabbed a buckskin shirt from a pile stacked on the table. Roughly, with none of the finesse of her sister, she yanked the shirt over his head. He swallowed the shout of pain that threatened to escape and shook his head to push back the dark tunnel that appeared.

"Tell me the situation, fast?" he said through gritted teeth.

She nodded and leaned close to whisper. "Three brothers, mean as sin and as desperate as an old bear with no teeth. The oldest, Linc is always leering at Viola like she's the last piece of Christmas pie."

"Can you get to the barn without being seen or heard?" Hunter asked as he took his sidearm from his concealed holster in his pants and checked the load.

As Beatrice shook her head, he fired off another question. "The side of the house?"

"Yeah," she whispered.

"Good," Hunter answered. "Go and wait on the side of the house. Don't show yourself until I signal you to. And take another gun if possible."

With a quick nod of her head, Beatrice disappeared through the bedroom. He offered up a silent prayer. *Lord, I know I screwed up before. Please be with us now and protect us. I'm weak and not up to this right now, but You say, when I'm weak, You are strong. I guess I'm relying on that promise, Lord.*

"Can we come in?" The man asked a second time, his voice holding a thread of annoyance.

As Hunter hobbled towards the door, Viola glanced back while she answered the snake's question. Surprise overrode the fear coming from her eyes when she saw Hunter coming. He picked up the pace.

"Linc, I'm sorry. I just can't let you in right now," Viola said, turning her response to the intruders. "I could pack up a sack of food for you, if you'll wait outside."

"I don't want a sack of food." The man spat with barely contained anger. "I told you, we have news, and I intend to share it. So put to practice your good Christian hospitality, and let us in."

Hunter reached Viola and eased the shotgun out of her hand. She shook her head, but Hunter chose to believe she directed it at the jackal at the door instead of Hunter. Moving up beside her, he stayed hidden behind the door.

Hunter couldn't stay upright without Viola's help, but he didn't want the men on the other side of the door to think him weak. "Hold me up?" He whispered to Viola, grinning when she responded with a slight nod.

He tucked Viola's arm around his back and opened the door, keeping the shotgun hidden behind it and his sidearm resting upon Viola's upper back. There before him were three rough-looking men. While the man up front had a face that appeared hard and angry at the world, the other two just looked weary. All three were dressed in threadbare clothes, their hair and beards long and scraggly. The one standing closest had a crazed look about him that gave even Hunter chills.

Taking on the calm control that got him through hundreds of missions, he said, "I believe the lady said you couldn't come in."

Shocked anger coursed from the man as he spat out. "Just who the hell are you?"

"A friend of the family. Well a bit more than that, huh honey?" Hunter answered casually, smiling down at Viola, her eyes widening as he quickly winked at her and turned his attention back to the men. "Vi's not up for entertaining today, so you boys best be heading on out."

"I don't care if she's up for entertaining or not! I came to give her news, and I'm gonna do it." Linc seethed.

"By all means," Hunter replied. "Share your news, but you aren't forcing your presence where it's not welcome, friend."

"I'm not your friend, you fool," Linc exploded, "and I expect Viola'd want to be sittin' down when I give her the news her pa and brother are dead."

Viola sucked in a breath and leaned more into Hunter. Linc wore an expression of both gloating and loathing. The two brothers shuffled a bit behind Linc. The youngest one appeared nervous as a cat getting ready for a bath. Hunter couldn't place the emotion that crossed the taller brother's face before returning to the blank, stoic stare he'd worn so far.

Hunter narrowed his eyes and with a cold voice he said, "You've delivered your news, now I suggest you head out."

"Oh, I don't think so," Linc countered with contempt. "Viola and that sister of hers will need protection now with their menfolk gone, and I don't expect some dandy of a man is going to be up to it."

Hunter tightened at the dig. If he wanted, he could break this little weasel in two, then dispatch the two brothers. The bigger one might give him some trouble. He was taller than Hunter's own six-two frame by at least three inches and built like a WWF wrestler, but Hunter had taken down men bigger with more training than some back hills mountain man. But now wasn't the time to get his ego up. He didn't want this to turn ugly, what with the ladies in the middle of it and him busted up.

"Oh, I don't know," Hunter replied with a tilt of his head. "What do you think, sweetheart? Think you're safe with me?"

He glanced down and watched as a beautiful blush rushed upon Viola's face. Instead of bowing her head shyly, she gazed up at him in adoration. Oh man, he was in trouble. He beamed big as he gazed down at her.

"I believe I'm as safe as a body can get," she said, her lips lifting coyly back.

"Sweetheart!? She's ... but ... I," Linc stuttered, drawing Hunter's attention back away from Viola's beautiful face. "She's mine, and no two-bit newcomer is going to take her from me," Linc said as he reached for his holster.

Before he could even reach his gun, Viola stepped into Hunter's side, wrapping her arm firmly around him. She didn't hide her face in his chest like he expected, but gave him the stability he needed to stand and defend against the men. Hunter cheered inwardly at her grit.

Hunter brought the sidearm over her shoulder pointing it at Linc's chest where he stood in front of them. Hunter swung the door open and aimed the shotgun at the brothers standing behind and off to one side. Everything froze in suspended motion. Linc glanced from the cocked and ready weapons to his brothers to Viola, indecision warring on his face.

"Well, shoot, you see here, Sweeney, I may be a newcomer, but I'm well accustomed to protecting what's mine and what's precious to me."

"Viola's mine," Linc said in suppressed rage. "I've worked too long and hard to give her over to some passerby. I don't even mind used goods, as long as I get what's coming to me."

"I've never been yours, Linc. Never," Viola said, anger lacing her voice with strength.

"You've gone too far," Hunter replied, his voice hard as steel. "Viola is a lady and you will remember to treat her as such. You and your brothers will leave. Now."

"Leave it for another day." The tall brother's voice rumbled, his hands held out casually from his side in surrender.

Linc stared at Hunter in an open challenge, his face frozen in a cold and harsh expression. He'd seen lots of anger in fighting against those who threatened freedom, but he'd rarely seen such demonic rage as what played upon Linc's face. Hunter silently prayed for God's protection even more fervently.

"You have two choices," Hunter said with authority. "Leave now or be shot. Sure, your brothers may just get peppered with buckshot, but at this distance it won't be pretty and more than likely will get infected. You, however, will die, and I won't have to unload all my rounds to do it. You see, I've killed before. More men than I can count, in fact. I don't mind doing it again."

"Come on, Linc," the youngest brother pleaded, his uncomfortableness since the beginning turning into downright spinelessness. Smart man.

Linc tore his gaze from Hunter and sneered at Viola.

"You just remember what I said. Your pa and brother are dead, and no newcomer is going to keep you safe, despite what he says. You're mine," Linc added with a lecherous glare. "I'll take you however I can get you, even with this man's stink on you. No way I'm giving you up when everything is now working into place. You and what belongs to you will be mine."

"Linc, I'm sorry if I ever gave you the impression I was interested in furthering our relationship. It never was my intention. However, if you ever come back here, you'll regret it. Leave, Linc, and don't come back. I pray you find a life of you own, a life worth living, because this life you've chosen is doing nothing but tearing you apart," Viola said, showing much more compassion than Hunter was willing to extend.

The large brother grabbed Linc's arm as the other brother scurried away. Linc hesitated a second more than turned and stomped to his mangy horse. He jumped into the saddle and kicked the poor beast into a full gallop with his brothers close behind him.

As Hunter stepped back into the house with Viola propped under his arm, all strength and energy seeped from him. His last conscious thought was to tuck Viola safely to his chest as he fell like a brick into darkness.

VIOLA SHRIEKED in surprise as Hunter's arm tightened around her and they fell to the floor. He held her close to his chest, taking all the impact with a grunt. Beatrice raced through the door with her gun drawn.

Her eyes widened. "What in the world happened?"

"I don't know," Viola replied as she tried to shift away from Hunter. "One minute he was scaring off the Sweeneys, the next he was falling like a felled tree. It was shocking, really, how all energy and strength left him." She grunted and pulled from his side. "Grab his guns and help me out of here. My dress got stuck underneath him."

Beatrice holstered her gun, shut the door, and walked to where Hunter trapped Viola. "He was impressive, wasn't he? I've never heard someone be so nonchalant and commanding at the same time. I wish I could've watched it instead of just listened."

Beatrice took the guns from his hands, but when she tried to roll Hunter over, his arm tightened like a vise around Viola and he mumbled, "No. Safe. Keep safe."

Beatrice moved away and his arm loosened. Viola tried to push herself away and his arm tightened again with him mumbling about her being safe.

"Oh, bother. What am I supposed to do now?"

"It looks like you're stuck, sister." Beatrice chuckled

"I can't be stuck. I have too much work that needs to get done." Viola huffed.

"Well," Beatrice said. "What if you lean away from him, and I'll try to pull your skirt out?"

Viola nodded and rolled away from Hunter a little as Beatrice reached between them to pull on the dress. Hunter pulled Viola close, trapping Beatrice's arm between them.

"No, stay. Safe. Keep safe," Hunter mumbled.

Beatrice started laughing hard. "Well, this is awkward."

"Beatrice, stop laughing," Viola said. "This isn't funny."

"This, dear sister, is wildly funny," Beatrice said.

Viola peeked at her and broke down laughing. They

were stuck there with Beatrice's arm pinned between them. With Hunter's strong arm anchored around Viola, she was safe ... maybe even cherished. She silently thanked God for this time of laughter, this time of peace, and this man beside her. She laughed until tears streamed down her face and she couldn't breathe.

As Beatrice's laughter calmed, and she wiped her tears on her sleeve, she said, "All right, my knees and back are aching, pinned in here like this. What if you real sweet like tell him you aren't going anywhere and you're safe? Perhaps he'll ease up enough to get my arm out."

"It's worth a try," Viola said as she calmed the last of her giggles. Taking a deep breath, she spoke in what she hoped was a convincing voice. "Hunter, I'm not going anywhere, and we're safe now."

Hunter breathed a sigh of relief and loosened his arms. Beatrice pulled her arm out and rubbed her arm and her lower back. Viola was lying flat on her back with Hunter's arm under and around her. She wondered if there was anything she might do from here. Knitting or even mending?

Just as Viola opened her mouth to ask Beatrice to bring her the mending, Hunter's arm began to tighten again. He curled his arm beneath her, pulling her close to him until her head rested on his shoulder. She self-consciously placed her hand upon his chest, and he sighed in contentment, placing his other hand upon hers.

"Well, this is embarrassing and inappropriate," Viola muttered.

"It's kind of sweet," Beatrice said as she went to the table and finished chopping the herbs for the stew. "Besides, he's doing it subconsciously and no one's here."

"I guess so," Viola said, attempting to relax.

"It must be nice to feel so, oh, I don't know, treasured." Beatrice sighed.

"I don't know if he feels that or is just obligated to protect me is all," Viola said, trying to control the elation that being adored by this man caused.

Beatrice snorted. "Just try to convince yourself that."

"It's true," Viola said. "We've barely met him, and he's been unconscious most of that time. There's no way he feels anything for me beyond an obligation to return the kindness of us bringing him here and patching him up. He just seems to be the protector sort."

"Believe what you want. I'll give you he's the protector sort. It seems to exude from him. However, I guarantee that if it were me pinned beneath him, he wouldn't be snuggling up close and smiling like the cat that stole all the cream."

Viola craned her neck to peer at his face. He looked quite satisfied and relaxed, which sent her heart skittering. Her face heated in a blush as she laid her head back down and sighed in confused frustration.

"It's just not possible," Viola muttered.

"Why not?" Beatrice asked. "Mama met Pa one day, married him two days later, packed up all the belongings she fit into her one trunk and left Pittsburgh and the grand life she had there to move here to Pa's home. They were in love. It's possible, and you know it."

"I guess you're right." Viola mumbled.

She remembered all of the happy memories of her childhood. Her parents had loved each other immensely. She'd always known that she wanted to look at a man and have him look at her the way her parents had gazed at each other. There'd been such a longing and tenderness within their glances, even after all their years of marriage and troubles. She often wondered if it hadn't been for her and her siblings, if Pa would've just curled up beside Mama and died alongside her from heartbreak. The silence seemed to fill with the heaviness of sadness.

"Do you reckon Pa and Orlando are dead?" Beatrice asked into the oppressive air, the question landing like lead upon Viola's chest.

"I don't know." She forced the words from her lips. She took a deep breath and continued with a confidence she didn't have. "I know that the Sweeneys are a bunch of weasels, so I'm not going to put much thought into what they said until I have real proof."

"I guess it wouldn't do much good to worry about it anyway, at least until we know the truth," Beatrice said, as she turned her back to Viola and sniffed, wiping her hands across her eyes.

As the sadness threatened to overwhelm her, Viola prayed, "Father God, You alone know the truth, and You tell us not to worry. Even if what the Sweeneys say is true, You'll always be beside us. Thank You so much, Lord, for bringing Hunter here when You did. One or more of us would've probably been killed if Hunter hadn't been here to diffuse the situation. Thank You for Your obvious strength that coursed through Hunter in his time of weakness. Please continue to heal him and make him strong. And please keep pursuing the Sweeneys so their hearts turn away from the evil they've allowed to course through them to the goodness that is You, Lord. Amen."

"Viola, why don't you just try to sleep a bit since you

aren't moving for a while. I know you were up all night caring for Hunter, and I'm sure you're tired."

Viola grunted in resignation. "If my other hand was free, I could at least do mending or knitting."

"This is God's provision for you to take a much-needed rest." Beatrice laughed. "Besides, it's not every day that you're forced to snuggle up to a good-looking man who's taken it upon himself to be your knight in shining armor. Take a rest. The work will still be there when he wakes up."

"Fine, I'll rest." Viola huffed. "Though it goes against every grain of my body."

Viola relaxed and closed her eyes. She figured resting her eyes couldn't hurt, though a nap would be better. While Hunter's arms around her warmed her like no blanket could, she knew she wouldn't be able to sleep.

CHAPTER 9

HUNTER WOKE to every inch of his body screaming to him in pain, but the screams faded to whispers by the pleasant touch of someone snuggled up next to him. He breathed as deeply as his busted ribs allowed and became enveloped with a sweet fragrance. Viola. He opened his eyes, raised his head and wondered what miracle could've possibly happened to have Viola's head resting upon his shoulder and fingers intertwined with his upon his chest. He loved that she was there but couldn't imagine her just laying down and taking a nap in the middle of the day, curled up next to him, no less.

Everything came rushing back with clarity, focusing his mind to access the situation. He noticed his guns on the table, surprised they had gotten them from his hands. Something that smelled delicious bubbled on the stove. Other than that, the place was calm and quiet, except for the soft breaths coming from Viola.

The door opened, and Hunter tightened his embrace around Viola, preparing to protect her against an intruder. Beatrice came in and smirked towards him. She carried an armful of wood, setting it onto the stack next to the stove.

She drew near and whispered, "Glad to see you're up."

"What happened?" he whispered back.

"Pure loco, but after the Sweeneys left, you took about three steps then fell like a chopped tree." Beatrice chuckled showing him with her arm how he fell, sound effects and all. "Somehow, you kept from squishing Viola flat. However, you pinned her dress under you."

"How'd you get the guns from me?"

"Oh, there was no problem taking your guns from you. You gave those up right quick," Beatrice said in mock disgust. "Getting Viola from you, now that was a different story."

"What do you mean?"

"Well, every time we tried to get Viola up, you'd pull her in tighter than a bear with a fresh kill." Beatrice laughed. "She'd roll away. You'd pull her back. I put my hand between you to pull her dress free, you pulled her so tight to your side that my hand got stuck and went numb. Every time you'd mumble some nonsense about keeping her safe."

Hunter's face heated in embarrassment. He hadn't blushed since high school. This place was crazy. He had to get back to his time before he turned soft. Freely giving up his weapons. The Unit would disown him for sure.

"It wasn't nonsense." Viola spoke as she shifted to look into his face and all thoughts of getting back to the future vanished. "I thought it was chivalrous."

Beatrice rolled her eyes and moved to the stove. Hunter stared into the eyes of emerald staring up at him and just about drowned. How she found him chivalrous when he kept fainting like those silly goats he'd seen on YouTube was beyond him, but he'd prove himself to her one way or another.

"I didn't hurt you, did I?" he whispered, rubbing his thumb across the back of her hand.

"No. It was a shock, falling like that." Viola sat up, pulling the sleeves of her dress down. "But you kept me tight to your chest and took the brunt of it, I'm afraid."

"Good, that's good," Hunter said, unable to pull his gaze from her face.

"If you two laze-abouts are done gazing into each other's eyes or such nonsense, the stews done," Beatrice said.

"Good. I'm starving," he whispered, his voice husky.

Viola blushed a bright red. Hunter smiled, reaching his hand still her hand that picked at her sleeve. She shivered, the blush deepening.

VIOLA TRIED to concentrate on eating the stew, but she couldn't get the look Hunter had given her out of her mind. Like he was starving, but not for stew. He appeared as if he was starving for her, but that was ridiculous.

"Viola, you feeling okay? You're looking a little flushed." Beatrice stared at her with concern.

Viola glanced at Hunter, noticing he smirked at her knowingly. She glanced down at her stew and took a big bite. Darn that man and her body's infuriating reactions.

"It's good that you're well enough to eat at the table." She tried to redirect the conversation.

"I need to get out of that bed as much as I can," Hunter said, digging into his second bowl of stew with relish. "I still have a long way to one-hundred percent, but I want to be up and about when I can be."

"We'll need to change your dressings after we eat," Viola said.

Hunter nodded as he shoveled another spoonful into his mouth. They sat in silence as they finished their meal. Hunter ate the entire bowl and cleaned up the bowl with his bread.

"This is by far the best grub I've had in years," Hunter said as he put the last bite of bread in his mouth. "If this is how we eat all the time here, I'll be fat before you know it."

Beatrice shook her head in amusement. "There's too much work to do to get fat. If you don't eat hearty for the work you are doing, you end up starved and bitter like the Sweeneys."

"What's their story, anyway?" Hunter asked, leaning his elbows onto the table.

"They came out here about three falls ago, slapped up a shack and started bragging to everyone how they were gonna make it rich in mining. Well, I guess Linc bragged," Beatrice said, playing with her coffee cup on the table. "Just about froze to death that first winter, and best anyone can tell, found nothing that first summer. It doesn't seem they did much mining at all, the lazy coots. Simply stayed in that shack when they aren't lurking around."

"What do you mean 'lurking around?'" A shiver ran down Hunter's back.

"Well, at first it didn't seem like much," Viola

answered. "Pa and Orlando started noticing tracks where they'd been or would catch glimpses of one or two of the Sweeneys in the woods. They wondered at first that it was a coincidence, that possibly they were prospecting in the same areas Pa and Orlando were going. But it became obvious it was more than that."

"Yeah, I'd call stalking 'more,'" Beatrice said with contempt.

"They were stalking your Pa and Orlando?" Hunter tried to understand the Sweeney's motives.

"Those idiots thought they could best Pa and Orlando by sneaking around." Beatrice snorted. "Once they figured out what those skunks were up to, they lost them when they wanted to."

"What's Linc's obsession with you?" Hunter asked Viola.

She shrugged, but Beatrice answered before she did. "He's been eyeing her for the last two years, ever since we first met them at the trading post, remember?"

Viola nodded and shivered at the memory of Linc taking her hand in his and declaring she was the prettiest woman ever to grace the earth. His hands had been cold and sweaty, and he'd had a gleam in his eyes that made her feel filthy. Pa had shown up at that moment and led her away, warning her to avoid the Sweeneys at all cost. Her fingers turned cold at the memory, and she cupped her coffee in her hands, hoping it'd help warmth to return. Hunter narrowed his eyes at her.

"Has he ever done anything like he did today before?" Hunter asked, his eyes intense upon her face. "Or made his intentions known regarding you?"

"I've hardly spoken a word to him or his brothers in

the last two years," Viola answered. "I did not give him any indication that I'd be interested in furthering our acquaintance."

"After we all noticed his attention directed toward Viola, Pa and Orlando made sure he didn't have any opportunity to be chatty with her," Beatrice added.

Hunter sat quiet for a minute, twisting his mug back and forth on the table. He stared into the cup, his face deep in thought, so she got up to clear the table while he contemplated. When the table was clear and the dishes were soaking in the sink, she refilled everyone's coffee and sat down.

"What I want to know is what your family has that he wants?" Hunter asked, looking from Beatrice to Viola. "It's obvious this goes beyond some messed up stalker obsession with you, since you say that they spend all their time following your dad and brother. If it was simply you he wanted, they would've been hanging around here, where I'm assuming you stay most of the time, not trekking all over the mountains."

Viola shook her head in concentration, then gasped when she considered the Sweeneys might know about her family's mine. "No. They can't know."

"It's not possible," Beatrice said with ease. "They aren't smart enough."

"What's not possible?" Hunter asked, looking between Viola and Beatrice.

"But what if they did?" Viola asked.

"I'm telling you," Beatrice said, "they just aren't that smart."

"Would one of you please tell me what's going on?" Hunter said, sounding frustrated.

Viola and Beatrice glanced from each other to him and back again. Viola raised an eyebrow silently questioning Beatrice about telling Hunter, which Beatrice answered with a negative shake of her head.

"Bea—"

"No, Viola," Beatrice said in exasperation. "No one's to know."

"I think with the current situation, Pa would under-stand us telling Hunter," Viola said. "How's he to help us if he doesn't have all the information?"

"Exactly!" Hunter said in triumph, causing Beatrice to glare at him.

"You yourself said that God must've brought him here for a reason," Viola said, furthering her case. "If God finds him trustworthy and honorable enough to bring him all the way back here to us, shouldn't we trust him as well?"

"Fine," Beatrice said, turning a sharp eye to Hunter. "But if you betray us, I'll hunt you down and gut you."

"Fair enough," Hunter said. "Now will you tell me what's got you so fired up?"

Viola shook her head. "I'm thinking the Sweeneys must've realized that we have a gold mine. They just must not know where it is."

"That would be a Sweeney for you." Beatrice snorted in disgust. "Instead of finding a way of their own or going where there's work, they slink around the mountains for two years trying to take what's not theirs."

"Isn't it public record when someone claims a mine?" Hunter asked.

"It's public record when you claim land, but you don't need to disclose that you've found anything," Viola explained. "Most people are so plumb excited that they struck it rich that they tell the whole dang world. Pa didn't want it to be public knowledge, so he went along like he had before, trapping and trading pelts for supplies like he'd always done."

"Couldn't the Sweeneys have just researched the land records to see where your mine is?" Hunter asked.

"They could've and maybe even tried, but we own property all up and down these mountains," Beatrice answered. "Granddaddy moved out here in his early twenties, and Pa was born and raised here. They'd been claiming and buying up property as soon as they could, wanting to keep the mountains they love as untouched as possible, knowing people would start flooding in as soon as they realized the potential."

"The truth is, the gold's pretty much all mined out," Viola said, shaking her head. "Pa found the gold by accident about twenty-five years ago, so even if the Sweeneys found it, there isn't anything left worth much. Pa still goes there to get the 'fever' as he calls it out of him, but he hasn't found any more veins. Most all the gold was sent back to my mother's father for him to put in banks or invest. We only kept a little bit hidden here for incidentals."

"So they've been following your dad and brother around for two years and now show up here," Hunter pondered aloud. "What caused them to change tactics?"

"Maybe Robert and William got sick of Linc's wild goose chase," Beatrice said.

"Could what he said about your dad and brother be true?" Hunter asked.

Beatrice shrugged, slumping into her chair. When Viola began picking at the table Hunter knew they both were hesitant to admit there might be truth to the Sweeneys' claim. Hunter reached over and took her hand in his.

"I guess it's possible." Viola sighed again, then straightened her shoulders in resolution. "But I'm sure not going to believe it until I have more proof than the word of a Sweeney."

Hunter gave her hand a squeeze before letting go. "We need to be diligent until we have proof or the Sweeneys return. Linc will not give up that easily, and now that he knows I'm here, he's not just going to ride up to the front door again."

"He's too yellow-bellied to do that." Beatrice's mouth tightened, as if she tasted something bad.

"Thank you, Hunter, for stepping in like that," Viola said. "I don't know what would've happened if you hadn't come to the door, but I know it wouldn't have been good. I worry about Linc. Something doesn't seem right with him."

"He's definitely got a few screws loose," Hunter said.

Viola looked at him, her forehead scrunching in confusion. Some of the words he said baffled her. He shook his head and shrugged.

"Sorry. It's a saying from my time that means he's not all there in the head," Hunter said. "And if that's the case, we'll have to be extra careful. Don't go anywhere without a weapon and don't go out of the sight of the house without all of us present. It'd probably even be best if you didn't go to the barn or for water alone."

"That would be too much hassle," Beatrice said. "They aren't going to hide out in the barn, and even if they did, the animals would give them away in an instant."

"You don't know that, Beatrice," Viola said. "If they snuck in there in the middle of the night, by the time we went in, the animals would probably all have calmed down. Even though it'll be a pain, I think it's smart to do what Hunter says."

"I could always bunk down in the barn," Hunter suggested. "You could bar the door and then both the cabin and the barn would be protected."

"You aren't bedding down in the barn in your condition." Viola glared over at him. "How do you expect to get better in that smelly old thing? No, you'll stay right in the front room. I don't like the idea of us separated at night, anyway."

Beatrice snickered. Viola glanced over at her in confusion. As understanding dawned on her, Viola's heat scorched up her neck and cheeks.

"Well, I don't like the idea of being separated at night either, sweetheart," Hunter said saucily, throwing her a wink.

Viola's blush raced the rest of the way up to her hairline. She pushed away from the table and went to the stove, muttering to herself. Beatrice laughed so hard Viola hoped she fell out of her chair. Viola heard Hunter's deep chuckle as she grabbed the coffeepot and brought it to the table, refilling everyone's mug.

"She walked right into that one, didn't she?" He joked.

"You could say that again." Beatrice laughed, pointing her finger at him. "You should've heard her talking about taking off your clothes yesterday."

"Oh, really?" Hunter wiggled his eyebrows up and down.

"I did nothing of the kind, Beatrice, and you know

what I meant," Viola said turning to the sink and slamming clean dishes onto the counter as she washed and rinsed them. "This conversation is inappropriate, and you know it. You two are taking innocent comments and twisting them into something they aren't."

"Lighten up, Viola," Beatrice replied. "We're just teasing. We know you didn't mean nothing untoward."

"I know," Viola said, her shoulders loosening up. "It's just that I seem all in a dither since we found you, and I'm not this way."

"I don't think you've seemed in a dither," Hunter said. "In fact, I think you've both handled me popping up here half dead after somehow traveling through time quite well. Add to that the Sweeneys visit, you've done better than any woman, and most men, I know back home."

Viola shook her head, placed the last dish on the counter to dry, and came to sit down again. "You know," Viola said, "I've been thinking about you traveling through time. Please, don't take this the wrong way, but I think we might need to hide your stuff until we can figure out a way to get you back."

"Okay," Hunter said, nodding his head. "You've got my attention."

"Well, everything you have is just so different from what we are used to. Even the weapon you pointed at Linc is far more advanced than any gun we have —"

"I'd love for you to show me how it works, if you don't mind," Beatrice interrupted. "Your other gear as well. It's all so fascinating."

"I don't mind showing you." Hunter nodded at Beatrice before turning back to Viola.

"It's just that I don't think we should let it out where

you are from." Viola motioned at Beatrice. "While we are accepting of the idea, most people won't be. It could just add more problems onto the ones we already have."

Hunter nodded in agreement. "I see what you're saying. So what's your plan."

"Well, I've been mending Orlando's clothes that he left here." Viola pointed to a pile of clothes in a basket next to the rocking chair. "The only problem is that I think you're taller and broader than he is. So I will need to let out seams and cuffs. It won't be difficult for me to mend, but it might be hard for you to try things on to adjust fit, given your injuries."

"The easiest thing at the moment would be a shirt that buttons up the front. That way I don't have to lift it over my head to get it on and off," Hunter suggested. "I can tell you have lots of guns, but most of them I have minimal experience with, if any. Can you teach me how to use them, and do you have more pistols?"

Viola smiled her approval at the mention of them teaching him. Maybe he wouldn't be one of those men who thought women couldn't take care of themselves. Shoot, Voila thought, her and Beatrice had been on their own for what seemed forever now. While it was definitely nice to have a man around, it wasn't a necessity.

"I can have you a shirt made by tomorrow." Viola wished her mother had been able to teach her more sewing. Maybe then she could get his shirt finished faster. "We also have more revolvers we can get for you. Plus, I don't think it'd take long for you to learn them or any other gun you wanted."

"Perfect," Hunter said as he rubbed his face. His countenance held a weariness like he was weighed down. "I think if you want to swap out my bandages, we should get me over to the bed. I'm fading fast."

After he had hobbled over to the bed with Viola's help, he sat down, his shoulders slumped. She helped him take his shirt off to check on his injuries. Before he laid down, he looked at Beatrice, who was busy putting away the dishes.

"Beatrice, do you think you could pack my gear in my bag and find a place to hide it where we can still get to it?" Hunter asked.

"No problem," Beatrice answered. "I know the perfect place to put it."

"Great. Thanks," Hunter said, then turned to Viola. "You wouldn't happen to have a pair of pants in that pile you've already mended, do you? If she's packing away my gear, I should probably strip off these pants as well before I lay down."

Viola walked to the pile, trying to keep her face from blushing again, and brought back a pair of buckskin pants. "I'll just turn around so if you need any help or get off balanced, I'll be here to help."

Hunter chuckled. "Sweetheart, when I'm around you, I'm always off balance."

Viola sighed and listened as fabric rustled behind her.

"I'm decent." Hunter grunted as he laid back on the bed.

"Let me get you some tea for the pain before I change your bandages," Viola whispered.

Viola hurried to get the tea, trying to be as quiet as possible. Viola marveled at all Hunter had been through and his strength of character that didn't have him lashing out or outwardly upset. Even admitting he'd need their help in learning about this life here showed the kind of man he was deep inside.

Viola peered over at Hunter where he laid watching her. What would it be like to be married to a man who put his pride aside and admitted his weaknesses? Should she even consider such a possibility with a man God might sweep back to his own time? His eyes softened as she brought the tea over. She probably shouldn't, but that didn't mean her mind wouldn't mull over the idea on its own.

CHAPTER 10

FOUR DAYS AFTER THE SWEENEYS' visit, Hunter stood at the door, staring out into the dark pink that pushed the curtain of night away to day. He exhaled, knowing that the longer he waited, the less he'd want to do what needed to be done. All night he'd laid in bed, contemplating his next step of action.

He'd been so confused what to pray for, part of him knowing he should pray to go back home and part—a bigger part, if he was honest—wanted to pray that God had brought him here for good, to start a new life. A life with Viola. But those thoughts made him feel guilty. How could he possibly be okay with never seeing his brother, Chase, again? How could he be so selfish to not desire to be back where his responsibilities, friends, and family were? In the end, he just prayed that God would give him direction and peace with whatever happened.

Late the night before, he knew, without a doubt, that if he didn't try to get back to his time and try today, the guilt of wanting to stay would eat at him. If God sent him back, he'd thank God for the experience and try to get back into his life. But if God kept him here, he'd stay with the peace of knowing this is where he needed to be.

A delicate swish of fabric and a soft "Oh!" turned him from the sunrise painting the sky to the woman that had been rapidly pushing the darkness that shrouded his heart back so that a vestige of hope appeared. As if the weight of his failures wouldn't weigh him down like a soaking cloak that would eventually suffocate him. Would he accept it if God sent him back away from her?

"I didn't realize you were up," Viola said, hurrying to the stove. "Give me just a few minutes and I'll have breakfast started."

Hunter watched her hustle to stoke the fire and move the tin coffee pot she'd prepared the night before over the heat. He moved to the table and grabbed the back of a chair, squeezing it for help when the words he needed to say lodged within his throat.

He cleared the lump of words where they stuck and forced them out. "I need to go back to where you found me. If you and Bea can take me today, I'd be appreciative."

He watched as her hands slowed and her shoulders slumped. Slowly she turned to face him, leaning back onto the worktable.

"Are you sure that's wise?" she asked, her voice shaking. She cleared her throat and continued, her voice solid again. "What I mean is, do you suppose you can handle the ride? Your ribs are still healing, and your fever left not two days ago. Plus, you can hardly put weight on your ankle. Don't you think it'd be smarter to wait another week until you are stronger?"

"No, I can't wait. Not even another day," he answered,

feeling horrible when she flinched as if he struck her. "Viola, the not knowing if I'll be going back home or here for good is weighing on me like a ton of bricks. I need to know."

Her eyes became glossy with unshed tears as he spoke, and he turned away from the searing pain her emotion caused within his heart. He walked back to the door, hearing her sniff once and the slamming of metal as she moved pans around. Did she believe he wanted to get away from her? Was she more worried about being here without male protection against the Sweeneys? No, that couldn't be it since Beatrice wouldn't hesitate to shoot, and Viola was just as brave and strong. They could take care of themselves if need be. Maybe her tender heart just worried he'd hurt himself more with the trip? Or possibly she cared for him, like he was coming to care for her. He couldn't contemplate the reasons for her reaction or else it'd throw him into more turmoil of vacillating between hurt and his desires. No, he'd decided. He had to know, because he just wasn't strong enough to stay here one more day to risk being ripped away back to his time later.

"I can't be in limbo any longer, Viola," he said as he peered upon the sky now shaded light pink and orange. He whispered to himself, "My heart can't take leaving you if I stay any longer."

"I understand," she answered, her voice strong now. "I'll make a quick breakfast and pack the saddlebags for the trip."

"Trip? What trip?" Beatrice asked as she walked through the bedroom door, tying a rawhide strip to the end of her braid.

Beatrice's buckskin pants and faded calico blouse

seemed a contrast to Viola's light green dress, which he realized was one of the few she had. These sisters were night and day. Strong in their own ways, stronger than most women he'd ever known. Yet where Viola embraced the elegant beauty of being a female in her dress and mannerisms, Beatrice clung to the clothes and trappings more manly, though no one would ever consider her a man. He hadn't once seen her in a dress and wondered if it was for simplicity sake that had her dressing so contrary to this time's norm or was there another reason?

"Hunter needs us to take him back to where we found him today," Viola said as she cracked eggs into a pan sizzling with butter. "He wants to see if he can get back to his time."

Beatrice looked from Viola, whose shoulders were stiff as she thrashed the eggs on the stove, to Hunter as he rubbed his hand across his neck in frustration. The tension was palpable in the air.

"You up for this? It'll be a long, rough ride." Beatrice eyed him with doubt.

"Yep." He answered as confidently as he could, hoping his own doubt wasn't blaring to their ears.

Viola huffed and stirred the eggs faster, mumbling under her breath. Beatrice smirked at her as she walked up to him.

"All right," Beatrice warned. "But if you think for one minute that I will haul your carcass anywhere because you're too stubborn to wait until you're healed more and you end up fainting like some liver-lilied city dandy, you'd better think again. I've already done that once. Next time, I'll leave you for the mountain lions."

"Okay," Hunter answered. "No passing out, I promise. Can you get my gear from where you hid it?"

"Fine," Beatrice said, before turning to face Viola. "Viola, I'll get the horses saddled up and the barn chores done."

Viola slammed another pan on the stove and started slicing ham into it, saying. "Fine."

Hunter decided taking Beatrice's normal testy attitude would be better than trying to converse with Viola. He hightailed it outside to the barn with a mumble of helping "gather eggs or something." His years of military training and avoidance of most women had done absolutely no good in preparing him for the constantly shifting and changing field of operation pertaining to Viola. His best bet was a retreat on the double.

VIOLA SLAMMED the pan of eggs onto the cooler spot of the stove to keep them warm as she heard Hunter mumble something ridiculous about helping gather eggs. Which was fine by her since she didn't want him in the cabin with her anyways. Which was a complete and utter lie. She wanted him to be in here with her, forever. Her eyes teared up again, and without him watching, she allowed one to slip down her cheek. She harshly wiped it away with one hand while flipping the ham with the other.

Viola was being ridiculous. She understood his desire to return to his time and family. If she was in his position, she knew she'd do the same thing to get to her family. So why did his request to go back to where they found him stab through her heart so viciously and rip it from her chest? She imagined if she glanced down at her dress there'd be a gapping hole where her heart had been.

She had known this day would come. Of course he'd have to try to get home, but couldn't he have the decency to wait a little longer so she might squirrel away more memories of him to lock in her mind for the loneliness the mountains brought? The loneliness that now bared down like never before and threatened to consume her before he'd even left. She moved the ham to the back of the stove with a shove and started wrapping jerky and leftover biscuits for the trail, her motions shaky with anger and sorrow. She hoped he was as miserable as she was, that he'd long for her like she knew she'd long for him when he disappeared. Would serve him right for putting her through this misery.

Viola stilled, sucking in a shocked breath. How could she possibly want him to hurt this way? What a selfish, petty creature she was turning out to be. She pulled out a chair from the table and sat in it hard, the anger that had moments ago consumed her seeped through her feet into the rough floor below.

"Oh God," she cried, placing her face in her hands in shame. She sat in the chair and prayed for forgiveness, for her broken heart, and for peace with whatever happened when Hunter attempted to return home. She breathed in deeply and blew out hard, cleaning all heaviness that she'd accumulated in her selfish huff from her.

She stood up and moved to her room to change into her riding clothes, resolved to handle Hunter's leaving with an attitude that would please God. As she unbuttoned her dress with shaky fingers, her whispered prayer of "Help me," was one she knew she'd repeat a million times over that day and possibly into forever.

HUNTER SAT on the horse behind Viola as he stared at the base of the mountain that had sent him plunging into the past. His palms sweated, and he clenched his hands to keep from pulling Viola close to his chest, grabbing the reins and spurring that horse as quick as it could go back to the cabin. But he kept his hands resting on his thighs, where they'd stayed glued the whole ride except the time or two he'd needed to hold on or fall off. Though he'd wanted to hold on to Viola the entire way, he'd held back, keeping whatever distance he could between them for her sake, not wanting to give her hope of his feelings or memories she'd regret if he left.

Oh, who was he kidding? He'd kept his distance for his sake as much as hers, if not more. When he and Beatrice had returned to the cabin, breakfast sat on the table, and the provisions packed, Viola acted like it was just another ride in the woods. Like she was ready to send him off with a smile, a wave, and a hope-your-life-turns-out farewell. And didn't that make him want to grab her and shake her until she mourned for the potential loss of each other just as much as he was.

Hunter rubbed his hand down his face. He was a mess. He simply needed to focus on what they came here for and deal with what God had planned after.

Viola pulled to a stop and pointed to a depression in the ground where the snow runoff was eating away the earth. "That's where we found you."

"Okay," he replied, taking a deep breath of her sweet cinnamon smell and capturing it into his memory before he leaned forward, pressing into her as he dismounted.

Hunter limped a little closer to the spot where he'd been found while Viola and Beatrice dismounted and tied their horses to a shrub. He stared at the side of the mountain and the indention that would, in his time, be a ravine. Taking long, deep breaths, he attempted to slow his racing heart. He hadn't been this sick-to-his-stomach nervous since his first mission out of Basic. Viola walked up to stand beside him and his stomach turned to a rock.

"I-I can never thank you for all that you've done for me," he whispered hoarsely.

Viola touched his arm with her slender hand. "I know God will bless you wherever He takes you, Hunter," she said with such conviction he thought he might break-down and cry.

He put his hand over hers and gazed into her eyes as she gave him a watery smile. He squeezed her hand, cleared the dust that in no way resembled emotion from his throat, and turned his attention back to the mountain.

"I'm going to climb up the mountain a bit and slide into the depression." Laying out his tactical approach as he would with his squad, he distanced himself from the emotions churning within him.

"That's a wonderful plan." Beatrice snorted as she said the sarcastic reply. "Might as well break more ribs and sprain the other ankle while you're at it."

"Why don't you just walk over where we found you?" Viola asked after giving Beatrice the look his mom used to give him and Chase to keep quiet.

Hunter shook his head. "The way I see it, you two

were walking everywhere I had been to help me up and didn't go anywhere, plus I don't know where I transported back here. So, if I start up there a bit and slide down, it'll be more like when I fell from the top."

"I guess that makes sense," Viola said with hesitation.

"Why don't you go all the way to the top?" Beatrice asked smartly. "I'd even give you a push to re-enact the lion's swipe."

"Beatrice!" Viola gaped.

Hunter rubbed his chest and shook his head. "As tempting as that sounds, I think I'll pass. Besides, I distinctly remember coming to that depression, which in my time is a ravine, and thinking it would hurt."

"Well, you have your plan, so get on with it then," Beatrice said in a tone that told Hunter she didn't have time to stand here and watch him stare at his task. He knew that tone since he used it often on new recruits.

He turned from the mountain and grabbed Viola's hand. "Thank you. Both of you. I probably would've died without you. It's really been a pleasure to get to know you two, and I'm glad I was able to help you, even if it was just a little." He glanced between them, lingering on Viola's green eyes.

Viola threw her arms around him in a hug, whispering "Good-bye," in his ear. He peered at Beatrice who stood behind Viola. She nodded her farewell in the brusque manner he was growing accustomed to. He pulled away from Viola, gave her one last nod, and turned to the mountain.

He adjusted his pack on his shoulders and limped up the mountainside about thirty feet. He squatted down, putting his good foot under him and holding his bad ankle out in front of him like a guide. He hoped to slide down on his foot, using his hands to keep him upright and keeping his bum leg from being hurt worse. Shifting and getting comfortable as long as possible without looking like, how did Beatrice put it, a liver-lilied city dandy, Hunter knew if he didn't slide now, he might never. He heart beat like a machine gun in his chest.

He gazed down at Viola, her hands covering her mouth in worry and her eyes shining with the longing he felt within himself. He willed himself to turn from her and focus on the dirt and rocks before him. With a final prayer for strength, he pushed himself into a slide.

The talus rock and loose dirt slid fast beneath him as he raced down much quicker than he'd anticipated. When he was a second away from the depression, he chanced one last look upon Viola before he might never see her again. She had Beatrice's hand in a vice grip between hers, her eyes closed tight and her lips moving as if in prayer. He hit a rock that was solid, breaking his concentration on her and pulling it to his head-first dive into the depression. Well, shucks, this would hurt.

CHAPTER 11

VIOLA SQUEEZED Beatrice's hand so tight between her own she thought she might break it. Her eyes closed so she wouldn't have to watch him slide and get hurt. She'd wanted to keep her eyes on him, soaking in his image until the end, but her heart couldn't take it, so she'd closed her eyes the second he had slid. She muttered prayers of safety and strength, hoping that God would answer and keep him from further harm.

The sound of him sliding down the mountain was loud and monstrous, as if the whole mountain was sliding down with him. Then there was nothing but the sound of small pebbles racing to catch up. Beatrice whooped, and Viola's eyes flew open to a cloud of dust so thick nothing appeared before her. Willing it to clear, she squeezed her sister's hand harder and harder, holding her breath for fear of what she might not see.

A shuttering cry came out as the dust settled enough for her to look at a crumpled heap at the base of the mountain. She let go of Beatrice's hand and raced to

Hunter's body. She slid to a stop beside him and fell to her knees, rolling him over. When he groaned in pain, she burst into tears, no longer able to keep the emotions at bay.

"Where do you hurt?" she asked wiping her tears between touching his face, arms and legs, thankful that she could touch him, no matter how inappropriate it was.

He groaned and sat up, his voice raspy. "No where new."

She helped him out of his backpack, wincing as he hissed a breath in. She pulled her kerchief out of her pocket and tried to wipe the dirt from his face while tears streamed down hers. The pain of seeing him hurt and the relief of seeing him still here was just too much for her to keep in the stupid things.

Hunter reached up and wiped the tears from her checks and whispered, "Viola, I'm okay. It will be okay."

Viola took a shuttering breath in, steeling her emotions and tucking them within as Beatrice led Cocoa up to them. Hunter squeezed Viola's hand, and she smiled at him.

"Well, you going to sit there all day, or are we going to head back?" Beatrice asked in a surly tone.

"Bea, let him catch his breath," Viola said in exasperation. "He just tumbled down a hill, for goodness' sake."

Hunter rolled to his knees and started to push up, grunting in discomfort. Viola moved to his weak side and wrapped her arm around his back to help him up.

"I'm ready." Hunter huffed when he was standing, his arm wrapped around her shoulder as he leaned into her.

"You sure?" she asked, peering up into his handsome and filthy face.

He gazed down at her in a way that had a hundred butterflies fluttering for release within her stomach, making her nauseous and excited at the same time. How could one look have her knees trembling and her brain frozen in a comatose state?

"Let's head back," he said, his voice husky.

Viola mounted Cocoa as Beatrice helped Hunter move closer to the horse. Viola slipped her foot out of the stirrup and reached down to help pull Hunter up. He positioned his good foot into the stirrup and swung up behind her with a grunt. Viola tried without success to not relish the feel of Hunter close behind her as they waited for Beatrice to mount Firestorm.

"Let's go home," she shouted.

"Home," Hunter breathed behind her as he wrapped his arms around her waist and pulled himself against her.

She sighed in happiness, leaning into him. He placed his cheek upon her head. In the breath that fanned her ear, she thought she heard him whisper, "Thank you, Lord" as he pulled her even tighter.

LINC SEETHED JUST AS VEHEMENTLY a week and a half after being chased from Viola's side as the day it happened. In fact, if he thought about it, he was even angrier now than he was then. That man, with his smooth words and hands all over Viola, would pay.

William moaned in the saddle behind him. Linc sent a scathing glance his way. His brother was still black and blue and probably had some broken ribs from where Linc had beaten him the week before. He deserved it, acting like the spineless chicken he was in front of that stranger cozying up to Viola. If William had been the fearless Sweeney he should be, if he'd shown some solidarity, that man may have backed down. Linc had let the rage loose on William, and he still wished, at times, that Robert had gone ahead and let him beat his weakling brother to death.

Smoke drifted above the trees up ahead. Linc turned to his brothers. "Let's go see who it is. Might be Orlando."

He turned back around, not waiting for a response and headed to the camp ahead. When they got close, he pushed down the rage and put on the cordial face that tricked folks into talking. It was growing harder and harder to do, though, with the rage building constantly inside him since seeing Viola's new beau. But he forced the anger deep down. He had a part to play and things to get done.

"Hello, camp." Linc hollered when they got close.

"Hello, yourself," a friendly booming voice answered. "Come on up to the fire, friend."

As they cleared the trees into the camp, Linc inwardly groaned. It was the simpleton called Jack. Though Linc knew he wasn't really a simpleton, the man's incessant talking always got on his nerves.

Jack motioned towards the fire with the mug he had in his hand. "Come, join me. The grub's just getting done, and I'd sure enjoy the company."

Linc swung from his horse, tied him to a tree, and followed his brothers to the campfire. Sure enough, the old trapper had a pot of beans simmered at the edge of the fire.

"The good Lord told me I'd be having guests." Jack

chuckled. "Good thing too, otherwise all I'd have for you boys would be some jerky."

"Jerky would've been just fine." Linc smiled, hoping his contempt didn't show.

"So what have you boys been up to?" Jack asked, looking into each of their faces and lingering on William's with an expression of concern.

Before he could ask William what happened, Linc said the first thing that popped in his head, "We are just coming from the Thomas' cabin."

"Oh, really," the old man said smiling fondly. "And how are the good sisters doing?"

"Not good, I'm afraid. Viola has let herself become quite the hussy," Linc said.

"How so?" Jack questioned, pulling back in shock.

"She has a man staying with her," Linc answered, trying to keep his voice calm with a tinge of disgust instead of the rage he felt. "She was hanging all over him while allowing him to call her inappropriate pet names like sweetheart and fondle her right in front of our very eyes. He was staying with her in the cabin with no other menfolk around that we could tell."

"Is this true?" Jack asked Linc's brothers.

When they both nodded, though not looking up, Linc smiled inwardly and continued his story. "In truth, I haven't seen such lewd behavior since stopping over at the brothels in Denver on the way out here."

"Glad I ran into you boys," Jack said as he pulled on his beard in concentration. "I'm heading north to take a message from Chief Johnson at the White River Agency to the girls' uncle Trapper Dan. I'll add it to my message that he needs to make beaver and see to those girls quick like since you say the Thomas menfolk are off."

"That's a relief." Linc said in feigned consolation. "I sure have been worried about the state of her soul since leaving there.

"It makes me mighty nervous not going to check on them myself, but this message from the chief is important and needs to get to Dan quick," Jack said, shaking his head in disappointment as he took a drink of his coffee.

As Jack droned on and on like a ninny about all the changes at the Ute agency and how he'd been tasked with finding Trapper Dan to get his thoughts on the situation, Linc tuned the idiot out. He could care less about the Indians. If it was up to him, those Utes would be moved off that prime farming land so whites could take advantage of it.

Something Jack had said nettled Linc's mind, though. The crazy coot's comment about leaving Viola with that stranger staying at her cabin got Linc to thinking. Something had been off about that man who'd spoke so carelessly about killing before. Something dangerous. Now that he thought about it, Viola had most likely been coerced to say those heartless things that had sliced through Linc's heart and left him to die. The thought of the man's arm wrapped around Viola sent a shiver through Linc. At first he thought is was jealousy, but now he recognized it as fear. Fear for his Viola. He owed it to Viola to go back for her, to take her from that precarious environment, and save her from that strange man. She'd be so thankful to him, she'd do anything he asked. With that thought, a grin stretched across his lips and a planned formed in his mind.

~

VIOLA GLANCED up from the laundry she was scrubbing on the washboard to where Hunter stood hanging the clean clothes on the line. She couldn't believe only a week had passed since that day at the mountain. She shook her head at the sight of a man doing laundry. Her pa and brother had certainly never hung clothes for her. She sobered as Hunter winced and brought his hand to his side. While he was healing well and much quicker than she expected, the way he occasionally winced when he moved or stepped told her he was more sore than he let on.

"Hunter, you don't have to do that," Viola called.

"For the hundredth time," Hunter called back, stretching his chest before reaching for the next item to hang. "I'd rather be doing what you all call women's work than sitting on my butt all day. I'd dust, mop, and cook all day if it keeps me out of that bed."

Viola went back to scrubbing the dress she had on the washboard and hummed as the memories of what they'd talked about all the days and nights since he'd arrived passed through her mind. She smiled at the amazing outcome of the trek to where he'd come to this time. She'd thanked God a million times over and more for allowing Hunter to stay. While he hadn't held her again, their conversations had created an intimacy between them that simultaneously frightened and elated her.

They'd talked about him being a high-ranking member of the elite and highly confidential military unit called Delta Force, about the danger, the intensive training and skill set that had distinguished him above the rest, about him commanding his team through more successful missions than any other Delta Force team up to that time. He'd joked about their importance to keep what he told them secret since his missions contained sensitive information and how his team would rile him to no end about being pushed down a mountain by a "kitty cat". At first he'd been hesitant to talk about it all. Maybe he worried the violence that had surrounded him the last ten years of his life would frighten her and Beatrice. However, once she'd talked to him, she'd never questioned his motive or morality. His every memory shared seemed saturated in his burden to rescue the innocent and protect the precarious freedom of the future United States that those of her time took for granted. Every memory shared made her heart more tender to the amazing man that he was.

Their conversations had moved to family, and they'd shared stories of their childhoods. She smirked at the memory of him mock shuddering when she told him their mother had named them after characters by her favorite author, Shakespeare. Hunter confessed when he'd had to study Shakespeare in school he'd read the sonnets, hoping somehow the poetry would get him noticed by the girls. It had surprised her they shared the experience of losing parents and feeling the pressure of raising a sibling. But the conversations she cherished the most were the ones late at night after Beatrice went to bed, when they talked about their dreams, about God and their fears. It was in those times she opened her heart completely, and she hoped and felt as if he had too.

Hunter hobbled over with the basket and plopped down on the grassy bank of the stream. He scratched at his beard that was growing, then laid back with one arm wrapped around his ribs and the other crooked behind his head. She thought he looked handsome in the buttoned cotton shirt she'd made him and buckskin pants she'd adjusted to fit him. He appeared as comfortable in the clothing of now as he did in the clothing he'd worn when he got here. How crazy to think after less than two weeks of knowing him, she felt as if her life would never be complete with him gone.

Not wanting to dwell on how she'd survive if God took Hunter back, she asked, "Would you like me to shave your beard?"

Hunter opened one eye and regarded her skeptically. "You ever done that? I thought mountain men had rugged beards and never cut their hair."

Viola laughed at his wariness and description. "Well, some of them never shave or cut their hair, I'll give you that. However, Pa and Orlando have me shave and trim them every spring."

Hunter hesitated. "So you've shaved your dad and brother once a year. That's not much practice."

"It's up to you." Viola shrugged, pulling the last dress from the washtub. "It certainly wouldn't itch if I shaved it."

"I thought the idea was for me to blend in." Hunter opened both eyes to look up at her. "Won't the other men here think it's weird if I'm clean shaven?"

"There are plenty of men who shave, even here in the mountains, besides—" She shrugged shyly, looking at the dress she was wringing to dry. "—I rather enjoy being able to see your face."

Hunter sat up, eyeing her with interest. He rubbed his

hand over his scruffy short beard and nodded. "Okay," he replied with a slow grin. "I'll let you shave this fur off."

Viola heart raced, and she wondered if she made a mistake in offering. It was one thing be close to help an injured man, but an entirely different thing to shave a healthy man. A man who stared at her like she was cake waiting to be devoured and who's crooked smile made her light-headed and brave at the same time. Viola shook her head at herself as she went to fetch the shaving supplies. This definitely was a mistake.

CHAPTER 12

THIS WAS A MISTAKE, Hunter thought as he sat on the homemade stool Viola had brought from the barn. The laundry flapped in the wind and the birds sang in the trees. With the creek bubbling next to him and the song the bloomers and birds were making, Hunter should be relaxed.

Viola ran the straight razor back and forth over the leather strap, the scraping sound sending tiny shivers of fear skittering across Hunter's skin like a tiny army of spiders raced there. She tested it and nodded in satisfaction, making him gulp. She placed shaving soap into a cup and frothed it until it looked like whipped cream, then stepped up to him.

As nervous as he was about letting someone scrape a sharp razor across his neck, he couldn't help but notice the intimacy of having Viola do it. Sure, she'd been taking care of his wounds, her fingers leaving trails of fire everywhere she touched, but this spoke of what could be a life-long action, something she'd do often when he convinced her to take a chance on someone who knew next to nothing of this time and marry him.

Hunter wasn't sure if he should worry about his easy assimilation into this time and lack of desire to return to his. It near broke his heart that he'd never see his brother Chase again. Hunter figured he'd always worry about how Chase was doing, especially with the way Hunter had disappeared. After their parents had died, Hunter had watched how Chase had skirted the edge of the wild side. Thankfully he'd never fallen into anything drastic like drugs or alcohol, but he pushed the envelop of danger, always trying the next big stunt. Hunter had been glad when it seemed like Chase was beginning to settle down, making some money investing and seeming to make peace with life instead of flirting with death. Hunter hoped him being gone didn't push Chase over the edge, but Hunter knew deep within him that he'd never return to the future again. He was home, plain and simple, and this was where he would remain to the end of his days, Lord willing.

Viola stepped up to his side and began putting the foam on his face. His lips turned up at the idea of her being this close the rest of his life.

Shaking her head, she chuckled. "You continue to smile like that, you'll wind up with soap in your mouth."

"Sorry." Hunter peered into her eyes and grinned even bigger. "I can't help but to smile when you're this close."

She huffed and rolled her eyes, a soft pink rising up her neck and cheeks as she turned to put the cup of soap down. She draped a towel over her arm and grabbed the razor. Her shoulders seemed tense, and as she raised the razor her hand shook.

"Lord." Hunter elaborately prayed, hoping to dispel her nervousness and tension. "Please still Viola's hands so she doesn't slice my neck open before I kiss her. Amen."

"You're incorrigible." Viola glared mockingly, the blush now adorably red, her hands now still as she lifted the blade.

"Thank you, Lord," she whispered, her honey cinnamon breath wafting over him.

She guided his head where she wanted it, then with a rhythm that soothed him, began gliding the razor down his face. She worked confidently from one cheek to the other. When she got to the front of his face, she leaned over his knees. Presented with an opportunity he didn't want to refuse, he opened his knees and pulled her closer by the waist. Viola started and gazed into his eyes, but when he thought she'd look away shyly like she always did, she didn't. She stared at him openly, somehow conveying her reciprocation of all he felt for her. She smiled, leaned into his leg a bit and finished shaving his face.

Viola did once last swipe at his neck with a flourish, wiped the blade clean on her towel, and closed the blade and tucked it into her apron pocket. She took the towel from her arm and wiped his face clean.

"Not a scratch on you." Viola teased, a twinkle in her eyes.

She started to pull away, but Hunter held tight, spreading his hands up her back. He tried to think of some smart-aleck remark, but all he could think about was her and her lips and how much he'd wanted to discover if they tasted like honey and cinnamon. She allowed him to pull her close, her heart beating rapidly against his hand pressed to her back.

When she placed her hands on his shoulders, he leaned the rest of the way to her. "Thank you." He whispered, his voice low and gravelly.

He tentatively pressed a kiss upon her lips. When she sighed and leaned further into him, her arms circling tight around his neck, he deepened the kiss. This was where he belonged, melded within her embrace. He breathed her name as he feathered kisses along her cheek and down her neck, sinking his hands deep within her hair. She grabbed his face in her hands, bringing his mouth back to hers, and kissed him with such passion his heart raced faster than it had on any mission he'd ever had.

"So, this is what you two do while I'm off slaving away in the barn mucking stalls?" Beatrice's question skidded into Hunter's mind as Viola ripped away from him with a gasp, her hands flying to her cheeks.

Hunter glared at Beatrice, hoping she saw how much he didn't appreciate her intrusion. She smirked and shrugged. She turned to Viola, raised an eyebrow in question, and placed her hands on her hips.

"I'm sick of eating deer. I'm going to go hunting, see if I can scare up a rabbit or two," Beatrice said, her tone all business as if she hadn't just interrupted the most amazing moment of Hunter's life.

"I still have the sheets to wash," Viola said, turning to pick up the basket. "I'm not going to be able to go for awhile."

"I'll go by myself, like I always do," Beatrice said, turning towards her horse that stood saddled and hitched to the corral.

"Okay." Viola said.

"No," Hunter said at the same time as Viola. Hunter glared at Viola when she disagreed, which she returned with a cock of her eyebrow.

Beatrice huffed and crossed her arms. "I'll be alright. I won't go far and will be back within a few hours."

"It's not safe for you to be out there without someone watching your back," Hunter said, standing from the stool. "We'll all go."

"I'm not leaving this laundry. The water's hot and ready. I don't want to have to set this up again tomorrow and the sheets need a good scrub," Viola said, her fingers tightening around the basket as if she thought he'd pry it from her fingers and toss her over the back of a horse or something.

Hunter exhaled and rubbed his hand over his forehead and eyes. Both ladies wanted different things, both had valid points and yet both couldn't be done at the same time without living someone alone. He was going to make someone upset when he made his decision. This was why he loved the military. With the army, you were given orders, and you followed. In real life, that didn't work out so well.

"Beatrice, why don't we go first thing tomorrow morning before the sun rises? That way we can finish the laundry and still get meat." Hunter asked, hoping his voice sounded as convincing as he planned.

"I'm going, Romeo, just like I've always gone. Who do you think watches over us when our father and brother aren't here?" Beatrice asked, her shoulders tight in agitation.

"Beatrice, I don't like you going off to the woods alone

right now, either." Viola said, Hunter finally glad she'd come to his way of thinking. "If anything, it'd be better if I stayed here at the safety of the house while you two went hunting. No one can sneak up here in broad daylight with the way the house is located. I'll get the rest of the laundry done, keep a vigilant eye on the horizon, and wear my holster at all times."

Beatrice nodded like the idea was smart while Hunter shook his head so hard he thought it might pop off. "No, no. I don't want us separated. When the unit is together it's stronger."

Viola walked up to him with a look of compassion on her face that made him itchy. She placed her hand upon his arm, causing his muscles to twitch with anxiety. "Hunter, this is our life here. We can't wait for the situation to be perfect or safe to do the things that need to be done. What we can do is assess the situation and pick the most logical approach."

"But—"

"Both these chores need done." Viola talked over him, which was another thing that he wasn't used to in the army. "Pa set this homestead up so we wouldn't be surprised by unwanted guests. Now we know the Sweeneys are up to no-good. If they show up, I'll just bar myself in the house. There's no way they can get in with the bar on. However, Beatrice needs to go hunting, and out there, she's more open to attack. She needs your extra eyes right now, not me."

Hunter didn't like it, wanted to refuse the logic, but he knew Viola was right. If he didn't go with Beatrice, she'd go anyways. This wasn't the army where he could command people to do what he thought best.

"I don't like it. I still think we should all stay together, but I agree Beatrice shouldn't go alone," Hunter said, doubt thick on his heart and in his voice.

"It'll be alright, Romeo," Beatrice said. "You'll be back in no time to continue wooing your Juliet."

Viola glared at Beatrice. "Beatrice, really."

Beatrice walked to the barn with a laugh. Viola reached for Hunter's hand and gave it a squeeze. How could he just leave her here?

"Please," Hunter begged, knowing his voice sounded pathetic. "Be safe. Keep vigilant."

"I promise, I will." Viola squeezed his hand one more time before letting go and heading for the cabin.

Hunter watched for a second before moving to the barn to help Beatrice saddle his horse, though he knew she didn't need his help. These two women could take care of themselves without him, so why had God brought him back? Maybe he was wrong, and this family wasn't why he was here. Was he making his own way, blazing his own path again, focusing on what he wanted instead of what God wanted? As Hunter stepped into the shadowed barn, a chill spilled over his head and slid down his neck causing him to shiver, and it had nothing to do with the cooler barn interior.

LINC PEERED from the spot him and his brothers had camped out to keep watch on the Thomas cabin. As he witnessed Viola and that man kissing passionately right in the open field beside the stream for all the world to see, Linc could barely suppress rage bubbling hot and blinding. Whatever decency had remained in his heart turned cold and hard as Linc realized that the woman that was supposed to be his wife was happily throwing herself at another. The coldness spread from his chest to his limbs, and he vowed he'd make her pay for her indiscretion.

The only thing that held Linc back from going in their with his guns drawn and firing was his superior intelligence that told him to hold off and wait. They had a plan, and it would work.

"She don't look too upset to be with him," William the Idiot said.

Linc glared at his youngest brother, wishing Robert wasn't between them so Linc could whack the stupid right out of the little fool. William noticed Linc's anger and cowered behind Robert. Perhaps Linc should just shot William and put Linc out of his misery. How they shared blood was beyond him.

Linc's rage turned to glee as he watched unbelievingly as Beatrice and the interloper rode off across the field and into the woods leaving Viola home alone.

"Looks like the Good Lord is smiling down on us today, boys," Linc said cheerfully. "We go get my bride now without anyone to get in our way."

Robert gave him a doubt-filled look while William curled more into himself like a baby. It was a plumb shame Linc was the only Sweeney with brains. He pulled hard on the reins and took off towards his future, towards his reward. As they rode closer, he swore he heard the angels singing down upon him in encouragement.

～

Viola wrung the last sheet tight as she hummed the tune to *Beautiful Dreamer*, a song her brother had heard from some trapper once. She knew she acted ridiculous singing over a hot wash pot, her hands scalded red and cracking from the boiling water and harsh lye soap. She probably appeared a fright wearing her oldest dress stained from years of use and her hair stringy with sweat plastered to her face.

Viola couldn't seem to draw one ounce of worry over her appearance as the memory of the scorching kiss replayed over and over again in her mind. Hunter hadn't cared that she looked like a wet hen on a rainy day. He'd dug his hands right into her hair, the heat of the kiss practically consuming her right there next to the creek. If it had continued much longer, she would have needed to throw herself into the water just too cool down.

Viola stopped humming and fanned her face with her hand at the thought of swimming with Hunter. Their clothes soaked and plastered to their bodies as he pulled her close for another kiss. Maybe she should suggest a nice swim when Hunter got back.

Viola shook her head at that senseless notion and sang loudly as she hung the sheet on the line. "Beautiful dreamer, wake unto me. Starlight and dewdrops are awaiting thee."

A horse whinnied a return. Viola glanced around the sheet. Viola's stomach dropped to her knees so fast she almost vomited. While she was off daydreaming, the Sweeneys had ridden up. She hoped she could make it to the cabin without them noticing her.

Viola skirted around the sheets, keeping them between

her and the Sweeneys as long as possible, then dashed for the cabin. The loud clip clop of horses footsteps as they came into the yard warned Viola she didn't have time to lift the heavy bar to the door. She took off to her father's bedroom, racing to the book shelf that stood against the back wall. She released the secret lever and squeezed into the cave hidden behind, pulling the shelf closed behind her. Viola unholstered her gun as she heard the front door crash open.

"Viola, dear, I've come to rescue you!" Linc's yell squeezed her heart in fear.

Viola backed two steps further into the cave, her only light the sliver coming from underneath the secret door. The gun shook violently in her hands. She pointed it to the floor, not wanting the thing to go off accidentally in her unsteadiness. She took a deep breath, let it out with a prayer for help, and focused her attention on the sounds coming from other side of the bookshelf.

"Viola, girl, come out. We don't have time for you to act silly and hide," Linc said, his loud voice sounding cold and harsh.

Viola strained to hear the deep voice that spoke to Linc, but it was too low to discern. The sound of glass breaking caused her to jump. She listened as Linc moved through the cabin, explosion of noise following his footsteps. The sound muffled for a minute, and Viola hoped he'd left. Yet, with a loud growl from the cabin, she realized he had simply been in her and Beatrice's room. She shuddered at the thought of him being in there, touching her things. The crashing got louder as Linc moved into her father's room.

"Where is she?" Linc bellowed as the bookcase shook

with his violence, the thud of books hitting the floor sounding through the wood.

Viola heard the low, steady voice of Robert speak. "She's not here, Linc. Let's go before the other two get back."

"She's here you idiot. Where else could she be? I saw movement by the clothesline," Linc said, as the wood in front of her rattled again.

To Viola's horror, the bookcase popped open an inch, causing light to point a line right to where she stayed frozen in the cold cave. Robert stood before the crack, his eyes widening in shock as he peered at her. He stepped quickly to the crack, pushing the case flush to the cave wall with a soft click.

"What was that?" Linc's question shuddered the air from her chest. Would he find her now? Would she have to unload the pistol on him, scarring her soul from taking his life? If he found her, she knew she wouldn't hesitate ... at least she hoped she wouldn't hesitate. She prayed she wouldn't find out.

"Just what do you think it was, Linc? You're throwing things around like a child throwing a tantrum, things falling left and right. I just caught this bookcase from falling on your fool head." Robert's voice, firm and harsh as he lied to his brother, confused and elated her. She held her breath as Robert continued. "Viola's not here, and I'm leaving. I'm not about to be caught here when the Thomas's come back and find this place trashed."

Viola heard heavy footsteps walk away. She let her breath our slowly and quietly took another in, listening, waiting. A loud, anguished roar full of rage and hurt sounded from the bedroom. Viola cried out in fear and quickly covered her mouth with her hand to stifle the noise. An eternity passed before feet stomped out of the cabin with another roar. As Viola heard the horses's muffled retreat, she fell back against the cave wall, collapsed to the floor, curled into a ball, and sobbed.

CHAPTER 13

THE ANXIETY that sat heavy on Hunter's chest since the moment he and Beatrice had left the homestead now howled and gnawed at him like a two-hundred pound lion. They shouldn't have left Viola alone. Now that the hunting responsibility was fulfilled with the small elk laid across the back of his horse's rump, the desire to kick into a full-out gallop proved almost overwhelming.

How was he ever going to survive in this time? He had always longed for the simple, uncomplicated life of long ago, a life where your focus stayed on surviving the elements, far from the constant intrusions and distractions of the future. But this time held it's own distractions, mainly a beautiful blonde, with eyes as calm as mountain lake water and a tender heart that made Hunter go all macho and insist on protecting her.

Hunter shook his head at the idiocy his thoughts were creating. Back home, he wouldn't have hesitated in leaving his wife or girlfriend home alone, a woman who probably would have less skills at protecting herself than

Viola did. So why was he suddenly pulling this chauvinistic stunt, practically thumping his chest and dragging her away by the hair? In truth, Viola and Beatrice could probably take care of themselves better without him, since he wasn't adept at operating the firearms here. He also knew almost nothing of farming or ranching or whatever it was they did with their land and animals. He was just an extra body, and a broken one at that.

As Hunter and Beatrice rode into the homestead yard, Beatrice whipped out her revolver and scanned the area. Hunter's focus sharpened as he pulled his own gun out. The sheets flapped on the line and the wash pot still sat on a fire that had died low. A lone sheet laid piled in the dirt by the line. Everything was quiet—too quiet.

Hunter dismounted fast, sending a sharp pain up his bad leg, almost bringing him to his knees. He gritted his teeth through the pain and raced to the cabin where the door stood wide open. He flattened himself to the side of the door and took a deep breath, willing his training to the forefront. Beatrice landed on the opposite side of the door and glanced at him. Hunter pointed to himself and gave hand signals he'd go in first, then she'd cover him. She nodded her head, and he breached the room.

As Hunter scanned the front room for intruders, he noticed the cabin's floor was littered with stuff, like a cyclone had gone through and ripped everything loose. Hunter motioned for Beatrice to check her room while he went to the other bedroom. The same disorder greeted him there but no Sweeneys. No Viola.

"Viola!" His yell ripped from his chest as he turned in the bedroom doorway, peering for her in the corners of the front room as if she'd pop out from under the scattered books or crawl from beneath his bed. He knew they shouldn't have left her. Now the Sweeneys had her. Beatrice looked about to say something as she pointed behind him, but he held his hand up to stop her. Anger at himself and at her filled him so much he couldn't look at her, let alone hear any excuse she might give. She put her hands on her hips and glared.

As a bellow began to build within his chest he heard a soft click behind him. He turned, raising his gun when the most beautiful vision walked out from behind the bookcase that stood against the back wall. Viola. Her face smeared with dirt and tears. Her hair loose and tangled. She stood there alive, not kidnapped by a crazed man. A sob ripped from her as she launched herself across the room at him. Hunter holstered the gun and met her halfway, pulling her tight to him as her body shuddered in his arms.

"I thought they'd got you," he hoarsely whispered. "I thought I had failed again, lost someone else."

"What happened?" Beatrice asked from the bedroom doorway.

Viola pulled back, but just far enough that she could look at Hunter and Beatrice, which Hunter thought was wise since he wasn't sure he could let her go yet. "The Sweeneys showed up while I was finishing the laundry. I didn't have time to lift the bar. I barely made it into the cave."

"They just trashed the place and left?" Beatrice asked in doubt.

Viola shook her head. "It was the oddest thing. Linc was in this room raging. He threw books off the case and accidentally sprung the lock, opening the case an inch. I knew for sure he was going to find me and I was going to have to kill him." Viola shook her head again, her forehead scrunching up in confusion.

"What happened?" Beatrice asked the question screaming in Hunter's head.

"Robert stood by the opening, his eyes wide in shock. I know he saw me. He stared straight into my eyes. Next thing I know, he's stepping up to the case and pushing it shut. When Linc asked what Robert was doing, Robert lied and said he stopped the bookshelf from falling on Linc. Robert then said he was leaving, that I wasn't here and he wasn't about to get caught when you all returned."

"Why would he do that?" Beatrice asked, her voice dripping with skepticism.

"He's not quite sold on his brother's scheme," Hunter answered, brushing the hair from Viola's face, running his thumb across her dirty, tear-stained cheek.

"Maybe Robert will talk Linc out of this insane obsession," Viola said as she peered up at Hunter, the fear still evident in her eyes. He wished he could wipe that away as easily as he could the dirt and the tears.

"Linc's loco. He's not giving anything up this easily," Beatrice said as she surveyed the cabin with a huff of disgust. "Did he really have to destroy the place? That polecat left a mountain-load of work behind on top of butchering that elk. Let's move you two. We don't have time to stand around, staring into each others eyes."

Viola stepped out of Hunter's arms, holding his stare with hers as she did. He trailed his hand down her arm and squeezed her fingers. He wanted to hold on forever but knew he didn't have that privilege yet. As she pulled her hand from his and walked away, the sunlight from the open door turned her hair to spun gold. He knew he couldn't claim her as his now, but he determined that distinction would be his the first chance he got.

～

As VIOLA and Beatrice got to work picking up books, Hunter turned towards the back of the room at the hole exposed behind the bookshelf.

"Are we just going to ignore the gaping hole in the back of the cabin?" Hunter asked. "Inquisitive minds want to know."

"We can show you that later. There's too much work to do," Beatrice said as she headed towards the door outside. "Hunter, come help me hang that elk up in the springhouse before it gets too warm."

"Fine, but when we are done with that, we are barring the door and you two are showing me what's in the secret passageway." Hunter made his way through the mess, grabbing Viola's hand and dragging her along on the way out. "You're sticking close to me until my heart rate and my nerves are back to normal."

Viola sighed and squeezed his hand in hers. He led his horse to the springhouse, which was really a small shed built up against a small cave that he'd been told stayed cool all summer. The entire time they worked at hanging the meat, Hunter's mind roamed to that opening at the back of the cabin. He'd always been intrigued by secret passageways. He remembered begging his parents to build him one in-between his and Chase's room. One weekend, while his mom had been out of town on a conference, him, his dad, and

Chase had built a secret door to connect their two bedrooms. That weekend, and the surprise on his mom's face when she returned, remained one of his favorite memories.

Now a secret room no one cared to mention before begged to be explored, and he was stuck outside wrestling with an elk. He wasn't going to allow the fact that he hadn't been told about the cave pinch at him, at least not much. He tried not to inwardly pout that in all the hours of time him and Viola talked, not once did she mention a hidden passageway.

"I need to know if there's enough ammo for me to practice shooting? I'm good with my gun I brought with me, but these old six-shooters are cumbersome, and I want to be comfortable handling them," Hunter asked, hoping if he talked, his mind wouldn't obsess over why he hadn't been told.

"Don't worry. We have plenty," Viola said, as she closed the door to the springhouse after him and Beatrice finished.

Hunter wasn't sure his idea of plenty and hers would match, but with the elk hanging, he pointed his feet towards the cabin.

"We need to put the horses up," Beatrice said, her tone chiding.

"The horses can wait five minutes … I'm about to bust at the seams with anticipation." Hunter glared at her, daring her to contradict him.

Beatrice rolled her eyes and walked towards the cabin. "Well, let's get to it. Those Sweeneys left us enough work for a whole week. We don't have time for childish whims of exploring."

"Really, Beatrice, do you have to be so rude?" Viola quickly glanced to Hunter.

Beatrice turned, a sparkle of mischief in her eyes. She snickered as she jogged to the cabin. Hunter looked at Viola, winked, and took off after Beatrice. When he got to the cabin, he waited for Viola to enter and barred the door. He followed her to the bedroom, the swish of her skirts almost distracting him from the mystery awaiting.

Beatrice reached for a lantern hanging on an iron hook right inside of the hole. She struck a match along the wall, lit the lantern, and then held it up, revealing a tunnel that led into the heart of the mountain. The sharp scent of the match's sulfur mingled with the musty scent of underground.

"What most people don't know is that Pa's primary reason for building here was so he'd have access to this cave without having to leave the house. It's strategical, just not in the way people would think," Viola grabbed his hand and pulled him towards the entrance.

Her voice bounced off the walls as they walked through the tunnel. It amazed him when he ducked in and immediately stood up straight. The roof of the tunnel was about six inches from his head and the width was a good five feet across. The musty, earthy scent of a dry cave instead of the dank smell of a moist one tinged the air, and the temperature dropped the further they walked in the mountain. About fifteen feet in, the tunnel opened up to a cavernous room.

Beatrice walked to the center and hooked the lantern to a chain that hung from a metal hook hammered into the ceiling. How anyone had gotten the chain up that high baffled him, with the rough walls and the near vertical slant of them. With the place lit up except in the farthest corner, he saw crates and crates of items organized along the walls and upon shelves that lined through the middle of the cave like their own personal mercantile. Labels described every crate as if he stood in the archive of some museum. Hunter willed his brain to shut his mouth from gaping like a caught trout. This cave was the best secret room he'd ever found.

"Pa never wanted to be caught unaware," Viola said from next to him. "He always said if we got holed up in the cabin, whether from weather or miscreants, he didn't want to worry about not being able to survive. He said if a man grew roots, he should be able to protect it, whether the threat was natural or man-made."

"Sounds like a good idea," Hunter replied as he walked further into the cave and took inventory.

"The crates along the walls are all filled with ammunition." Beatrice turned and pointed as she beamed with pride. "The shelves on the inside are food stores, fabric, bandages, and extra medicinal herbs and whatnot that we gather during the year. And the best part is, if you follow the crack in the back corner, there's a fresh spring that comes out of the mountain and runs into the lake. The crack's tight, so only Viola and I ever go back, though you could make it if you needed to. We have an endless supply of water, enough food to last half a year or more, and enough ammunition to wage a war."

Hunter peered at the number of crates stacked as high as he could reach around the entire perimeter and wondered at the ingenuity and forethought put into this amount of storage. Thousands of rounds had to be stored here, and with the dry atmosphere of the cave, the ammunition wouldn't be compromised and left useless. His military mind immediately went into overdrive.

"Can the water be tainted?" he asked as he walked around the wall, cataloguing what he saw.

"No, Pa searched for years for the source to make sure it couldn't be tampered with. He never found where it began, and if he didn't find it, there's no way a knuckle-headed Sweeney will find it," Beatrice said.

"What about where the spring leaves the mountain? Can that be followed into the cave?"

"Nope, it runs for a few feet through the cave then disappears through a hole I couldn't even get my head through. Pa searched for where it comes out the mountain and his best bet was that the spring feeds somewhere into the lake. Wherever it goes, there's no way into here," Beatrice answered.

"How'd your Pa get all this in here without anyone noticing?"

"We didn't bring it in all at once," Viola explained. "This has been years of gathering. Pa traveled each summer to a couple of different forts or trading posts located throughout the mountains. He'd hook up the buckboard, load the thing up with furs, even though driving the wagon is tricky with no good trails, sell the furs, stock up to the hilt on supplies, and sneak everything into the cave. He'd make sure food and household goods stacked visible on the top so no one watching would notice the ammo."

"And going to different forts kept people from putting it all together." Hunter whistled in admiration.

"We also use the springhouse for the storage of the items we use every day, like our milk, cheese and whatnot, so anyone visiting or coming and going won't wonder how we keep things fresh," Viola added.

"So even if you shot a whole case of lead for that Colt Navy you've got strapped to your leg, we'd still have more than enough to hold off those lowdown, dirty polecats," Beatrice said.

"This is fantastic," Hunter said rubbing his hands in satisfaction.

He peered across the shelves at Viola. Her face shone in the soft lantern light with pride. This was more prepared and more thoughtful than most people ever were in his times, and that included all those apocalyptic nuts he read about. *Lord, please, help me be the man worthy of her. Help me protect her. To protect them.*

CHAPTER 14

AFTER HOURS of straightening and salvaging the items Linc had ravished, Viola, Beatrice, and Hunter sat at the table. Thankfully, she'd put a roast to simmer on the stove. All they had to do was slice some off and make sandwiches out of the leftover morning biscuits for supper. Even though they all sat in silence, the exhaustion of the day pulling all their shoulders down, Viola knew they still had a lot to discuss.

"I guess we should get to the serious stuff, so we can get to finishing up with the chores," Beatrice said. "I'm not one for sitting around chatting over coffee, so let's be out with it and move on."

Hunter sat up in his chair and pushed his mug away. Viola could see his demeanor shift to one taking command. He'd trained for ten years for situations like this. She remembered him telling her his ability to assess the situation, and neutralize the problem. While she knew her and Beatrice didn't need him here taking charge and making orders, she praised God for the comfort she felt because of Hunter's presence.

Hunter looked at both her and Beatrice, his face set in serious lines. "We all understand that we haven't seen the end of the Sweeneys, but what we don't know is when they'll show their ugly heads again."

"In the past, they haven't stuck around very long," Viola replied. "We'd see them one day, then not see hide or hair of them for months."

"Just because you didn't see them didn't mean they weren't there," Hunter said. "Linc seemed adamant that you were his, and someone that obsessed is liable to stalk in the bushes and spy on you. He may have been watching you for days."

Viola shivered and wrapped her arms around her middle. The idea of Linc watching her caused vomit to rise into her throat. She peeked at Hunter and wished she could move closer to him, have him wrap his arm around her.

"So he's sulking around," Beatrice said. "That'll make it that much easier to put an end to him when he messes up. I say we take this fight to him. Both Viola and I can ghost around in the woods. We can track them come morning and finish this by tomorrow evening."

Hunter shook his head. "It's not that easy, Bea. We can't know where he is after all this time. He could have circled around and is watching as we speak. If we go after him, that'll make it that much easier to take us out one at a time until he gets what he wants. Viola and, we're assuming, your mine."

Hunter pushed his hand through his hair. Frustration fairly pulsed from him. Viola reached her hand over and patted his where it clenched on the table. He quickly grabbed her fingers and held them, his thumb running over her knuckles.

"If there were more of us, it wouldn't be a big deal," Hunter said. "We could go off in pairs and be kind of safe, or we could go confront them head on and probably come out on top. But, with only the three of us, I don't like the odds.. No. Until Orlando gets here to back us up, we stick together. No one is alone out of the house, ever."

Beatrice mouth fell opened, and she shook her head. Viola knew Hunter's plan would chap Beatrice's hide, but it would be necessary.

"Ever, Bea," Hunter insisted. "If we need to go to the barn, either we all go, or the one who stays behind bars the door. Have to use the outhouse? Guess what? The buddy system never lets you down. That way the Sweeneys can't get any of us alone. I'd rather we all go, but I'm hoping that the bar on the door will keep them out. Whoever is inside can look through the peephole before opening the door."

"I can't do it," Beatrice retorted. "The Sweeneys won't get the drop on me, and I'm not giving up my freedom."

"Would you rather die?" Viola asked, anger at her sister's selfishness making the words come out harsh. "What if they kill you? What if they take you as a warning or for ransom? I can't think of you not being here or getting hurt because of me. No, Beatrice, you will do as Hunter says. He knows what he's doing. And when it's time to act, he won't hesitate to include us in the plan."

Beatrice stood up so fast her chair crashed over behind her. As she stormed out of the house she ranted, "If we hunt down those skunks like I said, then we wouldn't have to worry about them anymore."

Viola turned, pulled her hand from Hunter's and sighed. As she moved to stand, he motioned her to stop. He stood up and moved to leave.

"Bar the door," he said. "I'll go see if I can cool her down."

Viola nodded, knowing she should talk to Beatrice herself, but not having the energy to do so. Maybe Hunter could get Beatrice to listen. All Viola knew was that if she tried to talk to Beatrice right now, she was liable to just get angrier. So she lifted the bar into place and went to clean the supper dishes, praying that God would give Hunter the wisdom needed to deal with her stubborn sister.

HUNTER WALKED TO THE BARN. The chinking and logs did nothing to block the banging and furious one-sided conversation taking place among the animals. He understood Beatrice's frustration. He wanted nothing more than to take the fight to the Sweeneys, and he knew he and the ladies might even get the drop on them. Yet to do so would put everyone in even greater danger. After the disaster in Colombia and his failure to Hope, he just wasn't sure if he could trust himself. He wasn't sure if God could trust him.

He paused at the side door into the barn, placing his forehead against the rough wood. Beatrice's angry rantings muffled through the barn wall.

"Lord," he prayed, taking one more deep breath,

wanting to feel God's presence, though Hunter knew he didn't deserve it. "Give me your wisdom."

He watched the sun shimmering on the lake. The mountains reflecting on the surface created a picture that took his breath away, huge and rugged yet softened by the unfurling of the aspen leaves that circled the middle of the mountains like a velvety skirt. In all Hunter's travels for the army, he'd never seen a place more beautiful. He took one more deep breath and went to face the maelstrom that was Beatrice Thomas.

Hunter opened the side door that led into the barn and let his eyes adjust to the dark interior. He admired again the sturdy log walls and efficient design that could hold five horses, the milk cow, and all the gear needed for living in the wilderness of the 1800s. The hay loft stretched out above and was low on hay. He was glad it was summer, and the horses roamed out in the corral.

Beatrice's voice sounded from above him. "So, the prison guard checks on the prisoner."

"Don't you think you're being a little dramatic? Permission to board, my lady?" Hunter asked with flair as he walked to the ladder.

"Permission granted, I suppose," Beatrice answered.

Hunter climbed the ladder, wincing with every step on his bad ankle. The dust and hay particles tickled his nose. He sneezed as he reached the landing, his ribs spiking with pain. His moan of discomfort changed suddenly to one of awe. Beatrice sat on a low bench facing a window that overlooked the vast meadow. The meadow blended into the aspen and pine laden forest that climbed up the mountains still capped in snow. The slowly setting sun finished the picture with light shades of yellow and orange just tinging the blue sky. Hunter knew within the hour the sky would be a riot of color, and this spot would prove the best seat for viewing the sunset.

"This is incredible," he said as he awkwardly walked half bent over to avoid smashing his head on the rafters. He lowered to the bench and settled with a huff. "This is unexpected. How did I not know about this?"

"Well, since it's on the backside of the barn and you've been stuck in the house laid up or making moon eyes over my sister, you haven't been up for doing much exploring," Beatrice replied, steaming with anger and frustration, and if tumbling back in time hadn't fried his instincts, also doubt and loneliness.

Hunter grunted. "Can't argue with that."

They sat in silence for several minutes. It was a comfortable silence that seemed to capture the serenity of the beauty before them. He took it all in, letting his eyes shift from shadows to light as he memorized the details. He tried to remain relaxed, but also kept his eyes sharp for anything that shouldn't belong, like a no-good Sweeney staking the place.

After at least a quarter of an hour, Beatrice sighed. "My pa built me this bench and brought the glass all the way from Denver one summer. I spent a lot of time up here thinking and, I guess if I'm being honest, escaping. He said if I was going to spend so much time up here mulling things over, I should at least have a comfortable seat and good scenery to make the mulling more enjoyable."

Hunter leaned over and bumped her shoulder.. "He sounds like a very thoughtful father, like something my dad would do. In fact, my brother Chase used to spend so much time in this tree at our childhood home that my dad decided he needed a treehouse so Chase would have more room to move around. They spent an entire weekend knocking that thing out. Secretly, I think it petrified my mom that Chase would fall out of the tree and break his neck, so to keep my mom from worrying so much, my dad built the thing."

"My pa's amazing." Beatrice's voice was airy with longing. "He understood I wasn't happy here, that I dreamed of leaving, so he did everything he could think of to make life here better for me. Things like this bench and sending off for books on every subject under the sun."

Hunter looked at her profile. "Why aren't you happy here?" Hunter asked, hoping she'd open up to him.

She sighed. "You aren't going to leave this alone, are you?"

"Bea, I'm not going to force you to talk," Hunter said, hoping his sincerity came across to her. "I just thought you might want someone to talk to who isn't family."

"It's so hard to explain," Beatrice replied. "The lack of people here almost drives me insane. I want to see more of this world. To find a way to bring joy to others and meet new people. I know that sounds silly, but it just gets lonely and depressing out here."

Beatrice picked at the seam in her pants. Hunter gave her the space she needed. If she talked, she talked, but he didn't want to push her too hard. She huffed as she picked up a stalk of hay and crushed it in between her fingers. The dry, grassy smell wafted to Hunter's nose. He had a sense that wasn't all, so he waited for her to continue.

"Honestly, I just feel like I'm not where I'm supposed to be. That this—" She gestured with a sweep of her hand to the meadow and mountains before them—"Isn't my destiny. But where am I supposed to go? We have no relatives I can go live with, and a single lady on her own is just not acceptable. I could go to college, but I have no desire to be a teacher or a nurse. So I'm stuck, and I hate that my discontent is viewed as such an oddity. Don't get me wrong. I love my family. I love the mountains and the freedom. I just wish there was more."

"I understand how you feel," Hunter replied. "I felt the same way back home. I liked my job, my brothers-in-arms. I loved when Chase and I could hook up on my vacations and go camping, surfing, or hiking."

Beatrice shook her head, her eyebrows pulled together in confusion. Hunter laughed, realizing something he said wasn't familiar to her. He shrugged. "Sorry. Ask me later about what I said that confused you, and I'll explain. Anyways, there was always a disconnect, a feeling like there was something missing. I tried not to dwell on it, but when I got here, I realized there had been a big part of me missing."

"I kind of don't think time travel is God's everyday answer to discontentment." Beatrice huffed.

"Yeah." Hunter pushed his hand through his hair. "You're probably right."

"And now, because of those lowdown, stinking Sweeneys, the freedom I love about this place is being ripped away from me!" Beatrice got more riled, ripping hay into pieces. "It's not right. I can take care of myself, Hunter. I don't need you keeping tabs on me or anything. I've wandered these entire mountains with nothing and no one but Firestorm, my Colt and my hunting knife. I've never come up against anything I can't handle."

"I don't doubt that, Bea. You are very capable," Hunter replied with sincerity. Feeling his lack of confidence rising, Hunter huffed in frustration and continued. "The thing is, I'm the one not capable. Not only am I still injured, every step up that ladder was painful, but I'm not good enough with the guns here yet. I'm not good enough, period. I can't keep her safe without you, Bea. I need your help here, and that's hard for a army grunt like me to admit."

"I don't know about that." Beatrice smirked, the anger and frustration fading a bit from her face. "You appear to be doing just fine."

Hunter shook his head in disagreement. His draw of the gun earlier when they arrived at the cabin had been clumsy, the heavy gun awkward in his hand. "No, that Colt is like drawing bricks from my holster with how unyielding the thing is. I'm totally, completely, and utterly at a disadvantage here. If we don't stick together, it could end up in another tragedy. I don't think I can go through that so quickly again."

"I didn't mean to eavesdrop during your conversation with my sister, but I heard you talking about your mission and that poor girl Hope. I'm so sorry," Beatrice apologized.

"Missions fail all the time," Hunter explained, ignoring the confused look once again gracing Beatrice's face. "It was bound to happen to us, especially with the level of danger and secrecy our missions required. We'd had other soldiers injured or killed, but we sign up for that, and even with those KIA ... I mean killed in action, our missions had always been completed successfully. Hope Isaac's family were civilians, missionaries in Colombia that the US government recruited as dignitaries. The government thought with their knowledge of the local culture and their way with the local people, the Columbian president, who is basically a drug lord, would be more open to communication with the Isaacs. The government was wrong."

Hunter pulled his legs up and placed his arms crossed upon his knees. He looked out the window and tried to keep the images of that horrible day from playing in his head, the images that rolled like a film stuck on replay every time he closed his eyes. He prayed at some point the memories would stop haunting his dreams.

"The Columbian cartel kidnapped, tortured, and held hostage the Isaacs. Nothing was traced to the Columbian president, though we all know without a doubt it was his directive that had them taken. We went in to get them, a quick in and out job. We had extensive intel, which isn't always the case. But when we got on the ground and in the thick of it, I hesitated at the worst time. I could feel God nudging me to move in, to engage, but I wanted everything to be perfect. My hesitation killed that poor couple and left Hope with no one."

"You don't know that," Beatrice countered. "They could've died anyway or possibly one of your men could've been killed or maybe even Hope."

"Maybe," Hunter replied, shrugging. "But I also know that I failed God when I failed to follow what my heart told me was His urging. I won't do that again. I can't always have things the way I want them. I won't always be able to control the outcome or even the process, but He is always in control and has my back. 'The Lord your God is in your midst, a victorious warrior.' That's from Zephaniah chapter three. My dad made me memorize it when I enlisted. I know sticking close and going in pairs chaps your hide. I don't want to take away that freedom you hold so dear, believe me I don't. But we have to go into this battle with a sound strategy. Our chances of us all surviving this is being smart, sticking together like glue and waiting for reinforcements."

"I'm going to go loco!" Beatrice pulled her hair in frustration.

"We don't have to stay at the house. We can still go hunting and what not. We just have to go together. Plus, it'll only be for a few weeks. As soon as Orlando gets back, we can reorganize and re-strategize."

"Then we take the fight to them," Beatrice growled.

"Absolutely," Hunter replied. "I don't want to be on the offensive for the rest of my life. As soon as we get all the information from Orlando, we find out just what those Sweeney's have to say for themselves. In the meantime, do we have a deal?"

"Sure," Beatrice answered. "You know, Hunter, I don't understand half of what you say sometimes. What happens to the English language in the next hundred or so years?"

"It gets botched, Bea, totally and completely botched," Hunter replied with mock sadness.

"See, you just made my point." Beatrice snorted.

Hunter laughed right along with her. Breathing out with relief, he gazed out the window at the incredible sunset painting the sky in brilliant oranges, pinks, and purples and thanked God again for the life he had fallen into.

CHAPTER 15

VIOLA STOOD at the sink washing dishes from dinner and butchering the elk, her movements slow with the weight of tiredness. She was thankful for the fresh meat, but, since they woke before sunrise to butcher it as early as possible, she was more thankful at the moment that the chore was done. Her shoulders slumped in exhaustion.

When Viola had fallen into bed the night before, fatigue made her eyelids so heavy they felt like bricks. She was sure she'd be sound asleep before Beatrice got settled. Yet sleep evaded her, skirting away like a skittish squirrel, only to leave the terror of the day to chase her every time she closed her eyes. Memories of Linc's angered yell echoed in her ears. The cold of the cave seeped into her skin. When she'd finally fallen asleep, Beatrice elbowed her shortly later to get up.

The sound of approaching hoofbeats sent Beatrice running to the window. Viola dried her hands as Beatrice gave a whoop of excitement and threw the door open. Viola ran out the door without hesitation, knowing

Orlando must finally be home. The smile froze on her face as River Daniels slid off of his paint mustang, embraced Beatrice in a side hug, then approached Viola with a hopeful hunger in his eyes.

He was everything she had dreamed about all last winter, all strength, confidence, and gorgeous to boot. Her breath caught as he stopped in front of her, much closer than a friend should. He raised his hand as he peered into her eyes and brushed the hair that was forever escaping from her bun.

"Viola," his deep voice whispered. "I've dreamed of seeing you again all winter long. I don't know how it's possible, but your more beautiful than the day I left you. I'm so sorry I've —"

"Vi, you going to introduce me to your friend?" Hunter's voice dripped with menace as his words pushed her into the present.

She stepped back, her face heating in the infernal blush. She glanced back at Hunter and gulped. His face was hard as stone as he stared at River, who'd gone rigid beside her. Hunter glanced at her and her heart clenched at the hurt and vulnerability he masked from everyone but her.

She cleared the rock from her throat. "Hunter, this is our friend River Daniels. River, this is Hunter Bennett."

Viola felt tension rolling off River, his body coiled, ready for action. She wasn't entirely sure what to do. Why couldn't it have been Orlando to ride up?

"What is this man doing here?" River's voice had an edge she'd never heard before.

"We found him injured with some broken ribs and a banged up ankle. He's been staying here healing," Viola answered, consciously keeping her hands from wringing in her apron.

"He doesn't look injured now. Why's he still hanging around?" River asked, accusation thick on his voice.

"After the Sweeneys showed up twice trying to take Viola, we decided to keep Hunter around. He's right handy in a situation," Beatrice said, throwing a wink at Hunter before looking at Viola with raised eyebrows.

"Are you alright, Toowutchun?" River turned to Viola, his face marred in concern as he grabbed her hand in his. His childhood nickname warmed her heart with a familiar comfort.

"I'm fine," Viola said.

"Why the new horse? What happened to Black?" Beatrice asked, rubbing the paint River had rode up on.

River turned to Beatrice, who had taken his horse's reins. "I have much to tell you both. Can we go in and talk?"

Viola pulled her hand from his and wrung it in her apron. Would they have the questions and doubts the Sweeneys had thrown into the air finally answered? Viola suddenly didn't want to go inside. She looked to Hunter where he still stood on the porch. He met her gaze with one of strength and encouragement. He nodded sadly at her, the expression somehow told her everything would be okay, even if the news was bad.

Viola walked towards the cabin. "I'll go put coffee on."

"I'll help River get his horse settled then be in," Beatrice said, her voice tinged with a subtle thread of fear.

Viola's legs felt wooden as she moved to the cabin, towards a conversation she wanted to run away from. Hunter grabbed her hand, stopping her as she passed.

"Viola … " he said, his voice tight with emotion. "Whatever happens, whatever this River fella tells you, I want you to know I'm here for you."

Viola nodded her head, her throat too tight for words to form. She pushed through fog that threatened to shut her mind down and walked to the stove. She went through the motions of making coffee as if someone else controlled her body. She didn't want to hear what River had to say. She wanted to run through the meadow and never return if it kept her from listening to words she feared would come from River's mouth.

Viola's hand shook as she reached for the coffee mugs, rattling the stoneware. Hunter's hand steadied hers as he stepped behind her and reached for the mug she held. The heat of him standing so close lent her comfort and strength. Without saying a word, he squeezed her shoulder, then started gathering mugs for the coffee. He then guided her to a seat as Beatrice and River came through the door. With one last squeeze on her shoulder, Hunter took a seat beside her.

As Beatrice took the seat on Viola's other side, Viola mentally shook the dread from her mind. She would take whatever information River had to tell with the strength her father and mother had raised her in. With that thought ringing through her head, she prayed for God to carry her in the moments to come.

EVERY MUSCLE in Hunter's body tensed as River sat down between Hunter and Beatrice at the kitchen table. Hunter hadn't missed the look of hunger that had been on River's face when he approached Viola outside or the look of happiness that overrode the look of shock upon Viola's face at seeing him. It didn't escape Hunter that River's glare as Hunter seated himself next to Viola could've scorched a man alive. Hunter wasn't about cower away with his tail between his legs just because some competition came into the picture. He needed to prove he could handle this time and be the man Viola needed.

He focused on River across the table, whose glare still hadn't left his face. He hated to admit that River was a much better looking guy than he was, but Hunter knew a bad attitude toward an old friend wouldn't ingratiate him to Viola. No matter what, he'd prove the better man and handle this new obstacle with the determination trained into him since high school.

Viola cleared her throat beside him. "You said you had some news for us."

River nodded. "Yes, I'm so sorry. I should've been here weeks ago, but Black stepped into a marmot hole and broke his leg. I was thrown and injured. Thankfully my grandmother's people found me and took care of me. I left the agency as soon as I could."

"I'm sorry to hear about Black, but I'm glad you're doing better," Beatrice said, placing a hand on River's arm. Hunter wondered what kind of relationship this man had with the Thomas family.

"I have a letter from Orlando he wanted me to deliver. Again, I'm sorry it took so long for me to get here. Orlando never intended for you to wait this long without news," River said, regret and sadness thick in his voice.

River took a folded paper from his pocket and extended it to Beatrice. She grabbed it from his hands and opened it, her hands shaking so much Hunter wondered if she'd be able to read it. He prayed for strength and courage for her and Viola. Beatrice closed her eyes and took a deep breath. When she opened her eyes, her hands had calmed.

She cleared her throat and began reading. "'My dearest Viola and Beatrice, It is with great sorrow that I write to tell you that Pa has passed on and is in Heaven with Ma.'"

Hunter watched as shock, anger, sadness, and finally loneliness flitted across Beatrice's face. Viola's shoulders started shuddering as she lowered her chin to her chest, tears falling onto her hands that twisted in her apron. Hunter reached over and grabbed Viola's hand. She abandoned destroying her apron and clutched both hands to his.

Beatrice continued reading Orlando's letter. "'I found Pa north of Rawlins in the mountains towards Green River. There is much business that needs to be taken care of before winter sets in. I am hoping that with me being able to hop on a train in Rawlins, I can take care of everything in Denver quicker and be home not long after River delivers this letter. It tears me up to do this to you both, to write a letter instead of tell you in person. But I can't risk a trip to Denver later and get snowed out for the winter'...That's the truth. I'd much rather him go now for a bit than be gone the whole winter."

River rubbed the back of his hand over his neck, his voice filled with sadness. "Orlando struggled deeply with what to do, felt terrible even writing the letter. He took it back from me three times before he finally decided to follow through and took the train to Denver."

"Were you with him when he found Pa?" Viola asked in a hoarse whisper.

River nodded his head sadly and shrugged. "It looks like your pa wrestled with a bear."

Something in River's voice was off. Hunter could tell he was lying, and he sharpened his eyes on River. When River glanced over at Hunter, he raised his eyebrow to silently show the man he knew there was more to the story.

"That's hogwash and you know it," Beatrice said. "Pa was just about the best mountain man ever. No bear would surprise him."

"I know, Beatrice," River replied. "I didn't believe it as well, but I saw him. Helped bury him."

Beatrice sighed and returned to the letter. "There's a bit more here. 'I know this will come as a shock. I promise, I'll be as quick as I can in Denver and hurry home. Please be careful. Always be on guard. Love your favorite brother, Orlando.'"

River placed his hand on Beatrice's where she flattened the letter to the table. "I'm really sorry about your pa. He was a good man, a great friend, and I will miss him until we meet again in heaven."

"Pa loved you like a son, River. He always cherished when you came to visit," Viola responded, sending a clench through Hunter's heart knowing her father probably wouldn't have approved of him with all he lacked.

River scrutinized the two ladies. "You two are taking this much better than I thought you would."

"We had a forewarning, of sorts," Viola answered.

"What do you mean?" River asked, concern lowering his eyebrows.

"Those lowdown, dirty Sweeneys came by claiming Pa and Orlando were dead and demanded Viola marry that skunk Linc," Beatrice replied, the anger of the situation still tainting her voice. "Hunter scared them away, though he was halfway near death from his ... accident."

River's eyes sharpened as he turned to Beatrice, his voice sharp with disgust. "When did this happen?"

"About a week and a half ago," Viola answered, shivering with the horrid memory.

"And yesterday those skunks came back. Linc tore up the place looking for Viola." Beatrice fumed explaining the latest situation.

As they told River of all that had been happening, Hunter watched River's face grow darker and darker with anger. He guessed he now had a strong ally that he might use to their advantage.

Beatrice snorted in derision. "Linc was mad as a hornet that Viola wasn't as easily got as he hoped. He seethed when Hunter confronted him, saying the Viola was his and no dandy newcomer was going to take what he'd worked so had to get."

"A Sweeney doesn't work hard for nothing," River countered. He took a deep breath and regarded Hunter. "Praise God you were here, Hunter. I can't imagine what would've happened if you hadn't been here."

"I'll tell you what would've happened," Beatrice replied harshly. "We would've been burying three dead Sweeneys is what would've happened."

"Beatrice." Viola's hand covered her mouth in shock. "How can you say that?"

"There is no way on this green earth that I would've ever let them make you marry that snake." Beatrice stared at Viola with determination. "I would've killed them all or died trying if they had forced you to leave with them."

"I'm glad I was here then." Hunter spoke as he placed his hands on the table around his mug. "Killing a man leaves a scar on your soul, one I hope you never have to bear."

"Are you saying you wouldn't do everything you can to protect your family?" Beatrice asked, pushing her chair back and standing fast.

Hunter looked at Beatrice, hoping all he felt showed on his face. "No, Bea, I'm not saying that at all. I'm blown away by your bravery and ability to push through the fear of a situation to do what needs done. When I asked you to take action, you never hesitated. But my hope and prayer is that you never have to bear the weight of knowing you took the life of someone, even if it was the only option available."

A heavy silence fell upon the room. Beatrice acted strong and unmovable, but Hunter had seen a vulnerability that might crack the thin veneer that she had created to protect herself. He prayed that if that ever happened, Beatrice would allow someone to help her.

"Sounds as if you're speaking from experience," River said with a weary tone in his voice.

"My scars are deep and numerous," Hunter replied, pain and regret saturating his voice. "Every single one of them was justified, but they burn my conscience, none the less."

"That's what separates a man following the will of God," River said, "and a man only after his own gain. I've seen men kill others because it was the only choice they had and struggle for years with knowing they had to send someone to the pearly gates through force. I've seen others take lives without a second thought. It's what separates good from evil, God-led from hell-bound. How is it you came to have so many scars?"

Hunter sat in silence for a minute, then replied, "I was in the military, a special elite branch. But I'm done with that now."

"What brought you to Colorado?" River probed.

Hunter peered to Viola, holding her gaze. "God did."

Viola lips tweaked up before she turned her eyes down keeping River from seeing her chuckle. Beatrice snorted in the corner where she paced and covered it up by clearing her throat.

River's eyes lowered to slits, clearly not liking the answer. "How'd you end up all banged up?"

"Well," Hunter said. "Let's just say I had a tangle with a lion, and he won."

Beatrice came to the table and slammed her palms to the surface, "Can we please get back to what's important?

The three of them glanced among each other in confusion. Beatrice threw her hands into the air and turned around, muttering to herself. Viola looked at Hunter. He gazed back at her in question and shrugged.

"If the Sweeneys knew about Pa's death," Beatrice huffed as she turned around and crossed her arms across her chest, "it's more than likely they had something to do with it. We should go get them, bring them to justice. Bury them before they can do more harm."

"Do you want justice or revenge?" Hunter asked.

"They're one and the same," Beatrice answered.

"'Vengeance shall be mine, saith the Lord,'" Hunter whispered, the verse he'd burned into his brain when the

182

atrocities he witnessed threatened to turn his heart to hatred.

"Haven't you been listening at all?" Viola asked, shock thick in her voice. "Violence never did any good and searching out the Sweeneys to make them pay for a crime we don't even know they did would be wrong."

"How could they have known Pa was dead if they didn't do it themselves?" Beatrice demanded.

"River said a bear got Pa," Viola answered. She took a deep breath before continuing. "He wouldn't lie to us if he believed different."

River grabbed his mug of coffee and stared into it. The move screamed that he was lying, and Hunter determined to know why before River left.

River twisted the mug in his hand, answering without looking up. "Some animal sure got your Pa. It's not a sight I wish to see again."

"But how did they know he was dead? Did you or Orlando tell anyone?" Beatrice fairly yelled. "At least let's go find them and ask what they found."

Hunter shook his head. "That's not strategically a smart scenario. Linc is unbalanced, and if we go in there and something goes wrong, we'd end up dead or, worse, one of you ladies might end up compromised. I won't risk that, even when I'm up to par."

Beatrice huffed in frustration, whispering something about not caring about scars. Hunter chose to ignore Beatrice's ranting and zeroed in on River.

"We could use your help, if you're up for it." Hunter threw out the challenge to River with a leveling look of expectancy.

River replied, "Anything for my friends."

"I need you to scout around, find out where they stay holed up," Hunter said, leaning forward in earnest. "I can guarantee that Linc will not give up easily. If you find them, when Orlando gets back, you can lead us to them. I'm assuming you're good at sneaking around without getting caught?"

River smirked. "I could cut the shirt off your back and you'd never know where it went to."

"Is that all we're going to do?" Beatrice exploded. "Sneak around and wait? We have the advantage now with River here. The extra man that puts us above the Sweeneys in numbers and you want to wait! We should go now and hunt those varmints down."

Hunter urged her to understand. "Viola is decent with a firearm and you can shoot a squirrel fifty yards out mid-jump from tree to tree with that bow of yours, but I'm not willing to chance it. If we wait for Orlando, we'll outnumber them five to three. There'd be no way for them to get away."

"Just because you doubt yourself, doesn't mean River and I couldn't get close enough to shut them down the instant we confront them. Waiting is the coward's way to finish this." Beatrice seethed.

"That's not fair and you know it," Viola said. "Shame on you. Hunter is thinking of this from every angle so all of us come home when this is over. Rushing into this is not only idiotic but will get someone killed."

River stood, walked to Beatrice, and grabbed her clenched hands, easing his palm into hers and threading his fingers through hers. "Easy, little one, Hunter's plan is sound, something your father would've approved of."

Beatrice yanked her hand from River's. Hunter recognized she was about to combust, but he didn't know how to stop the eruption.

"Little one?" She screeched, motioning her hands up and down her body. "It's clear no one has realized I'm a full-grown woman, not a child anymore. I also happen to be better than anyone here at sneaking around the woods and shooting any weapon. Waiting is just an invitation for the Sweeneys to attack, mark my words."

She stormed from the cabin, slamming the door so the floor shook. Her words sent a shiver of dread down Hunter's spine. Could she be right and waiting would only end in pain? Was he basing his plan on his weaknesses and lack of confidence? His shoulders dropped in indecision.

River stood up and headed toward the door. "Your plan is solid and the right one to take. She's full of grief and spitfire. I'll go calm her down and make her see reason."

Hunter replied, "Be careful. The Sweeneys might be just waiting to take us out when the opportunity comes."

"I'll keep vigilant and keep her safe, if only from herself." River spoke with conviction as he left the cabin.

Hunter hung his head as the door closed. He whispered, "Is she right? Would it be better to act now and catch them off guard?"

Viola bristled like a mama bear defending her cub. "No, your plan is the way we should move forward. You understand what you're doing. You've done this a hundred times and know how to go against an enemy force. She forgets that no matter how much more she thinks she knows about sneaking around in the woods, she's never been up against anyone out to get her. You have, against people more dangerous than we will ever understand. I plan on reminding her of that fact when she gets her head back on straight,"

Viola breathed deeply as she reached for the mugs and took them to the sink. Hunter knew she had to be hurting from having confirmation he father was dead. He stood, taking his mug to the sink.

"I'm really sorry about your pa, Viola," he said, rubbing his hand across her shoulders, wishing he knew how to comfort her.

She looked at him, tears suspended from her lashes. She nodded once, then threw herself into his chest, burying her face in his shoulder. Hunter wrapped his arms tightly around her, lending her his strength. Her shuddering body broke his heart. He prayed he would spend the rest of his life with her in his arms.

HUNTER WALKED OVER TO RIVER, who leaned against the corral rail. Hunter scanned the area, searching for anything that seemed out of place. Everything appeared as it should, and he didn't have the Holy Spirit giving him that sense he always got when things weren't right.

"You and I need to have a chat," Hunter said, leaning up against the fence next River.

"About what?" he replied without looking up from where he whittled a twig.

"You're lying," Hunter accused. "You're lying about their dad, and you're going to tell me why."

River nodded his head and sighed in resignation, "I knew you had the look of someone knowing. Was sure I couldn't get much by you." He tossed the twig in the grass, and sheathed his knife. He turned so he faced the corral, facing away from the house. "A bear ate Joseph up a fair bit." River shook his head. "Gruesome seeing him like that. I sure was sorry that Orlando had to be the one to find him. On the other hand, it's a blessing he was the one who did. Orlando, being trained as good as any doctor east of the Mississippi, better considering he'll also use the Indian medicines, noticed marks on Joseph's body that didn't match up with the bear attack."

"Marks? What kind of marks?" Hunter asked, his mind not wanting to know, but needing to understand.

"Marks like he'd been beat up, tortured," River answered, shaking his head in disbelief. "From what we could tell, Joseph had knife marks all over his body, but only in places it would've hurt, but not killed. That is except the one in the abdomen that probably killed him."

"You noticed this, even after the bear got to him?" Hunter asked in suspicion.

"I probably wouldn't have caught it," River said with regret. "But that Orlando is a mighty smart man. He also happened to come up on the bear and chase him off before the bear or some other animal dragged the body away."

Hunter shuddered. Seeing someone blown apart by landmines or RPGs had been bad enough, had given him nightmares for months. He didn't want to imagine what being some animal's lunch would look like and hoped he never did. Though, if he was to live here in this time and embrace the life Viola lived in the mountains, he probably would end up finding out.

"Does Orlando have any ideas who might've done it?"

Hunter asked, forcing his mind to move from the grim images.

"He had his suspicions." River nodded while answering. "And after what you all told me happened here, I have to say I'm inclined to agree with him."

"So you think the Sweeneys are behind this?"

"There's a good possibility, though in honesty I'd put my bet on Linc more than the other two. They probably just went along with him if they were even there."

"Yeah, but allowing an innocent man to be tortured and die brutally is as bad as doing the act yourself." Hunter seethed in anger.

River nodded his agreement and gazed into the corral at the horses that milled there. His brow furrowed in concern, and he breathed out so long and loud Hunter worried the man might double over in sadness.

"The Thomas's are like family to me. I've known them my whole life ... they are very special to me," River said, looking pointedly at Hunter. Hunter knew while the entire family was important to River, Viola held a special distinction to him. "You need to keep a sharp eye out while I go scout around. I'll be back no longer that two weeks."

"Don't worry," Hunter said. "I trained for this sort of thing for the past ten years. I won't let anything happen to them."

"I'll be praying for you," River promised. "And I'll be praying for the Sweeneys. God still has time to soften their hearts to Him. Let's pray they embrace it before it's too late."

"Pray that I can keep Beatrice from doing anything

rash while you're at it. I have a feeling she might not like my plan to hunker down and wait for reinforcements."

Both men chuckled a sorrowful laugh. Hunter knew River agreeing to help had everything to do with Viola. Hunter understood their temporary collaboration would end the instant Viola was safe. He planned to take every opportunity he could while River was gone to convince Viola that Hunter was the man for her. He figured it was probably an unfair advantage, but Hunter needed every advantage he could get if he wanted to compete with a lifelong history River and Viola had.

CHAPTER 16

VIOLA SAT BACK on her heels and ran her arm across the sweat racing down her face. Summers in the high country of the Rockies were short, but they sometimes got scorching. Today was a scorcher. There was no wind to rustle the meadow hay that was quickly stretching to the sky. No clouds to block the punishing sun, simply the clear light blue sky that reminded her of robin eggs. Some folks didn't believe a snowstorm might blow in tomorrow, though the summer storms rarely stuck. At this point a little snow wouldn't feel so bad and would get her out of the wretched chore of weeding.

She thought about her conversation with River earlier that morning before he left to find the Sweeneys. He'd kissed the back of her hand softly, causing a faint fluttering like a lonely butterfly flew around her stomach. He told her he'd be back to pick up their conversation of last fall. He'd said he knew the timing was horrible, but that he'd spent the winter thinking about her and the beautiful life they could build together. She knew life with River would be filled with friendship and a familiar comfort when her world suddenly seemed so foreign.

She watched as Hunter carried another two pails of water from the lake to water the thriving plants. His muscles flexed as he poured the water over the row of potatoes. The tiny flutter that had appeared in her stomach at River's touch seemed paltry compared to the flock of hummingbirds that raced in her gut every time she looked at him.

She fanned herself and huffed at her wayward thoughts. How was she to pick? Was the comfort of a life-long friendship the more reasonable choice or the excitement of a man she hardly knew? He glanced up and caught her staring. The scoundrel grinned knowingly and winked as a clod of dirt hit her in the arm.

"Would you quit lallygagging and get to work?" Beatrice said in mock disgust.

"Sorry Bea," Viola shrugged as she got back to work.

"I will give you that he looks mighty nice when those arms of his are working." Beatrice sighed, fluttering her eyelashes in exaggeration as she watched Hunter pour the next set of buckets.

Viola gasped and threw a clod of dirt Beatrice's way.

Beatrice snickered. "But the longer you waste time looking at him, the more weeding I have to do and the longer it takes to get the horrid chore done."

Viola focused on the weeds popping up in the carrots and yanked with a vengeance. She didn't blame Beatrice for being cranky. She was used to running out on her own, doing what she wanted, when she wanted. Shoot, Viola was sick of having to constantly look over her shoulder. But until Orlando got back from Denver, and they chased the Sweeneys off, her, Beatrice, and Hunter remained stuck together like peas encased in their pod.

"We're almost done with this row. It'd might be a good idea to stop anyway with the sun getting so high. It's not smart to be out in the heat of the day doing this," Viola answered.

As she moved down the row, she wondered if they'd ever be back to normal. Could they chase the Sweeneys off or bring them to justice for the death of their father, if they had anything to do with it? It would be next to impossible to prove without witnessing it. And who would they take them to? It wasn't like there was a marshal that wandered around, picking up outlaws. She guessed they could always take them over to Fort Steele and have the army take care of them. That was the closet thing to the law out here in the wilderness.

But what if the Sweeneys didn't leave? Would her family remain stuck in this tension of defense forever? Would she ever be able to go to the outhouse without taking a loaded weapon with her? Viola rolled her eyes at her ridiculous thoughts. They lived in the wilderness in the middle of the Rockies, for Pete's sake. Danger always lurked behind every boulder and mountainside. They would forever have to be vigilant or they would be dead. Period. And if the mess with the Sweeneys escalated that wariness, she guessed it made good practice.

Done chastising herself, she weeded the rest of the row of carrots in record time, the bittersweet scent of new growth and dirt filling the air as she threw the weeds into a basket she'd dump away from the garden. When she got to the end of the row, she pushed her bonnet off the top of her head and lifted her face to the sun. As hot and sweaty the day made her, she relished the dry warmth that symbolized the coming of new bounty and life.

~

HUNTER PULLED the Colt Navy from his holster in a quick, smooth sweep. Two shots so quick they almost sounded as one rang throughout the valley and across the lake. He slid the revolver back into the holster as he walked to the target on the knoll. He scanned the meadow and the forest, the shadows like old friends of his. The ladies were busy with the garden while he was the sentry, his job of hauling water finished.

His smile broadened as he stepped up to the target. Two holes, slightly overlapping each other and dead center, marred the surface. *Good*, he thought, *I'm almost good enough.*

Hunter walked back to his shooting point, scanning the area as he went. His gaze skipped over rocks and under trees, skidding past a clump of sagebrush and sliding back to it unconsciously. He stopped and stared at that brush. Something wasn't right about it. He studied the area around it, always keeping the brush in his peripheral before going back to it. Was the shadow darker under it? Was there a movement that shouldn't be there? His heart told him something was off, so he stared.

No movement was evident. No branches quivered. No shadow moved. After several minutes, Hunter took a calming breath and sent up a prayer for protection from what his mind said was out there, despite what his eyes saw. He turned, drew quick and shot three bullets in rapid succession. When he checked the target, it had three holes slightly away from the bullseye. He huffed in frustration.

A loud animalistic bawl coming from the barn had Hunter spinning, his gun in his hand before he even thought to go for it. Viola and Beatrice both stood from where they were weeding and took off for the barn.

"It's Maybelle," Viola shouted. "She's calving. Sounds like trouble."

Hunter took off in a sprint toward the barn after the girls, wondering if there would ever be a day that didn't have some kind of problem. Why he ever thought this time period would be less stressful was beyond him. His ankle didn't even hurt him anymore and his ribs only twinged with discomfort now and then. He pushed himself faster, reaching the barn right after the ladies. He skidded to a halt as a horrendous noise bellowed from the stall.

Beatrice walked into the stall, circling the cow while murmuring. Viola moved to the back of the barn and pulled items from a cabinet. She set large chains and clamps on the workbench along with rags and a rather wicked-looking knife.

"Hunter," Viola snapped him to order. "I need you to sharpen this knife with the whetstone. It needs to be razor sharp."

"Yes, ma'am," Hunter responded, barely suppressing the urge to salute.

"The calf may be coming out the wrong way." Beatrice called over just loud enough for them to hear. "She'll need help to get it out."

"Hurry, Hunter," Viola said as she passed him to get to the cow. "We'll need your strength."

As he put an edge on the knife, Viola and Beatrice led Maybelle into the center of the barn where they could get around her more easily. The cow's eyes rolled in pain, and she bellowed every time her body contracted.

"What can I do to help?" Hunter asked as he came around to the business end of things.

Beatrice had her hands deep into the cow, Hunter assumed checking progress, though on what he hadn't a clue about. Just another thing he was unprepared for. Useless. He wondered for the thousandth time why God sent him to a place he was so out of his element in.

"The calf's head is caught, turned backwards against its body," Beatrice said, the last getting cut off as the cow's body contracted around her arms. She grimaced and panted under the cow's horrendous bellows. When it finished, she pulled her arms out, wiping them on the fresh hay Viola had forked onto the floor before moving the cow.

"I can't get enough leverage to push the calf back and straighten its head," Beatrice explained as she looked at Hunter.

"So." Hunter gulped, trying not to have his sudden nervousness show. "I'm going in?"

"Yep," Beatrice replied curtly. "You're going in."

Viola placed her palm on his shoulder. Hunter wasn't sure if it was in encouragement or comfort, which proved he hadn't hidden his uselessness well enough. He glanced at her and nodded confidently.

"Tell me what to do," he said.

"Roll up your sleeves and come on over here." Beatrice waved with her still bloody arms.

He did as she asked then walked over to where Beatrice stood, and took a deep breath. He'd trained in every situation possible, except this one. However, that little tidbit of insight would not keep him from action. His training was the reason he'd succeed and adapt at anything, even helping a hurting cow birth its calf.

"Get your arm in there and push the baby back up the birth canal," Beatrice explained as sweat burst forth from his forehead. "Hopefully, the calf's head will straighten on its own, otherwise we will have to straighten it. After the next contraction, I want you to get your hand in there. You must push as even as possible and may need to use both hands. You won't be able to push during contractions, but we need to prevent the calf from descending any further if we can."

Hunter nodded, knowing anything he said wouldn't help the situation, and, honestly, he wasn't sure his voice wouldn't crack, which made keeping his trap shut an imperative. He watched as the cow's entire body contracted. He placed his hand on its rump to get the cow used to him. When the contraction was over, he took a quick, fortifying breath and plunged in. Hunter reached up the calf's feet and found the neck. He cringed when he touched the calf's head as it twisted back. He placed his hand on the shoulder and pushed the calf back with a slow, steady pressure.

Just as he'd gotten the calf on a slow and steady move, his arm became squeezed in a vice. The pressure pushed his arm up against the calf's body, so intense he didn't know how Beatrice hadn't cried out. He hoped he didn't. Sweat streamed into his eyes, his entire body tensing in response to the pain. He wiped his forehead onto his shoulder as the contraction let up.

He began pushing again. Inch by inch, the calf moved the opposite way of its freedom. After two more intense contractions, Beatrice reached her hand in with his. Her hand slid up his arm and circled over the calf's head.

"I think there's enough room that I can attempt to turn the head. I don't think it will do it on its own, and if we wait much longer, we'll lose them both."

Beatrice looked up at him, the green of her eyes deeper with her concern. There was a hesitance in her look, but her confidence overpowered it. A contraction wrapped its strength around their arms, squishing and smashing them together. Beatrice gritted her teeth against the pain, which forced Hunter to stifle the moan threatening to escape his lips.

"Okay," Beatrice said. "When this is done, I'm going to turn the head. Keep the body pushed back and be ready. I may need you to help me."

When the contraction let up pressure, Beatrice began turning the head. As she worked within the cow, her other hand slid up to grip the calf's head. She pulled hard, her entire body shaking with strain up against his.

"You got this, Beatrice." Hunter whispered.

The poor cow screamed in an even more terrifying sound that sent shivers up and down his body. He felt intense sorrow for all females everywhere, no matter the species. He glanced at Viola, where she was busy at the cow's head, whispering calming words and keeping her from laying down. Hunter shuddered at the idea of Viola giving birth in this wilderness, far from a hospital. Far from any help at all. He shivered again in fear.

A sudden excess of space and Beatrice"s sigh of relief had Hunter's attention back on the business at hand.

"Bring your hand out," Beatrice said. "I'll hold on to the hooves and pull it out on the next contraction."

"You sure you don't want me to do that?" Hunter asked as he moved his hand out with a sickening slurp of fluid.

"Nah," Beatrice replied. "Both my hands are already in here. It shouldn't be difficult now."

As Hunter wiped his arm on the hay, Beatrice braced herself and pulled. With a sudden gush, the calf slid out, landing right on Beatrice's lap. Maybelle sagged to her knees in relief, laying down in the hay.

Viola rushed over with rags and rubbed the calf's face whispering, "Come on, sweetheart. Breathe."

Beatrice vigorously rubbed its body, while Viola rubbed its face. Hunter kneeled down into the hay beside Viola. *Lord, please help this little one.*

Hunter felt slightly ridiculous praying for a calf, but he realized this was his life now. It was more grounded in the world around him than he ever imagined life could be. His muscles ached from pushing the calf, like they did every night when he fell into bed, exhausted from surviving another day in this wilderness, but he slept with more satisfaction that he ever had. He didn't miss the conveniences of the future all that much, though he would figure out a way to bring indoor plumbing into the cabin. The outhouse in the middle of winter was not something he was looking forward to.

The calf bawled loudly, and everyone chuckled in response. Hunter peered down at his filthy clothes and grimaced.

"It's a good thing you made me a spare set of clothes made, Viola," Hunter said. "Otherwise I'd be wandering around in my skivvies until these got washed."

Beatrice snorted as she wiped her hands on the hay. "That'd be an intimidating scene, you with your holster strapped over your underthings. Might just scare the Sweeneys away for good."

Maybelle mooed in agreement causing everyone to crack up laughing. Hunter shook his head. If only it was that easy.

~

LINC'S BLOOD ran glacier cold as he'd watched Viola's beau practice shooting his revolver. It did every time he saw the fluid motion of him drawing and the swift fire the gun belched forth. It seemed almost inhuman how quick the man could draw and shoot.

Nothing would deter Linc though. If anything, he now understood he needed to save Viola from this man she'd allowed to lure her in. Only a man who entertained with the devil himself could shoot like he did. Linc knew all about the power evil gave a person.

He laid on his back where he'd froze as the interloper's keen eyes penetrated right into his heart. He realized the man hadn't seen him, but it was obvious by the way he'd stared seemingly into Linc's eyes that he sensed Linc there. He had been so close to running, leaving his cover like a scared rabbit, but his pa had made him stronger than that. So he'd stayed still until they'd taken off into the barn.

Linc peered at the cozy homestead tucked against the mountain and sneered to himself. He was done hiding in bushes, waiting for an opening. His brothers weren't being any help. Robert flat out refused to help anymore, saying it was a fool's errand, and he wanted to quit the area. But he hadn't left yet, which meant Linc couldn't wait any longer.

If Robert was around when this all went down, he'd help. "Family stuck together, no matter what," pa always beat into them. Linc had a plan, and it was high time he followed through with it.

CHAPTER 17

VIOLA WATCHED Hunter where he stood just outside of the cabin door a step off the porch. He hadn't lit the lantern, so she only saw his silhouette against the dark sky as the sun was just lightening with day. He'd amazed her the day before, not hesitating to help with Maybelle. The only sign of his discomfort had been a slight raise of his eyebrows when Beatrice had commanded him to roll up his sleeves. How was it that he constantly rose to the need? He attributed it to his training, but she wondered if it was more his character. She figured he'd be the same amazing and focused man with or without the Army.

She walked up and stood beside him. She breathed in the calm of morning, the smell of dew on the meadow grass. The sparrows sang a wake up song in the trees. She breathed out, her breath dancing with the light breeze that blew strands of her hair in her face.

Hunter's hand came up and gently placed her blowing hair behind her ear where he left his hand to cradle her neck. She stared up into his face that could just now be seen in the morning light. His expression held such tenderness and longing she wondered if anyone had ever looked at her like that before.

"Viola," he whispered as he leaned down and captured her lips. The kiss was much more tender than the one they'd shared before that had blazed through her with a passion she never knew existed. Yet this one changed her at the core just as much, revealing the affection he held for her rivaled his desire. He angled his head and deepened the kiss, driving all question as who she belonged with out of her mind.

A voice boomed from the field, ripping Viola from pure bliss. "What in tarnation is going on here?"

Hunter moved quickly. In one motion he pulled Viola behind him, anchoring her to his back with his arm, while he drew the Colt Navy from his holster, cocking, and pointing it at the chest of the bear of a man standing before him.

"Another one of your admirers, Viola?" Hunter asked sarcastically.

Viola grabbed onto Hunter's shirt, her face pressed into his back in mortification. How was it that every time Hunter kissed her, they ended up caught in the act. And this time by Uncle Dan, no less?

"Viola Grace Thomas, you come out from behind this man and explain yourself," Uncle Dan bellowed, causing Hunter's muscles to tighten. "And for the love of all that's holy, you'd best lower your weapon, son."

Viola started to go around Hunter, but he tightened his arm, holding her in place. She huffed and pushed on it without luck. It held tighter than a steel trap snapped around its prey.

"You'd better explain why you're sneaking up on people," Hunter said, his voice cold and hard like it had been when the Sweeneys had stopped by. "Seems to be a quick way to get oneself knocking on the pearly gates, if you ask me."

Viola pushed harder on Hunter's arm as she said, "Hunter, it's all right. This here is Trapper Dan, our uncle of sorts."

Viola came around Hunter as he lowered and uncocked the Colt, though he didn't holster it. She placed her hand on his arm and glanced up at him in encouragement. She peeked at Uncle Dan and inwardly cringed at how furious he appeared. Viola had never seen the easygoing, man of God vexed before.

Hoping to clear the air and brush over the embarrassing situation, Viola smiled and said, "Hello, Uncle Dan."

"This man your husband?" Uncle Dan asked.

"No, sir," Viola said, clearing her throat before continuing. "He's a friend that's gotten injured, and we're patching him up."

"Doesn't seem so injured to me." Uncle Dan eyed Hunter up and down before looking back at her. "I've been hearing rumors about you I knew couldn't be true. Heard them all the way up in Wyoming where Jack found me."

"Rumors?" Viola asked, dread and shock coursing through her. "What are you talking about?"

"That you're playing house with some stranger, acting like you belong in a brothel rather than the good Christian woman I know you are," Uncle Dan said, sadness and disbelief lacing his tone.

"Just you wait a minute." Hunter spoke icily, placing himself in front of her. "I don't know who you are, mister, but you will speak respectfully when you talk to Viola. She's done nothing to warrant such a statement, and family or not, I'll not allow you to continue to talk about her that way."

At that moment, Beatrice came running out of the cabin, joy stretched across her face at the sight of Uncle Dan. She slid to a stop on the porch, looking between Hunter and Viola and Uncle Dan in confusion.

"'Nothing to warrant such a statement.' I sure as shootin' have reason to say such a thing," Uncle Dan bellowed, his face going crimson again. "Were you or were you not just kissing her so passionately that it appeared as if all the water in the world had dried up and she was the last source left to quench your thirst?"

Beatrice gasped and said, "Again?"

Viola buried her head in her hands in mortification, willing her sister to just keep her mouth shut. She hoped Uncle Dan was so caught up in his sermonizing that Beatrice's comment escaped him.

Uncle Dan continued. "You were lost your sinful display that had I not said something, you'd still be at it. What kind of example are you setting for Beatrice? What else has been going on under that roof you two have been sleeping beneath?"

"Nothing inappropriate has happened," Hunter replied, his voice commanding and sure. He continued, a hesitancy in his voice. "You're right. I allowed the kiss to go too far, though I don't regret it, but I would never disrespect Viola by going beyond a kiss."

"You're right about that," Uncle Dan responded cooly. "Because I'm marrying you two right here and now."

Viola shook her head and started to tell Uncle Dan that he was being ridiculous when she heard Hunter say, "All right by me, so long as that's what Viola wants. I won't force her to marry me."

She shook her head and looked at him in confusion as tears threatened to spill from her eyes. She shook her head harder.

"Hunter, no." Viola grabbed his hand and pulled him to look at her. "No. You don't have to marry me. We did nothing wrong. Just a little kiss is all. I won't have you marrying me because of that."

"I know I don't have to marry you," he said, turning towards her and placing his hand upon the side of her face. "But I sure would love to. I've been racking my brain trying to figure out a way to convince you to marry someone so unworthy as me. I love you, Viola, as crazy as that is, and I'd consider myself honored to be your husband, if you'll have me."

Viola gazed into his eyes and found truth and love and more emotion than she knew how to handle. Yet despite all that he had written on his face, doubt and fear weighed heavy upon her. How could it be that this man, who had so much to live for and experience back in his time, would love simple, plain her? And looming even larger was the possibility that God would take Hunter back when he'd had finished what he was sent here for.

Tears coursed down her as she whispered. "But what if you … you … leave?"

"I'm not going anywhere, Viola," he replied confidently, holstering his weapon and taking her hand.

"How can you be so sure?" She choked out while attempting to hold back her tears.

He stared down at her hand in his and brought it to his lips, kissing the inside of her wrist. "I can't explain it, but for the first time in forever I feel as if I'm finally home. God's given me such a peace about being here. I've had this emptiness within me for so long, a longing I could never explain. I've had God, and He's filled my life with so many miracles and blessings, but there just always seemed like there was something more. It's you, Viola. You are my more. You've filled that lonely place within my heart. I'm convinced without a doubt that you are the reason God brought me here."

He took her face in both his hands and wiped the tears that streamed down her face. Joy filled her so completely with his declaration that she could do nothing but stare and cry.

"So what do you say?" Hunter asked, a look of vulnerability passing over his face. "Think you can stand being married to someone so out of his element as me?"

"I have no idea what that means, but yes," Viola said with a laugh. "I'd be honored to be your wife."

Hunter grinned so large and seemed so happy she about burst from the joy of it. Then his lips were upon hers, and she melted like butter in a hot skillet.

"Good," Uncle Dan said. "I was hoping I wouldn't have to use the shotgun."

They all laughed as Beatrice grabbed Viola from Hunter's arms and squeezed her tightly in a hug. Viola returned the hug and allowed Beatrice to pull her into the cabin to get ready for the wedding. With one last look to Hunter who returned her gaze with a wink, Viola closed the cabin door and prepared for her life to change again.

~

HUNTER SAT in a chair at the kitchen table, watching his wife flit around the room, making a late breakfast. His wife. He covered his grin with his hand and shook his head. Never figured that would happen, considering he had never met anyone in his time that he considered wife material. All the guys in The Unit called him Priest, not because he was Catholic, which he wasn't, or even because he was a Christian, but because he didn't date.

Hunter still remembered the weekend his dad had taken him fishing to the lake they loved when he was a freshman in high school. He'd told Hunter that now that he was a young man, he wanted to have a chat with him about being a man. That weekend, while casting from the banks of the crystal clear lake or sitting by the fire, the smell of pine and cooked fish lingering in the air, his father had impressed so much upon Hunter's character and values. His father and he talked about duty and bravery, about what it meant to be a warrior of God. They'd talked about standing one's ground when others fell from the path. They talked about women and the responsibilities of being a husband.

Hunter's father had insisted, in his understated way, that God had made someone special, just for him. He was adamant that someday God would put someone in Hunter's life that was his match and just as convinced that dating, even casual, confused the spirit of the one who was yours and that often relationships progressed to things that should wait until two married. Hunter had taken that to heart, trusting his father's wisdom, and had prayed, almost daily, that God would open his eyes to the one who was his.

In high school, it'd been easy, what with him choosing to homeschool and enrolling in the Texas A&M ROTC program when other kids his age were still sophomores in high school. He'd double timed it and graduated in two years, and at eighteen had entered the Army as an officer, already recruited for Delta Force. During the first years in the Army, he'd been so busy training, he didn't care much about women, and after the missions had started and his parents had died, he'd spent every moment he could home with his brother, Chase. Besides, Hunter had seen the side effects of casual dating, the heartbreak, the slow decline down a trail of unfulfilled, or more often wrongly fulfilled, lusts. His father's wisdom had proved right.

His team members had razzed him at first, trying to set him up with women they knew when they hung out while off duty, but none of the women had set even a spark off in his heart. Lately, he'd started wondering if his heart wasn't warm enough for a spark to start. If all the violence that surrounded him, the cold control that enveloped him, had smothered any evidence of hope that someone would ignite a fire. It was crazy that the one who would set his soul aflame like a roaring wildfire would be a hundred plus years in the past.

Viola glanced over her shoulder at him as she cooked at the stove. Her sweet, innocent smile and joy in her eyes kicked up an inferno. He was glad he'd followed his father's advice, because from the very first moment, his soul had reached out to hers in ways he thought impossible. Now their experiences would be theirs and theirs alone, unfettered by memories of or comparisons to past women.

Trapper Dan was speaking about his winter travels, of trapping up in Wyoming and ministering to a group of miners here and there. While Hunter tried to pay attention, responding and asking questions when appropriate, the gentle line of Viola's neck or the gold that glinted in her hair or the sway of her skirt as she moved about the kitchen pulled his attention away. He couldn't wait to get her alone and breathe in her cinnamon honey scent, to taste those sweet strawberry pink lips again.

"Son... Hunter, you listening to me?" Trapper Dan asked.

"What? Oh, sorry Dan, my mind was wandering," Hunter cleared his throat as heat rose up his neck. Man, being married was proving to be distracting.

"I realize that you're just married and new around here," Trapper Dan replied in seriousness. "Believe me, I understand how distracting the one you love can be." Trapper Dan peeked at the portrait of Viola's mother that hung on the wall before clearing his throat and continuing. "But these here mountains are tough, willing to chew a person up and spit them out, and the people who live here are even tougher. Sure, most of us are decent enough people that we help and take care of each other, but those that aren't will take any little bit of distraction they can get to tear you to pieces. You have a family now, and they will need every bit of your focus to keep them safe."

Viola turned toward the table and began setting things it. When she and Beatrice had put everything on the table, Viola sat down beside him and slid her hand into his.

"You don't have to worry about us, Uncle Dan," Viola declared. "Even though Hunter is new here, I'm convinced he is more than capable helping us protect and run our homestead."

Hunter's heart swelled at the pride and conviction that saturated Viola's words. He prayed that God would help him to not let her down. He squeezed her hand and pressed his lips together.

"Well, if the way he reacted when I interrupted you earlier is any indication, you are in capable hands," Trapper Dan responded. "Let's pray. The breakfast looks delicious, and I'm starving for something other than beans and jerky."

As they ate, the ladies asked Trapper Dan about the people he'd seen. He caught them up on friends, the babies born and the families that had moved out. Hunter tried to focus on the conversation, but his lack of knowing anyone had his mind wandering. He stared at Viola who was laughing at a story Trapper Dan told about a newcomer's little boy's hand getting caught in a stump. She looked so beautiful, laughing, her hand covering her mouth as she shook her head.

"That poor boy." She hid her smile behind her hand. "How'd you ever get his hand out?"

"Well," Trapper Dan said, pausing with dramatic flair. "I told him if he ever wanted to get his hand out of the hole, he'd have to stop his crying and let go of the baby skunk."

"No," Beatrice said, laughter spilling from her lips. "He was holding onto a skunk?"

"He said he wanted a pet, and that the baby skunk was so cute," Trapper Dan said. "I knew he still had a hold of it from the caterwauling going on inside the log and the stench hovering over the area. When his mama realized the boy still had a hand on the critter, she blew her top."

All of them roared with laughter. He imagined a boy like Chase, dark brown hair and piercing blue eye, crying, covered in dirt because he didn't want to let go of his pet. It was something his brother would've done. Shoot, it was something Hunter would have done. The memory brought a sadness to his spirit that he'd never see Chase again. Never laugh at memories of escapades. Chase would never meet Hunter's family. Never hold his nieces and get in trouble with his nephews. Hunter's mood turned somber at the sadness of where his mind had travelled.

Viola's small hand slipped into his. She covered both their hands with her other and offered him a sad, knowing smile. He brought her hands to his lips and kissed them.

Viola cleared her throat and glanced across the table at Trapper Dan. "Uncle Dan, we have some bad news. Pa's dead." Viola's hands tightened around his, and her voice cracked as she said the last word. Hunter leaned closer to her, putting his arm around her shoulder.

"No," Trapper Dan said, shaking his head in disbelief. "That's not possible."

"It's true," Hunter said when both Beatrice and Viola didn't respond. "River Daniels was just here with a letter from Orlando stating so."

"How?" Trapper Dan questioned, his face crumpled in sorrow.

"River said Pa was attacked by a bear," Viola answered.

"That doesn't sound right." Trapper Dan shook his

head and pulled on his beard.

"It doesn't sound right because it's not what happened," Beatrice said as she pushed her plate away from her. "The Sweeneys had something to do with Pa's death. We just haven't been able to leave this place to confront them."

"The Sweeneys? What's this got to do with them?" Trapper Dan asked.

"They came here a few weeks ago, saying that both Pa and Orlando were dead. Linc expected to come here and leave with Viola as his wife," Beatrice said, her voice going cold with anger. "The only way they would've known Pa was dead was if they had something to do with it. And now that you're here, we can go get them and force them to tell us what they know."

Worry filled Hunter's heart. River had only left the morning before. There was no telling where he had gone off to. Would Beatrice accept the need to give River some time to find the Sweeneys and bring the information back to make a plan of attack?

Trapper Dan sighed regretfully and said, "Beatrice, girl, I wish with everything in me that I could help. And I'll come back as soon as I can to do that, but first thing tomorrow morning I have to go the the White River Agency and talk with the new Indian agent there. Chief Johnson sent a note that he needs my advice. I can't have him waiting on me any longer."

Hunter relaxed into his chair, glad for the time to allow River to return with reconnaissance. Hunter didn't want to go against the Sweeneys blind. He looked at Viola and smiled mischievously. He wouldn't mind a night or two with his new wife before going off to battle.

CHAPTER 18

BEATRICE HUFFED IN FRUSTRATION, made some excuse about taking care of the animals, and stomped out the door, slamming it shut. Viola glanced from Hunter to Uncle Jack.

"I'm sorry," she said, her voice rasping. "She's always been one whose emotions run fast, though most wouldn't think it by looking at her."

Uncle Dan reached his hand across placing it upon hers, tears shining bright in his eyes. "I'm sorry about your pa, Viola. And I'm sorry I can't stick around right now to help out. You are the daughter I never had. Beautiful and full of mercy, just like your ma. Thank you for puttin' up with an old coot like me."

"I love you too, Uncle Dan," Viola said.

Uncle Dan sniffed, stood up, and headed towards the door. "I'm going to go help your sister with the animals."

As Viola watched him go, Hunter's hand rubbed across her shoulders. He leaned close and put his forehead

213

against the side of her head. His breath tickled her ear as it blew across it.

"I'm so sorry about your dad," Hunter whispered, the soft breeze of his breath unlocking the vault she had locked her tears in.

She turned her head and peered into his eyes as a single tear tracked down her cheek. Compassion and love shone forth from him. He reached up and wiped the tear though another and another quickly replaced it. When they proved too many to catch, Hunter simply pulled her into his arms.

"Oh sweetheart, I'm so sorry," he whispered again, stroking his hand down her back.

Viola knew it was ridiculous and pointless to sit there crying, but when one's father died, she figured it to be a good enough reason. Not that the crying would bring him back or make things better. But as Hunter held her there in his strong arms, she realized he had made it better.

How would she have ever made it through this time without his strength? How would she know what to say to Beatrice to stop her talk of vengeance? Just having Hunter here to hold her helped her not experience such loneliness, like she no longer had to take on life and trials by herself. Though she hadn't been looking and didn't even realize she needed a husband, God sent this man from the future for her. It was unexpected, surprising, and too much to understand.

Viola pulled back from him, just enough to look into his face. He brushed her tears with his thumbs, the calloused skin rough against her cheeks and his fingers gently wrapping around the back of her neck.

Wanting to thank him for his caring, Viola leaned

forward and kissed him. She pulled away, exhaling softly as she stared at his lips. The right side turned up in a tempting tease, and she kissed him again, wanting to have this surprise husband of hers close. He matched her passion with his own, until, against Viola's wishes, he slowed down the kiss. He kissed her once, twice, three times before pulling her into a hug. She snuggled her face into his neck, his heart pounding through his shirt against her.

"How is it I just met you, and yet, I feel as if God connected our lives since the beginning of time?"

"My dad told me once that God had made someone special for me," Hunter said, combing his fingers through her hair, which she now realized had come undone. "He said that if I was patient, it would be obvious who that was. Lately I had worried that my life, who I've become, was too tarnished. That maybe I wasn't supposed to be with anyone because of it."

Hunter pulled Viola back from him, and she saw so much love there that she about broke down crying again. She relished the feel as he sunk his hands further into her hair.

He looked into her eyes and confessed, "I've prayed for you every day of my life since I turned fifteen. I prayed God would make it obvious so I wouldn't be swayed into something false." He chuckled and shook his head before continuing, "I just didn't think He'd make it this obvious. Maybe He thought only time travel would be a big enough sign for me. Despite that, and my lack of preparedness for this life here, I promise, you won't regret taking a chance on me."

"How could I regret marrying you?" Viola asked,

chuckling. "I would marry you even if you never learn a thing about living here and I have to push you down a mountain every few weeks to keep you here. I love you, and I'm not letting you go. Ever."

Hunter quickly pulled Viola onto his lap and she yelped in surprise. He kissed her digging his fingers deep into her hair. He trailed kisses down her neck and back up to her ear, whispering thanks to God between kisses. Her body turned hot and tingly in the strangest, most wonderful way. Her breath came quickly and her heart pounded like a stampeding herd of mustangs. Much too soon, Hunter pulled away, leaning his forehead to hers. They both breathed heavy.

"We need to stop before someone comes in," Hunter said, kissing her one last time. "Let me help you with the dishes."

Viola stood in a dazed state, having more help than she would like to admit from Hunter. How could the man possibly think of dishes at a time like this? She stiffly walked to the sink, having to lock her knees after they'd acted like plum pudding on the first step. She stared at the sink, wondering why she was here. Hunter offering her a bemused smile.

He kissed her on the nose, handed her the bar of soap and said, "Dishes, remember?"

"Of course I remember." Viola snapped, mortified a little kissing would put her in such a state.

She started shaving soap into the tub and allowed Hunter to pour water from the pan on the stove. Though, with his ribs still healing, she shouldn't let him lift such awkward things. When he threw her a saucy grin and a wink, she decided he had healed enough for the work.

With the water ready and utensils in the tub, Viola plunged her hands into the water and began to wash. After dropping the third fork into the rinse water with a splash, she turned to Hunter as he chuckled.

"What's so funny?" Viola asked.

"I'm wondering if you were so dazed and shook up after a little kissing," Hunter said, leaning in to whisper the last huskily in her ear. "What's gonna happen when I get you alone tonight?"

Viola gasped, her face blushing hot. Hunter kissed her on the base of her neck, scorching her skin with the contact. The spoons she was holding slipped from her hands, and she clutched the sink to keep standing.

Hunter smirked. "I can't wait to find out."

At that moment, the door swung open, and Beatrice came in. Viola blushed again and quickly turned back to the sink. Hunter playfully nudging her while he reached into the rinse water for the forks. Viola thank the Lord someone hadn't caught them a second time in one day kissing wildly.

"Hunter," Beatrice said as she came across the room, "don't worry about the dishes. I'll help Viola with them."

"All right." Hunter dried his hands on the towel. "I'll go fetch water from the creek."

He leaned over and kissed Viola on the cheek, gave Beatrice a hug while he whispered something in her ear, and walked out the door.

"I think you might have got yourself a keeper," Beatrice said, tying her apron on over the dress that Viola had begged her to wear for the wedding.

"Yeah, think so, too."

"Maybe God might drop me a husband off the mountain," Beatrice said.

"I don't know," Viola answered. "The possibility of it happening again is mighty slim."

Beatrice sighed and plunged her hands into the rinse water to grab the clean dishes. They worked in silence until all the dishes were clean, dried, and put away. After they both had hung their aprons on the peg, Viola pulled Beatrice into a tight hug. They stood there, drawing comfort from each other's presence, not needing words to express their grief. Viola supposed that was what happened when two sisters were as close as they were, but she thanked God they both had each other and promised she'd do whatever she could to make this time easier on her sister.

VIOLA SAT on the porch swing, the creak of the rope as it moved back and forth adding its music to the crickets that sang their ballads. The day had been long and trying, with thoughts of her husband's words and kisses distracting her throughout the hours. She rubbed her aching knee. It had swollen large after one of the wilder horses they corralled had kicked her out of spite. What chapped was she knew she was never to let her guard down around that ornery beast, yet there she had stood daydreaming.

The mug of coffee cradled in her hands didn't warm her as much as the arm that the man pressed to her side had draped across her shoulders. Who would've known that one could gain such comfort and security with the place of an arm? Who would've known that a caress could send such heat burning through her, as if lightning sprang deep within her body everywhere he touched? She wondered how her entire body didn't ignite in flames with her left side pressed to his. Would she even be able to survive the wedding night without combusting to ash?

Viola lowered her head to hide the telling blush that raced up her neck and face, shame racing up just as fast. How could she even be thinking such thoughts while they sat here telling stories about Pa? What kind of daughter was she that her thoughts would so quickly vacillate from dread and intense grief that her father no longer lived to joy and intense desire to know this man as only husband and wife would know? Her tossing and turning thoughts sickened and shamed her so much she pulled within herself as Beatrice and Uncle Dan told stories of Pa, hoping against hope that her traitorous mind wouldn't reveal itself to the others.

But despite how deep Viola tried to retreat, there was that arm draped across her shoulders providing such comfort and strength and hope, preventing her from pulling too far within. Life connected her to this fascinating man so much that she envisioned their very souls intertwined and braided together.

"I know he's rejoicing in heaven." Uncle Dan sniffed as he finished his latest story. "Seeing the Lord face to face and being reunited with his precious Victoria, and I should rejoice with him, and I am. I'm just sad I won't be seeing him again on this side of eternity."

The silence that followed was thick with grief and threatened to pull Viola further into darkness. She squeezed her hands around the mug, hoping the solidity of the object would keep her from buckling into the emotional torrent that, if she allowed to break the tenuous dam of her eyelids, would have seen her father running for the hills. As much as a woman's tears had made him uncomfortable, it'd be even more disgraceful and to the discredit of Pa if she allowed them to flow unchecked now. No, the one hard cry that her and Beatrice had in the cabin was enough to release the grief and hurt. Anything more would be self-indulgent and weak. Her father didn't raise weak women, but women strong enough to conquer these savage mountains to live a life full of love and hope rather than fear and timidity.

Viola leaned further into Hunter and placed her head upon his shoulder. This was where her love would blossom, within this man God had thrown back in time and down a mountainside. Here was her hope that life would be more than simply survival, would be abundant beyond anything she ever hoped or imagined. God in His mercy and grace and unending wisdom sent Hunter to her before she even knew she needed him. Not to take the place in her heart that her father's death was leaving empty. That place would always ache with the void of him. But even as the pain of that emptiness threatened to overwhelm, a new place in her heart filled, one she never realized was as cavernous as it was. One she somehow knew would only be surpassed by the love of God she held in her heart. The Lord giveth, and the Lord taketh away, Viola thought.

"Blessed be the name of the Lord," Hunter murmured jolting Viola's head around to his face, not realizing she had spoken aloud.

"Yes, blessed be the name of the Lord," Uncle Dan agreed. "Well, I believe I'll go find a place to light a small fire and study the stars. Beatrice, would you do this old man the honor of joining me? I sure have looked forward to our next discussion."

"I got a fascinating book this winter on stars and how people use them for navigation beyond what I've always understood," Beatrice answered as she raised from the chair she was sitting in on the porch. "I'll go get it and my gear."

As Beatrice closed the door to the cabin, Uncle Dan stood and reached out his hand to shake Hunter's. "Welcome to the family, son. I have a good feeling you'll fit right in."

Hunter stood, bringing Viola with him. He met Uncle Dan's hand with a strong clasp before pulling him into a hug that had so much thumping Viola worried Hunter's bones would come loose again.

"I'm honored to be a part of this family," Hunter replied, glancing at Viola and threading her fingers through his, causing her heart to beat wild and her arm to tingle.

Hunter turned back to Uncle Dan and continued, "Thanks for doing the ceremony for us and for not shooting me on the spot."

"My pleasure," Uncle Dan laughed before becoming serious. "Just remember, you don't live up to what this girl deserves and needs, you won't live at all."

"Understand, sir," Hunter said. "And you have my permission to do the honors if I ever don't."

Uncle Dan turned to Viola and pulled her into a bear hug. "I love you girl and know this one is a good one."

Uncle Dan pulled away and winked. As Beatrice and Uncle Dan walked to the barn to saddle their horses,

Hunter pulled Viola to his side and kissed the top of her head.

"I knew I liked that guy," Hunter's eyes gleamed as Viola peered at him. "He gave us the house to ourselves."

"Oh," Viola mouthed, her face turning red yet again as understanding and embarrassment came.

"Come on, Mrs. Bennett," Hunter said as he grabbed Viola's hand and pulled her to the house.

Viola limped after Hunter, aware that she might just find out if she would combust. Her heart raced in intimidating anticipation. She really wished her mother would've explained a little of what was about to happen. *Okay, Viola, don't get jumpy,* she warned herself.

CHAPTER 19

HUNTER CLOSED the door after he led Viola through, the loud snap causing Viola to jump. He would've teased her about how on edge she was if he didn't feel as nervous as a greenie on his first mission. He needed to keep his focus, remember that she'd lost her father, for Pete's sake, and push his desires down to the back of his mind, like he'd done the last fifteen years of his life. If he got through adolescence without giving into that lustful monster, he could get through this.

Though that wasn't when the lady of his desires was his flesh and blood wife. The wife he'd waited the last fifteen years for and prayed every day for. Viola, his wife, who was so beautiful of both face and heart that it hurt to look at her. Who was brave and intelligent. Who was faithful and trusting of God much more than he had been recently. He didn't deserve her, but he thanked God for delivering him to her. If he didn't stop thinking about how amazing she was, he would never control the desires that were pushing forward, and then where would he be?

With a wife who thought him a heartless, groping thug, probably.

Maybe. He remembered her blushes when he'd brushed her arm on the porch. Or the energy that seemed to leap from her to him where their bodies pressed to each other. How she'd held her breath when he'd shifted, then breathed a faint sigh of contentment when he settled her closer to him. Maybe she wouldn't think him so heartless and groping after all.

He pushed that idea away, determined to focus on Viola and what she needed from him. He pulled her to the table, grabbed the coffee mug from her other hand, and nudged her into a chair.

"Would you like me to put on the teapot for you?" Hunter asked as he took the mug to the sink.

"No, thank you," she whispered, her eyes riveted to the mar in the table she was scratching at. As he turned and leaned against the counter, she let out a deep breath, lifting her eyes to his before glancing back to the table, a faint pink coloring her pale cheeks.

"You've been quiet this evening," Hunter said. "Why don't you tell me what's on you mind, what's got you so agitated?"

Her face bloomed a bright red and her eyes grew large and round in her delicate face. Shoot, wrong thing to say. Hunter scrambled, trying to figure out something else to blurt before she started crying. Though she didn't look sad, more embarrassed, which confused Hunter even more. He probably shouldn't have avoided girls as much as he did, then he might have a clue what to do in this situation.

"Oh no," Viola replied, shaking her head. "You don't want to know what I've been thinking."

He walked over to the table, pulled a chair closer to hers, and slid into it, noticing that she leaned away.

"Please, Viola, I want to help you," Hunter whispered, grabbing her hand from where it picked at the table and pulling her hand to him. He rubbed circles with his thumb on the back of her hand, hoping to calm her into opening up to him.

"It's not right," Viola said. "I'd die if anyone knew what's been going on in my brain."

"Viola," Hunter reassured her, placing his other hand onto her cheek. "You can tell me anything, and I promise it won't shock me or make me believe less of you. Remember, I've been though a lot, have seen and been privy to circumstances of every nature. I can tell you're struggling, Viola. I felt you spiraling down deep out there on the porch. If you don't trust me enough to talk to me about it, I want you to let me go get your sister to talk to her."

"No, Bea wouldn't understand. I can't talk to her," Viola said looking down at her hand enveloped in his then back into his eyes, vulnerability shining from her face. "Promise you won't think less of me?"

Hunter would promise her everything he could think of if he could. He'd promise to keep her safe. He'd promise to love and protect her with every ounce of his being, to die to save her from harm. Shoot, he'd promise to race to the mountaintops and capture the wind if she asked. He cleared his throat, which had become thick. "Promise."

"I feel this intense grief for Pa, that I'll never see him

again or that you'll never meet him," she said, squeezing his hand. "He would've loved you."

"I can tell I would've loved him, too," Hunter replied, grief at the loss of a relationship that never was to be heavy upon his heart.

Viola mouth lifted a teary smile before confusion crinkled her brow. She pushed off of her chair so fast she almost yanked him out of his. She curled her arms around herself and started pacing, a limp in her step from where the cranky horse had kicked her.

"I don't understand," she said as she bit her nail and turned for another lap. "My emotions keep vacillating between sorrow for my pa and joy for having you. Intense pain that sears my heart to a fullness I never imagined was possible. There's something wrong, wicked even within me to be one moment on the verge of tears over my father's death and the next moment wondering if I'll make it through my wedding night without combusting in a flame from intense desire. How can I be thinking such things, longing for such things, when I just found out my father's dead? She turned again and pinned him with a look of confusion from across the room. "Is it because the Sweeney's told us about his death already that I'm so easily swayed or am I just a horrible, terrible daughter whose own selfish desires overshadow even her father's death?" A tear slid down her face before she brushed it away while muttering, "Stupid tears."

Hunter got to his feet nice and slow, not wanting to scare her but also needing time to process the fact that she just told him she desired him, to the point she was worried she'd burst into flames. He knew he had to keep his ego and own desires in check, or he'd blow this whole conversation to smithereens. *Lord, help me find the right words to say to her. Help me comfort her in a way that's Godly and true. Show me the way Lord. Please help me build the trust we'll need as a husband and wife to last as a foundation for the rest of our lives.*

He walked up to her, took her hand, bringing it to his mouth and kissing the inside of her wrist. She closed her eyes, her breathing rapid and shallow.

"I don't think you're wicked, and you are the complete opposite of a horrible daughter," Hunter stated, hoping she'd see the truth within his eyes. "I can't tell you how happy I am to hear my desire and love for you reflected in your words. I also understand how confusing that must be. The last few days has been full of life-changing events, a death and a wedding."

He paused, took a breath and sent a quick prayer heavenward before continuing. "I don't know if it will help you, but I'd like to tell you about a conversation I had once with our chaplain."

"Okay," Viola whispered, allowing him to lead her back to the table.

He scooted his chair even closer before taking both of her hands in his. He started his story. "We'd just got off a mission. It was one of the worst ones I'd ever had. Although the mission was a success in the big wigs' eyes, we came home with two of our fellow brothers dead. Men of honor. Men I loved like my brother. We were gathering our gear to go home, our commander giving us all some R&R to regroup ourselves, when one of the married guys in the unit said that he couldn't wait to get home to his wife and the comfort of their bed and her arms." He cringed when Viola gasped, forgetting that the people of this time were still sensitive to that stuff.

"Sorry," he continued. "People in my time aren't very proper with that kind of stuff, especially not in The Unit. I was a little taken aback by what he said as well, but confusingly jealous at the same time. I visited the chapel before I left, hoping that prayer would help straighten out my thinking. Chaplain Dave came in and asked me what was wrong. I told him what had happened. Told him the talk in the barracks upset and confused me. How could he have been so callous when our brothers weren't even cold in the ground? Chaplain Dave nodded in understanding before answering. He told me that God made us for relationships, relationship with Him and relationship with others. One of the strongest relationships ordained by God is the one between a man and wife. Often when we face death, we want to cling to the relationship that is closest to us, the one that would give us the most comfort. When my parents died, all I wanted was to be with my brother. When those two fellow men died, what I wanted most was to have someone to hold and to hold me. To comfort and, I don't know, prove that I was still alive. Of course, I didn't have that, so I went home to visit Chase and focused on my relationship with the Lord."

Hunter sighed, tracing her slender fingers in his, hoping what he was saying was helping and not confusing her even more. He peered into her face and saw unshed tears balancing in her exquisite eyes. He wished there was a way to help her, make it so she never hurt again. Hunter leaned forward and placed his forehead against hers.

"God brought me here for you," he whispered. "I'll do

whatever I can to make things better, to protect and help you."

He hoped he hid his surprise when she pushed him back and climbed into his lap, snuggling up against his chest. He pulled her as close as he could get her and wrapped his arms tight around her.

VIOLA SURPRISED herself as she climbed into Hunter's lap and wrapped her arms around him so she didn't hurt his ribs. Her boldness should embarrass her, never being in another man's lap but her father's as a child, but she wanted nothing more than to escape into the comfort Hunter gave. She needed bolstered by the strength that seemed to seep through his very pores. She exhaled as his arms tightened around her, pulling her close, and nuzzled her head into his neck.

"I'm glad the cloud of doubt that had been hanging over us since the Sweeneys showed up has cleared," Viola confessed. "Maybe now my stomach will stop churning with anxiety." She said wistfully and far too self-indulgently. "I just wish our wedding day wasn't wrapped up in all this mess. That Uncle Dan wouldn't have forced you to marry me, and we had found out sooner about Pa. Now a day meant to be beautiful will forever remain marred by ugliness."

"A lifetime of beautiful days are waiting for us," Hunter answered, his deep voice rumbling beneath her cheek. "We'll have our share of bad days, but I think having this difficult situation and turbulent start of our life together can only strengthen us."

He ran his fingers up and down her arm, sending those tortuous jolts through her body once again.

"Besides," he continued, "someday, we may look back on these last few days and realize they were beautiful, despite the tragedy."

Viola pushed away from him to peer into his face. "Do you think it's possible?"

He gazed into her eyes, and the assault on her arm stopped as he said with all sincerity, "Because I see beauty laced in it already. In the sun that shined through your golden hair as you stepped out of the cabin in your pretty green dress. Having Dan here to join us in marriage, a marriage I was trying to discover a way to expedite. In Dan, your family, being here to share good memories together, memories I'm glad I now have of a man I will always wish I'd met. You and Beatrice haven't had any time between when River showed up with that letter to today to really process and grieve. Dan being here gave you that. And in us, expressing what I felt since the first moment we met."

He winked and gave her a cocky half smile that had Viola's mouth tugging upwards. She lifted her hand and traced the side of his lips that hitched up, remembering how he'd looked as he'd kissed her in the faint morning light. She remembered the look on Beatrice's face when she had helped Viola get dressed for the wedding and the laughter in stories of Pa that had lifted her soul. Viola realized her heart had found what it was missing in this wonderful man from a different time.

Viola stared in his eyes and agreed. "I think you're right. Beauty laced through today, breathtaking beauty."

He turned his head and pressed a kiss to her palm. She was glad God had sent her this husband from the future.

Gathering her courage, Viola whispered, her voice huskier than normal. "I don't want the beauty to stop there."

Hunter peered into her face, his eyes darkening to a deep blue and his voice deeper than before. "What are you saying?"

"Take me to bed, husband," Viola answered, blushing despite her boldness.

"You sure?" he asked, his voice rasping.

"Positive," she whispered.

Hunter leaned forward and captured her lips in a kiss steeped in possessiveness. A fire ignited deep in her core. He slanted his head to deepen the kiss. The fire spread from her core to flow into the rest of her body. Viola gasped at the intensity, wondering when her hands had become fisted in his shirt. She shrugged, spread her hands across the fabric, feeling the muscles she could easily picture bunching beneath her touch. She leaned forward and kissed him with as much passion as he had given her, hoping she'd ignite a fire within him as well.

She shrieked as Hunter stood up and carried her across the room. "Wait! Your ribs!"

"My ribs are fine," Hunter answered as he squeezed her close. "Come on, wife. Let's go to bed."

The desire thickening his voice turned the fire within her to an inferno she wasn't sure she'd survive. One she was sure she'd relish.

CHAPTER 20

HUNTER LAID ON HIS BACK, running his hand through the hair he'd dreamed of caressing since the first day Viola had leaned over to check his ribs. Ribs that were now protesting the earlier exertion, not that he'd tell Viola. She'd have him back in bed for a week. However, if he could convince her to join him, it wouldn't be such a bad confinement. He warmed at the thought.

Her breath blew soft across his chest where her head lay. Her body warm where it pressed up next to him. This was what his dad had been telling him about. Hunter had never quite understood until now, this closeness of two people that transcended any other earthly relationships. He mourned for all those guys he knew that threw this away with one-night stands. This was such a sacred bond for two to have. He couldn't imagine sharing it with anyone but Viola. He thanked God He had provided the strength to overcome when Hunter's desires ran away from him.

What in the world was he going to do? He was

married, to a woman he'd met weeks ago, one hundred and fifty years earlier than he was supposed to be, a time as foreign as anything he'd ever encountered in the army. More so, if he was honest, with the antiquated weapons and lack of any amenities. He did not know how to earn an income in this time and this wilderness. How was he to provide for the wife he had and a child that may come just as quick? What if he failed as miserably in this time as he did in the mission to save Hope and her parents? He had even less control over circumstances here than he did back home. What if his brother went off the deep end without him there? He'd already lost their parents. Hunter had witnessed Chase's dance with trouble and victory over it. What if losing Hunter as well ripped Chase from his trust in God? What if God hadn't brought Hunter back to marry Viola, but only for a short period of time?

Hunter breathed out an unsettled breath and ran his free hand down his face. This was ridiculous, this lack of trust. He felt ashamed and weak-minded, like the wave being tossed in the sea like the book of James warned believers about in the Bible. Hunter placed his hand over his eyes and silently prayed.

"You will keep in perfect peace those whose minds are steadfast, because they trust in You." Hunter heard the verse from Isaiah chapter twenty-six being spoken within his heart, the verse his father had recommended he memorize when he first enlisted. Then followed just as quickly the verse in Isaiah chapter forty-two. The chaplain had suggested he read it after his parents had died and it now played through his head. *"When you pass through the waters, I will be with you; and when you pass through the rivers, they will not*

*sweep over you. When you walk through the fire, you will not
be burned; the flames will not set you ablaze."*

He sighed in relief as the peace of God settled upon his
spirit. Whatever this life brought, if Hunter kept close to
God, God would stay close to Hunter. This world and its
worries would not drown him in despair and worry if he
remembered God was with him, no matter what
happened.

"Thank You," he whispered, as all tension left his body.

Viola stirred and pushed herself onto her elbow, her
hair cascading over her shoulder like a tumbling river of
gold. Her brow wrinkled in concern and her eyes roamed
his face.

"Are you all right?" she questioned.

"Yea," he answered, his voice thick and husky. "I'm
fine."

And to prove how fine he was, he kissed her until all
traces of sleep disappeared.

VIOLA WOKE hot with what felt like an iron blanket
thrown on top of her. She wondered why Beatrice had
put so many furs on the bed when it was this late in
spring. Trying to push out from under the covers, she
found the blankets to be solid arms and legs that laid
heavily upon her and the heat the muscled chest pressed
against her back. Viola sighed in contentment and
allowed the arms to pull her even closer within their
embrace. She figured the heat wasn't so uncomfortable
after all.

As she settled back to sleep, she huffed in frustration

at the sun shining brightly on her eyelids. She sucked in a breath and sat up so quickly that Hunter flopped onto his back behind her. She pulled the sheet to her neck and stared out the window. The sun shone in all its glory through the calico blue curtains her mother had sewn years before, with the cheery white daisies scattered across them.

"What? What's wrong?" Hunter sat up, pulling Viola behind him on the bed with one arm as he reached for the revolver on the nightstand with the other.

"It's late," Viola answered as she pushed his arm out of the way. "The sun's halfway up the sky and I haven't even started breakfast, let alone the other chores. Uncle Dan and Beatrice could be here any minute. What if they come in and breakfast isn't done? Oh dear, how embarrassing."

Viola glanced back at Hunter, her cheeks burning at the thought of being caught again. Sure the bedroom door was closed, but her sister and Dan would know.

Hunter chuckled, drawing his hand up and down her arm. "Don't worry, sweetheart."

"It is late this morning." She huffed in frustration as she pointed to the window. "Just look at how high the sun is, Hunter. Now turn around so I can get out of bed and dress."

"I see the sun, and it's barely peeking its bright head over the mountains. It's just after sunrise and you know it." He teased, a roguish gleam in his eye.

"I haven't slept this late in years and only when sick." She shook her head in disgust. "I need to get up and stop lazing about."

"Oh, if I remember right, there wasn't much lazing about happening," Hunter replied. "In fact, I think we might just need to do a little more lazing about, it being our honeymoon and all."

"I'm not sure that's a good idea," Viola said as Hunter kissed up her shoulder and neck, her resolve weakening with each kiss.

"And why not?" He whispered against her neck, sending shivers up and down her spine.

A knock on the bedroom door ripped a gasp out of Viola. She heard Hunter groan then begin to chuckle. Viola turned and glared at him.

"We've got a problem," Beatrice said through the door.

"When do we not have a problem?" Hunter asked, grumbling as he hurried to put on his clothes.

"We'll be right out," Viola called to Beatrice. She turned to Hunter. "I told you it was late."

Viola stood and hissed. A sharp pain wrenched from her knee up her leg.

"Are you alright?" Hunter asked, grabbing her arm.

"It's just my knee," Viola answered then as quickly as her knee would allow got dressed and followed Hunter into the front room.

Beatrice stood at the door, her revolver drawn and her head turning as she scanned the yard. Viola could tell Beatrice was upset from the tightness in her shoulders and the way her free hand tapped upon her leg.

"Talk to me, Little Sister," Hunter said as he walked up to Beatrice.

Beatrice turned and glared at Hunter before moving out on to the porch and into the yard. "The corral's empty." Beatrice's voice clipped back.

Viola scanned the corral and around the yard, closing the cabin door. She scowled as she noticed the horses they kept there were missing. The gate to the corral sat wide open.

"Let's go check it out," Hunter said, his voice controlled, his face impassive as he scanned the surroundings.

Viola limped behind Beatrice and Hunter, cringing with every step and struggling to keep up. "Where's Uncle Dan?"

"He rode home with me to the rise in the meadow, watched to make sure I made it to the barn alright, then headed out to visit Chief Johnson. He said he'd be back as soon as he could be," Beatrice said.

"What about the animals in the barn? Are they missing too?" Hunter asked as they drew close to the corral.

"No. Maybelle and Cocoa are still in there and, of course, Firestorm was with me." Beatrice shook her head. "I'm so stupid. I didn't even realize the horses were gone until I headed to the cabin."

"Beatrice, you are anything but stupid. Distracted? Definitely, but never stupid," Hunter said with such force Viola smiled. His protective nature striking her as sweet when directed to her more than capable sister.

When they got to the corral Hunter spoke. "You two see if you can figure out what happened. I'll keep watch."

Viola nodded, and she and Beatrice got right to work. Was it finally time? Had the Sweeneys made a move? She hoped not, because she had hoped Orlando would be here when they did. As it was, they didn't even know how to contact River for help. Thankfully, they were more than stocked and ready for trouble. Worse case scenario, they'd bunker down in the house and wait the Sweeneys out.

"Hunter. Viola," Beatrice hollered, pulling Viola from her musings. "Come and look at this."

Hunter walked over to the gate where Beatrice had stopped as Viola limped close.

"Whatcha got?" Hunter asked

"It looks like the latch broke free," Beatrice answered, pointing to the latch that was hanging on the gate.

"Is that normal?"

"Well, it's not abnormal," Beatrice replied, scratching her head as she scrutinized it closer. "Could've been one of the rowdier horses pushing up against the gate. Buster is good at doing that, pushing on a gate until he busts it free. Hence the name Buster. We thought we'd figured out a latch that'd hold him, but I guess we were wrong."

"I might not have latched it completely either after Rowdy kicked me yesterday," Viola said.

Hunter inspected the latch that the horse had pushed open. He looked at the fence it connected to. He searched the ground. Viola's eyes followed every place he examined. Nothing seemed out of the ordinary. There were no clear footprints or markings that would prove that this was not a contrary horse.

Hunter took a deep breath in and relaxed his shoulders. "I remember a horse that always seemed to lean heavily on the gate, pushing on it throughout the day. I wondered what he was up to."

"We need to go round them up," Beatrice spoke Viola's thoughts, smacking her gloves onto her leg as she dragged them from her back pocket.

"Viola's not up for that this morning," Hunter said, pointing to Viola's leg. Viola crossed her arms in agitation that he was answering for her.

"I know she's not, but it's gotta be done. Not going is not an option," Beatrice answered, not even glancing Viola's way.

Hunter peered at Viola's face, then glared at her knee. "I guess she can ride behind me."

"I'm not riding behind you," Viola said, hot anger rising so fast she felt sure steam would blow from her ears. "My knee will just slow you down. Plus, with only Cocoa left, riding double will only do us harm. You two will go and get the horses. They wouldn't have gotten far."

"Great. I'll go pack some supplies," Beatrice said as she turned for the cabin and rushed inside.

"I'm not leaving you here. Don't you remember what happened a few days ago?" Hunter said, his neck turning red and his fist clenching in his free hand.

"Yes, you are." Viola answered. "The further those horses run loose, the harder it will be to round them up. I'll shutter the windows and bar the door. I'll only open it for you two, River, or Orlando."

"I can't leave you." The anguish in Hunter's voice and the desperation on his face whisked all of Viola's anger away.

Viola stepped close, resting her hands on his chest and tipping her face up to peer into his eyes. "I'm not going to be outside, busy with chores. I'll stay firmly locked inside, Hunter. I promise. I'll be fine. You have to trust that, to trust God."

He stared down at her with such love and devotion. Viola leaned into him, lifting onto her toes, and kissed him. He wrapped his arm around her and kissed her back, his misery evident in his urgent kiss and tight muscles that squeezed her impossibly close.

The cabin door slammed open followed by Beatrice's call. "Let's go."

Hunter pulled away and swept Viola into his arms. "I'm going to make sure all the shutters are locked, then I'll help you with the horses."

Viola allowed Hunter to carry her into the cabin without much protest. Her knee did hurt something fierce. Plus, she enjoyed Hunter's impressive strength. He set her down by the door and hurried to the bedrooms to lock the shutters.

When he came back into the front room with the revolver strapped in his holster and the Lancaster rifle in his hand, Viola's heart pinched. Maybe it wasn't wise to stay behind? Viola smiled past the doubt.

Hunter stepped up to her, ran his hand down her cheek, and kissed her passionately. When she thought she melt where she stood, he pulled away. "Bar the door."

Hunter strode out of the cabin heading for the barn. Viola closed the door slowly as her gaze lingered over her husband as he walked away. As she lifted the heavy bar and laid it into place with a loud thud, a weight of worry landed solid on her heart.

CHAPTER 21

Viola peered around the cabin with a huff. The place sparkled with a cleanliness she doubt it ever had experienced. Not that her family were filthy, but her anxiety had her scrubbing every nook and cranny until every speck of dirt vanished.

Viola glanced around, the walls of the cabin closing in on her. She realized it was irrational and that she should just find something else to do until Hunter and Beatrice got back. Her knee screamed at her from all the bending and walking she'd done, so she sat down in the rocker and pulled a shirt from the mending basket.

The sound of a horse coming into the yard had Viola standing before she even got settled. She limped over to the door, grabbed the rifle from where she'd propped it, and peeked out the peephole. A familiar horse rode up to the hitching post. Viola's fingers touched her parted lips. Orlando had finally returned home.

She propped the rifle against the wall and threw the bar off the door. Grabbing the rifle back up — her over-watchful husband would be proud of her diligence — she rushed out the door to greet her brother as fast as her aching knee would allow.

Orlando's look of happiness changed to one of horror as Viola was yanked back against a hard chest by an arm wrapped firm around her waist. Cold steel pressed to her temple.

"You came right out to me, sweetheart." Linc's voice rasped against her hair, sending a shiver down the length of her. "Throw your gun away Orlando, unless you want Viola to meet the same fate as your pa."

When Orlando moved to gingerly pull his gun from his holster, Linc aimed his gun and shot. Viola's world slowed and she screamed as Orlando fell to the ground. She struggled hard against Linc's arm, swinging the rifle up to hit Linc in the head. It glanced him on the forehead and he cursed. He grabbed the rifle and yanked it hard from her hands with his free hand and turned her around to face him. Blood poured from a gash on his right cheek, making him look even more sinister than normal.

"You'll pay for that, Viola," he whispered with menace. "Looks like you'll have to be taught how to treat your man properly."

Viola struggled, trying to kick his legs and claw at his face. Her infernal skirt kept her feet from making contact, and he contained her hands in his iron grip.

"Looks like we will have to do this the hard way," Linc said as he pulled his revolver from his holster.

Viola's eyes went wide in fear as he held it high above his head. She let out a short, piercing scream before his arm came down and everything turned black.

～

HUNTER WAS proud he'd been able to keep Viola's horse Cocoa up with Beatrice and Firestorm. While he wasn't a complete novice, his exposure to horses during his years in the Delta Force had been very limited. They'd followed the horses tracks the last few hours down a path past the meadow that snaked back into the mountains.

Leaving Viola, walking away had been the hardest thing he'd ever done. He knew he couldn't hover, knew retrieving these horses was important to life here in the wilderness. Yet disquiet had lodged in his spirit the instant his beautiful wife's face had hardened in anger and she'd demanded to stay behind. The further they traveled from the cabin, the more intense his unease became. Beatrice turned a curve ahead of him and disappeared, racketing his anxiousness up to the nausea level. He rounded the curve, bringing her back in view and whistled. She pulled to a stop and turned around, lifting her eyebrow up in question.

"Something's not right," Hunter said as he came up beside her. "My spirit is screaming that this is all wrong."

Beatrice cocked her head to the side and examined him. She closed her eyes and took a deep breath in. When she opened her eyes and released her breath, she nodded.

"Yeah, I feel the same. Let's ride up around this next curve right here. The trail opens up to another field. If we can't see the horses, we'll turn around and head home."

"Okay, but let's make it quick."

Hunter followed Beatrice on the skinny trail that was hardly wide enough for the horses to traverse. He could see a clearing ahead and hoped the horses would be there so they could head home. Hunter pulled up on the reins when Beatrice entered the field, took one glance around, and spun Firestorm around taking off in a run toward him. He yanked Cocoa around and raced down the trail they'd been traveling. He cursed the fact the trail was too thin to ride side-by-side, but he trusted Beatrice's instincts. Explanations to their wild ride back could wait. Several minutes later, though it seemed like hours, they burst into a meadow, and Beatrice came up alongside him.

"The horses were all there in a remuda so they wouldn't wander," Beatrice yelled. "Someone took them."

Dread fell heavy to the pit of Hunter's stomach. He'd done it again, moved against what he knew the Holy Spirit was telling him and left Viola unprotected and alone. He should've listen to his gut telling him not to go. Would this screw-up cost him much more than he ever thought possible?

He shook his head and shouted over the pounding hooves. "We ride as hard as we can. We'll need to go into the homestead smart, but we can't waste any time. When we get close, you go in with your gun drawn and ready for combat."

She nodded her head in agreement as she pulled forward to lead down another wooded trail. He sent up desperate prayers on the frantic ride back. They burst into the meadow that led to the cabin.

A horse stood in the yard with a man laying on the ground beside it. The front door sat wide open. Hunter's stomach constricted so fast and tight, he thought he would vomit right there on Cocoa's back. Beatrice arrived first, gun in hand and slide from Firestorm's back as the horse skidded to a stop.

"Orlando!" she shouted, rushing to the man rolling onto his side, blood running from his head.

Beatrice fell to the ground beside him and burst into tears as she helped him to sit up. He caught her in a hug and buried his face into her neck.

"Viola!" Hunter yelled. "Where is she? Viola!"

Orlando lifted his head, angst and wariness on his face as he narrowed his eyes at Hunter, "Who in the world are you?"

"I'm her husband," Hunter said, causing Orlando's eyes to widen in surprise.

"Linc took her. Was hiding behind the corner of the house and grabbed her before I could react." Orlando said as he pushed to his knees and touched his head where blood had clotted. "The snake shot me, knocked me out cold."

"Praise God he didn't kill you," Beatrice said, wiping her arm across her face.

Beatrice stood and walked to the porch where the rifle he'd left Viola lay haphazardly on the step. "Looks like she put up a fight," she said as she pointed to the churned up ground. "There's blood here."

Hunter dropped his head. He'd failed. God brought him back here for Viola, and he'd failed her and God in one stupid moment of not following God's urging. How could he have been that thickheaded to mess up so colossally? He straightened his shoulders. He'd find her. He'd make this right.

"Forgive me, Father," Hunter whispered as he walked with purpose towards Beatrice.

Beatrice glanced up from where she examined the

ground, her eyes pleading. "I'm so sorry. I should've listened to you. This is all my fault. I'm so, so sorry."

"I should've listened to what God was telling me," Hunter replied. "I had an unease in my gut and should've listened."

"This blood isn't hers," Orlando said from where he was examining the rifle. "There's blood on the rifle stock. She must've got a hit in."

"Why would Linc leave the gun behind?" Beatrice asked.

"If he was desperate to get her out of here or she wasn't cooperating, he'd not mess with grabbing the gun. At least I wouldn't," Hunter answered.

Orlando leaned the gun against the cabin wall and pointed at the ground while walking towards the meadow. He bent to examine something and stood up fast, weaving unsteadily.

"Linc carried her off. His footprints coming up are much lighter than the footprints leading out," Orlando explained.

"Can you track them?" Hunter asked.

"Yeah, I can track them," Orlando said.

Beatrice gave Orlando an easy nod. "If anyone can track them, it's Orlando. He's the best there is."

"Well, let's go get her back," Hunter said, his voice hard with resolve.

Hunter walked towards Orlando, who peered at him with skepticism.

"Just what has been going on here while I was gone," Orlando demanded.

"I'm your new brother-in-law, Hunter Bennett," Hunter

said as he shook Orlando's hand. "I married Viola after Linc Sweeney came here, claiming you were dead and bent on forcing Viola to marry him. The rest of the story will have to wait, though, since we need to work up a plan."

Orlando's eyebrows raised slightly as he glanced to Beatrice.

She shrugged. "Uncle Dan married them yesterday. It's been a hectic couple of weeks, to say the least."

The sound of hoofbeats fast approaching had all three of them grabbing their revolvers and turning to the intruder. Hunter holstered his weapon and took off running when he recognized River's paint. The footsteps following told him his family was quick to recognize the friend.

"Do you know where they are?" Hunter asked before River had even stopped.

"I know where Robert and William have been camping." River answered as he swung from the saddle. "Linc hasn't been with them, though I found tracks of a solo rider going into the camp just a day or two ago. I knew it was important for me to come tell you what I've found today, even though I was planning to wait longer."

"Praise God, He led you here," Hunter said, breathing a sigh of relief. "Viola's been taken and we need to get to their camp."

"What?" River rounded on Hunter. "What happened?"

Hunter seethed in his impatience. "We can chitchat about the details later. Can we get to their camp undetected, River?"

"Yes, without a doubt."

Hunter nodded and crossed to the house. "Tell me all

about the layout as we gear up. I want to be on the trail with a plan in fifteen. Then we're going to finish this."

Hunter rushed into the cabin, heading straight to the bookcase. He flicked the latch and glanced back as the shelf swung opened. River's mouth gaped wide, and Orlando shook his head in disapproval. Hunter could care less about family secrets at the moment. All that mattered was getting to Viola and bringing her home.

CHAPTER 22

Viola's head beat like a drum and her knee burned as if it'd been ripped from her body and put back on. Her face rested on a scratchy wool blanket that smelled of horse flesh and sweat. She laid on her side with her hands bound in front of her. Voices argued behind her, so she tried to remain still and breathe as if still unconscious. Focusing through the throbbing pain was a trial made easier as feet stomped her way.

"I'm telling you Linc, you shouldn't have taken her," a voice she assumed was Robert's said.

"She's mine, Robert, mine. I wasn't about to let some dandy come in and take her from right under my nose," Linc yelled back. A sound of metal being kicked echoed across the camp.

"Hey, those were my beans," William whined.

"Shut up." A slap punctuated Linc yell.

"Linc, calm down and think this through," Robert's steady and even voice urged. "That newcomer was not just a dandy, but a man who looked like he knew what

249

he was about with the way he pulled steel on us back at the cabin. He's not going to just let you take off with her."

Viola prayed that Linc would listen to reason. He'd let her go, and they would all move on from this. She realized it was a long shot, but she didn't think the prayer offended God.

"Are you going to help me or not, Robert? When they come running for her, we get the drop on them, then the homestead and the gold is all ours," Linc challenged.

Viola couldn't stop the soft gasp from escaping her lips. She relaxed her body and prayed no one heard her.

Robert answered, his voice moving closer to Viola. "I already told you after you killed Joseph, I would not help you do your dirty work anymore. I'm sick of all of this, Linc. It's no way to live a life, full of jealousy and hate. I'm ready for a life worth living."

Viola detected someone bending down next to her.

"What would you know about a life worth living?" Linc spat. "Don't you touch her. She's mine."

"I'm just checking her wound, so stop fretting. You left a welt the size of Texas on her head." Robert answered as he brushed the hair off Viola's forehead. "I want a life built on honesty and hard work. Don't you remember anything you learned in church when Mama would take us? "

As Linc ranted a raved about the all the good church-going ever did, Robert bent over her and whispered, "I will do all I can to help you, Miss Viola. I promise you that."

"Get away from her." Linc yanked Robert away, causing Viola to flinch. "Oh good, you're finally up. Now we can get moving again. The sooner we get away from here, the sooner I can make you mine."

Viola's eyes flew open, and she scooted away as fast as she could without her hands. Linc grabbed her by the arms and yanked her up, causing pain to radiate from her head all the way to her fingers. He pulled her close and leaned in to kiss her, making Viola almost vomit again.

"I don't think so," Hunter's strong voice thundered into the clearing.

Viola's knees gave out as Linc spun her around and pulled her back up against him.

Righteous indignation flared through Hunter as he moved into the clearing from his spot behind the trees where he'd listened as Linc ranted at his brother. Hunter lifted his Colt to aim at Linc.

Hunter realized things would happen fast, past experience had proved that, but the whiny brother surprised him when he stood quick and drew. Before Hunter even reacted, an arrow flew through the air, hitting the gun from the brother's hand.

"My gun!" The youngest Sweeney yelled as he gaped with rage from his gun that now laid on the ground to Beatrice who'd already knocked another arrow. "You're going to pay for that, missy."

"I'd suggest if you don't want anything more precious shot, you'd get your hands up and keep them there," Beatrice answered, cold and even.

"Shut up, you imbecile," Linc yelled at his brother.

Hunter focused all his attention back on Linc, who'd

pulled Viola in front of him, placing his gun to her temple. Hunter blocked everything else out, knowing his team would worry about the other two, though from his peripheral, he Robert had his hands in the air, not willing to help his brother.

"Let her go," Heat flushed through Hunter's body and his muscles quivered.

Linc sneered and chuckled, pulling Viola tighter against him.

"Linc, you're outnumbered four to one. You'd be smart to let her go," Robert said, his voice placating.

"Never, and you're gonna have a time of it explaining to Pa how you betrayed your family when you meet him in hell." Linc spat at Robert, spittle running from his lips and rage burning in his eyes.

"That's just it," Robert said with a sad shrug. "I'm giving my life to Jesus, like Mama always taught us, so I doubt I'll be seeing Pa again."

"Coward," Linc yelled, pressing the gun harder into Viola's temple.

The rage on Linc's face and and the shake forming in his hands told Hunter the situation bordered on spiraling out of control. A sudden sense of peace breathed through his body, and he glanced into Viola's face. Terror and pain swam in those beautiful green eyes, but he also saw her confidence in him there as well. He knew without a doubt that she trusted him to get her through this. The peace of God rooted solid within his feet as he lifted his gun higher.

"Last warning, Sweeney, let her go or pay the price," Hunter warned.

"I'd rather die first," Linc said, a sinister gleam entering his eyes. "And I'll take Viola with me."

Linc shifted the gun ever so slightly and Hunter didn't wait a second longer to react. He took aim and pulled the trigger. Time slowed as Linc and Viola dropped to the ground in a heap together. Hunter ran up to them, sliding in next to where they landed. Viola's frantic scream and kicking legs from where she laid pinned beneath Linc's body filled Hunter with such relief his throat constricted tight with unshed tears. He helped her get untangled and pulled her to him. Hunter captured her face within his hands and wiped the tears streaming down her cheeks, fully aware tears flowed down his.

"I thought I'd lost you," he whispered placing his forehead to hers.

"How in the world did you make that shot?" Orlando asked as he looked up from where he crouched next to Linc, the bullet wound seeping from his forehead.

"God," Hunter replied, "and a lot of practice."

Hunter turned to the Sweeneys. Robert's hand laid on Willaim's shoulder, who stood rocking back-and-forth, staring at Linc's body. Hunter wondered if what he'd overheard was true or if it was another game being played.

"I listened to what you said. Was Linc the one who killed Joseph Thomas?" Hunter asked, keeping his eyes on Robert's face for any sign of deception.

"Yeah." Robert looked down, running his hand through his dark hair. "We all had a part in getting the jump on him, but the plan was to get him to tell us about their mine. I never planned on him getting harmed, wanted none of this actually. William and I left to hunt up some game after we'd captured Joseph, and when we got back, Linc had already killed him."

"He didn't simply kill him, he brutalized him," Orlando said firmly.

"That was the most disturbing thing I'd ever seen." Robert shuddered. "I never imagined Linc had gotten so desperate, but I'd seen the rage in him growing for some time. With that though, I realized I was done with his schemes, but after what Viola said to us back at the cabin that first day, I knew I had to figure out a way to help if I could. So I kept William with me, refusing to go slink around with Linc and prayed for God to show me the way out. I never meant for things to get where they did. I'm sorry for all we've put you through. When you are ready, we'll go willing to Denver with you to turn us into the Marshalls. I just ask, though he doesn't deserve it, that you let us bury Linc before we leave."

Hunter glanced from Viola to Beatrice to Orlando. The grief on their faces was stark, varying in their expressions. No matter what they decided, he would support his family in whatever way he could.

Orlando stepped forward and stared directly in Robert's eyes and stated, "Yes, you helped Linc in getting Pa, but, if what you say is true, and I believe it is, then you didn't kill him. There's been enough evil and hurt between our families. I'm ready to be done with it. God calls us to rise above evil and to forgive those who sin against us. If you promise you're through with chasing after foolishness, I'm okay with letting you live out that life worth living you were talking earlier about."

"But we deserve justice for our part in this," Robert insisted.

"All of us deserve punishment, Robert, but like God gave us grace and mercy for our sins, we want to show you the same." Orlando encouraged as he put his hand on Robert's shoulder.

Hunter had never seen such Christian faith in action. The forgiveness Orlando gave, despite the horrendous crime done to their father, humbled him. He looked forward to getting to know his new brother-in-law after they got back home.

"I promise," Robert vowed. "William and I won't be bothering you anymore. We'll head out as soon as we get things finished here and you won't have to see us again."

Hunter wondered if William thought the same thing, considering the leering looks he was sending Beatrice's way. Hunter motioned for River come over.

"Why don't you and Beatrice go round up the horses and meet us back at the cabin?" Hunter asked as River came closer.

"Good idea," River stated as he grabbed Beatrice's arm and pulled her away. Hunter chuckled as he heard River ask in awe, "Where did you learn to shoot like that?"

Hunter turned to Viola and pulled her close. He was ready to go home. He was eager to finally start this new life God blessed him with.

VIOLA LEANED into Hunter's side as he pulled her through the forest. She figured he was taking her home, but she was still in such shock that she couldn't quite process everything yet. It amazed her that the whole ordeal finally seemed over. They'd get to live their lives, a life without the constant shadow of doubt that had blanketed the last weeks.

Viola let Hunter help her onto the back of Cocoa. He mounted up behind her and she leaned into him as he steered them toward home. She didn't talk, just cherished the touch of his strong arms around her and the scent that represented him, pine and leather and a hint of grass. She knew she'd never feel safer than when she was with him, and she hoped he finally realized he proved more than capable to do that job.

The fast clip of a horse's footsteps told Viola that Orlando approached. The mercy Orlando showed to Robert still overwhelmed her with love and pride. She rejoiced evil would ruin no more lives and prayed Robert and William embraced a life rich in Christ.

She peered over at Orlando as he pulled even with them. She thanked God that He had saved Orlando. It was obvious from the blood that still caked his hair and saturated his shirt that he'd been injured by the bullet. Viola figured since he seemed to be riding alright, he was fine for the moment, though she'd want to look at the wound when they got home. He also appeared rough around the edges from his travels and needed a good shave, but he remained handsome with his blue eyes shining with seriousness.

"You have a lot to tell me about since I've left, sister of mine," Orlando joked, smiling over at her and raising his eyebrows to Hunter.

"Orlando, you have no idea." Viola laughed.

"We have a long ride home," Orlando replied, then eyed her and Hunter skeptically. "There's not a baby on the way, is there?"

"Not yet," Viola said, eyeing Orlando sternly at the improper implication. She then smiled and added coyly, "But I hope there will be soon."

Hunter inhaled sharply behind her. Without warning, his arms loosened from around her waist. She turned. Hunter's eyes opened wide in shock and his body dropped from behind her with a thud as Hunter fell off the horse.

EPILOGUE

Hunter beamed at the baby wrapped snug in flannel that he held in his arms. His son Chase Joseph had thick blonde hair that curled upon his head. He had insisted on being there for the baby's birth, and he was glad he had. He never imagined he'd help birth his baby in the middle of the mountains trapped by feet of snow and miles of nothing and no one. But then again, God had required him to do a lot of things he never thought he'd do.

Viola sighed in the bed, so Hunter crossed to sit on it with her. As he leaned up against the headboard, Viola rested her head against his arm and stroked their son's hair as he slept.

"Isn't he perfect?" she announced.

"Yeah, but he takes after his mom that way," Hunter replied, kissing her on the head.

She beamed up at him. His breath left his lungs in a whoosh. Praise God for sending him back here to this beauty, how full his life was now that he had her and their

258

son. He kissed her, hoping to convey some of his aston-
ishment.

"How are you feeling?" he murmured.

"Better than you did when you fell off the horse when
I mentioned having babies," Viola sassed.

"Hey now," Hunter muttered. "We agreed never to talk
about that."

Viola laughed and snuggled in closer, replying with
sleep in her voice, "If I recall, you begged, but we never
actually agreed."

Hunter knew she was right. No amount of cajoling
would make them forget that event. He wondered how far
down history the family story would pass, and if his great
grandkids would laugh about the day he fell from his
horse in shock. He chuckled and figured he would make a
history full of stories while his figured this life out here in
the Colorado wilderness. Hunter hugged his family
closer. He would embrace the gift God had given him full
on without regret or doubt.

Made in the USA
Middletown, DE
24 December 2019

81804765R00158